Heaven's Kingdom: Tuck's story.

A Guy of Gisborne prequel

L. J. Hutton
Published by Wylfheort Books 2020

Chapter 1

St Mary's Priory of Ewenny, Abergavenny, Wales
The Year of Our Lord 1174

Tuck knelt in the choir stalls at the great priory at Abergavenny and did his best to focus on the office going on up at the high altar. It was Lauds, the morning prayers, and once again Brother Cedric was mangling the Latin something shockingly. Why did the prior not do something about that? Surely by now Brother Cedric ought to know what the proper forms were? And yet at least once a week, when it came around to Cedric's turn to lead whichever office it was, he always made such a shocking mess of the Latin. Perennially idle rather than incapable, Cedric epitomised – but was not the only example in the priory of – an indifferent Norman nobleman's son who would really rather have not been there, but had had no choice in the matter. It was still disrespectful, though, in Tuck's eyes, having been brought up with a more Celtic perspective.

Lord, forgive me my sin of pride, Tuck prayed, casting a furtive glance heavenwards and hoping that the sub-prior wouldn't catch him doing it. *It's not about whether I could do it better, but that he does You no honour, and surely that's what we are here for? Cedric's bored yawning and muttering surely makes a mockery of this office.* Then ducked his head again before Humbert caught his eye.

Sub-prior Humbert was the bane of Tuck's life, watching him with a most unchristian fervour, to Tuck's mind. And Humbert was just a bit too keen with the spanking of the young oblates too.

Thank you, Lord, for sparing me his judgement when I was really young, Tuck offered up next and from the heart. And he had been lucky. He'd come to Ewenny Priory as an oblate, one of the earliest young children to be given to God at this monastery, back around 1160 when the priory had only just achieved conventual status, and the community of monks was in its infancy. That meant that he had had the kindly and very learned Brother Rhys teaching him – a man filled with joy by the acquisition of knowledge and learning, and for passing it on. But that meant that for Tuck, Latin was like a second language, having learnt it as a small child – or rather a third language, since he spoke both English and his native

Welsh – and because of that, Brother Cedric's dire mangling of the holy words grated on every nerve.

God's hooks! Tuck found himself seething despite his best efforts. *Don't you know that's supposed to have the genitive ending? It's 'servant* **of** *God', so it's possessive and that means the genitive, not the accusative! How could you not remember that? You had a tutor mostly to yourself all through your childhood. You didn't have to sit in a class with ten other boys, all older and far ahead of you in their studies, to learn your verbs. Yet we all learned. Brother Osric is no scholar, but he's learned it the right way, and so has poor Brother Rufus – and he's been half-blind from birth and so cannot read! So why can't you?*

Granted everybody went through the services by rote, rather than reading it, except for the odd remembrance service which would only come around once a year. But the normal offices which came around week after week, month after month, were repeated so often they were known by heart – so after all these years, surely Cedric knew that? Others, even most of the novices, did so, why didn't he? Why didn't he care?

…Lord forgive me that mental outburst, Tuck hurriedly tacked on, *but this is all supposed to be to Your glory, so he should get that bit right! We're supposed to be pure of intent and praying for the benefit of everyone around here, isn't that what Brother Rhys taught us? We fight the spiritual battles, the nobles fight the earthly ones, and the poor people work the soil to keep our bodies and souls together. If I ever meet a demon, I hope I should acquit myself well in our people's defence…* then his train of thought was shattered by a loud snort from Cedric as he fell asleep mid-chant and woke himself up with his own snore, and heard the resulting giggles from some of the smaller oblates.

Then out of the corner of his eye he caught Sub-prior Humbert, from his position opposite them, beginning to scan the row of stalls where Tuck was, and ducked his head a little more. Like their prior, Father Augustine, Humbert was another aristocratic Norman monk sent over to supposedly bring culture to this border institution, and equally filled with arrogance and disdain for the local men like Tuck. Brother Rhys could have run rings around the both of them when it came to learning, yet he had never risen beyond schooling the novices, and to Tuck's mind, St Mary's had lost its holiest brother on the day that Rhys had died two years ago. So much so, that lately he was almost daily wondering how much longer he could stand being cooped up in here.

While he had been filling his mind with wondrous things, Tuck could accept that he was seeing nothing of the outside world. But once Rhys had died, and all of his extended learning had come to an abrupt halt, Tuck discovered that the monotony of the monastery had the ability to drive him mad. All the joy had gone out of the scriptorium with the arrival of Brother Eustace from Normandy eighteen months ago, and as Tuck felt little Brother Simeon flinch beside him, he knew that Eustace was behind them with that damned whippy cane of his that he so liked using on the youngest brothers.

He'd only tried it once with Tuck, who even back then at seventeen, was only a handful of years younger than Eustace, even if he was far below him in status. Finding the cane being ripped out of his hands, snapped in two, and then looking up into Tuck's furious eyes as this supposedly lesser brother towered glowering over him, had been enough. Not that Tuck had got away with such disobedience, but the banishing of Tuck to hard labour in the monastery's fields had had quite the opposite effect on Tuck to that which was intended. Far from becoming cowed by the hard work, Tuck had set to with relish, enjoying every moment he could at being out in the fresh air, and listening to the spring calls of the birds in the trees, and the burgeoning growth in the fields. Being part of the outside world for whole days for the first time in his life had been a joyful revelation, as had the chance to talk to the more worldly lay brothers more at length, and having to return to the now stifling atmosphere of the scriptorium only made Tuck worse. So much so that before long he was outside on punishment again, and working with a willingness he found it impossible to summon up for what was designated as his proper work.

Go on, Tuck found himself thinking as Cedric droned on, *put me on punishment again. Please! For the love of God, let me out of here!* Because more and more, Tuck was becoming convinced that if God had a plan for him, then living the rest of his life like this wasn't it.

As they all trooped back out of the church and across to the refectory, where some very stale bread and extremely weak small beer awaited to break the brothers' fast, Tuck's one and only true friend, Dafydd, sidled up to him and whispered,

"Another mangled office!"

"I know," Tuck hissed back. "How does he do it? How does he make such a mess of something he must have heard every day for decades? Didn't I hear someone say he'd been a monk for thirty years now?"

Dafydd had to wait until they had passed the lurking figure of Humbert before he replied, but when he did he shocked Tuck to the core.

"Well I've had it," he declared. "I'm making a run for it at the first chance I get!"

Just in time, Tuck managed to stop himself from halting in his tracks and gawping at Dafydd, but had to ask, "Where will you go?"

It certainly wouldn't be back home. Dafydd might not have come into the monastery quite as young as Tuck, but that meant that he had very clear memories of the father who had died, and the mother who had been forced into a loveless marriage with the Norman lord who coveted their little manor on the river Wye. There would be no welcome home for Dafydd there, especially as word had come last winter that his mother had also died.

"I'm going to join the rebels," Dafydd declared, "the sons of Deheubarth!"

"You'll have to be prepared to fight," Tuck warned him, fearful that his idealistic friend was having visions of serving as some sort of priest to the rebels, and knowing that Prince Gruffydd would have no need for a holy man of Dafydd's inexperience. It sounded like a grand adventure planned here in the safety of the monastery, but Tuck had enough common sense, and had listened to enough from the visitors he helped the infirmarer with, to know that the reality might be very different.

"Oh I know that!" Dafydd, replied with a grin. "I've no intention of heading back into any place like this ever again! Come with me, Tuck! You're a big lad – I bet they'd welcome you with open arms."

However, Tuck could only sigh. "No, Daf', that life's not for me. I have this feeling that God has a purpose for me that he hasn't shown me yet, but the life you're heading for isn't it, of that I'm sure."

By now they were inside the refectory, one of the few places where talking was openly permitted for a short while, and seeing Dafydd's stubborn scowl, Tuck knew that he was going to have to explain in more detail.

"Look," he said, drawing Dafydd aside once they had collected their simple breakfast, to a dark corner where they wouldn't be noticed. "If you go on the run, what are they going to say? What description are they going to give, eh? That they're after a lad of medium height, light-brown hair and hazel eyes? That's like half of Wales – or at least round here!"

He gave Dafydd a little shake. "Now look at me. I've topped six feet since I was in my mid teens, and that all by itself puts me a full head taller than the vast majority of men. And with jet-black hair and an olive complexion? Black hair with white skin, yes, that's very Welsh, but not

4

with my height it isn't, either. I'll stand out in a crowd like a great big, dark thistle in Brother Ioan's herb garden! On your own you stand a chance, but not with me with you."

Dafydd's face fell, and Tuck knew that he was bitterly disappointed that his friend wouldn't be coming with him.

"You should go," Tuck said kindly. "You're as stifled in here as I am. Don't worry, I'll find my own way."

But throughout the day, Tuck went about his tasks mindlessly while his thoughts were far away. He remembered Dafydd being brought to the monastery ten years ago, not only because the boy had sobbed his heart out for the mother who had been in hysterics herself at their being parted, but because of the questions it had raised in his own mind about himself.

"Why did my mother hate me so much as to give me away when I was so little that I can't even remember her face? What did I do so wrong?" he recalled his younger self asking Brother Rhys, and the kindly Rhys answering,

"It wasn't you, Tuck. A wicked man came and got you on her, see? And her family wouldn't have you around. You were too much of a reminder."

That hadn't been much consolation even back then, but it had been some years later, when Tuck was thirteen and already head and shoulders taller than the other boys, and a clue of a very different kind had come. A fine Norman lord had come to the priory to stay for that night, on his way to visiting the de Braoses at their other castle aside from Abergavenny over at Brecon. He and his entourage had clattered in through the gateway just as the boys had been released from their afternoon classes, and were dispersing to their other chores. Peering down at the boys from off his fine white horse, Tuck had heard him say,

"Who's that boy? Some lord's get, for sure! No mistaking the Norman turn of *his* features! Whose is he?"

And the prior of the time answering, "We have no idea, my lord. He was brought to us by the servant of a noble Welsh family from north of here. They said he was here to provide repentance for his father's sins."

The Norman lord had thrown back his head and guffawed nastily at that. "Noble Welsh family? *Pfhaa!* No such thing! And his mother may have been some Welsh bitch with pretensions of grandeur, but his sire was pure Norman, I'd wager my best hound on that! *He* wasn't the one who thought his sins needed a squalling brat to provide repentance for,

I'll be bound – that'd be *her* family. Either her husband wasn't best pleased at his overlord warming his wife's bed before him, or the father had plans to marry her off to another of those By-Our-Lady heathen curs, and the man wasn't willing to take her with a whelp already at her heels. *Ha-ha-ha!*"

Tuck's height, even back then, had given him a clear view over the other novices' heads of the brothers all wincing at the lord's coarseness, and lack of tact at referring to one of their own kind as a 'heathen cur'. Everyone here knew that Christianity had lingered on in Wales after the Romans had gone; and that meanwhile England had slipped back into worshipping heathen gods for centuries, before blessed St Augustine had been sent direct from Rome five hundred years ago to reconvert them. For weren't there several sacred little churches around here that could date their foundation back to long before St Bede, of reverent memory, had written his history of Christianity? Those ancient monks had stood up to Augustine once he got as far as the border, that every novice also knew from the writing of the great Bede, needing no help back then from that earlier pompous abbot from across the sea any more than the local brothers did now, and they resented the slurs against them by Norman lords. But Tuck had also caught many of the brothers looking at him, then at the lord, and then back again, as if seeing something connecting them. Certainly enough that he had taken himself off to the priory fishponds to stare at his reflection in the calm waters, needing to see for himself what it could be.

And what he had seen on that day hadn't pleased him. Oh yes, there was something very similar about his boyish features to that pompous lord's. The colouring was there for a start off. That olive skin which stayed dark, even in dull, wet Welsh winters, and was unknown of locally, especially topped by a mop of dark tight curls, for Tuck had been too young back then to be tonsured, being only just on the cusp of becoming a novice. But there had been something else. The set of the jaw-line and the eyebrows too, and they made Tuck wonder whether he had just been given a horrible glimpse of his unknown father – for if not this man, then surely it had been one of his family who had done the deed, and by then Tuck was old enough to have heard of rape and what it meant.

"I'm *not* Norman, I'm not," he had hissed to his reflection. "I'm *Welsh*! Whoever you were, Father, I disown you. I'm of my mother's people! I'm *Cymry*!"

And now several years later, Tuck knew that that had been the day when he'd first felt as though he was neither fish nor fowl. He wouldn't be accepted out with the ordinary Welsh lads in the farms and fields, but he would never be welcomed into the aristocratic Norman world either. But somewhat worse, something in that mongrel blood which ran through his veins wouldn't let him become subservient, no matter how hard he tried, and Tuck had tried so very hard to be obedient and humble to no avail. At some point a strain of the wild Celt would rise up in him whenever he saw an injustice – please God it wasn't Norman arrogance, he often prayed – and at that point, even if he could manage to keep quiet, it was as if his thoughts were written all over his face.

Two nights later, Dafydd went on the run. It had been a night of gusting winds which rattled the priory's wooden window shutters and doors, creating enough of a racket that the sound of someone slipping out of the dormitory wouldn't be noticed. Not that Tuck thought Dafydd had lingered long enough to see if anyone had raised the alarm. He'd spotted that his friend had rolled something up and stuffed it under his blanket to give the form of a sleeping figure in the dim light, for the brothers only had one meagre candle in a lantern at the end of the dormitory to light their way down to Matins in the depths of the night. Stumbling down the steps to the church, all of them half asleep and chilled to the bone by the icy drafts whistling through the buildings, everyone had been too busy pulling their own robes tighter around them to look about, much less take notice of a bed back at the far end of the dormitory. The placing of Tuck and Dafydd up the farthest end from the door – because they hadn't been trusted not to creep out in the night and get up to mischief – became the very thing which allowed Dafydd's escape to go unnoticed. And even Tuck hadn't seen or heard him leave, being merely the only one to notice that he had gone by Matins.

Come the morning, Sub-prior Humbert was vicious in his condemnation of Tuck and the half dozen other brothers who slept at the far end, yet all of them could swear on the Holy Bible that they had seen and heard nothing. And for that Tuck was grateful. His friend had no doubt gone as soon as everyone was asleep after Compline, and it had only been when he'd officially been missed at Lauds, some nine hours later as it fell at this time of year, that the alarm had been raised.

By now, Dafydd was hopefully far away from here, since all he'd had to do was keep the sunrise at his back all the way, and he would be deep within the Welsh princes' territories soon enough, even if it wasn't necessarily the specific prince he hoped to serve. Yet Eustace and Humbert had found the metaphorical stick they had long been looking for to beat Tuck with. He must have known, they told Prior Augustine over and over again. He was lying, they said. And yet Augustine had looked into Tuck's eyes as he had placed his hand reverently on the great jewel-covered Bible, which was kept chained to its lectern up by the high altar, and knew that Tuck was telling the truth when he said that he had not known when Dafydd had left. What Augustine was less sure of was whether Tuck had know that Dafydd had had such a thing in mind, for Tuck would not openly lie, but had been very careful to say only that he had known that Dafydd had been desperately unhappy.

When the abrasive Humbert and Eustace had eventually been dismissed from Augustine's office after the umpteenth attempt to get Tuck punished harshly, he regarded Tuck with dismay.

"What am I going to do with you, Tuck?" he asked. "Your faith isn't in doubt. Indeed I suspect that you have more devotion to God than many of the senior monks here. But you do not fit into the monastic life. That has become very clear over these past few years, and it's not getting any better as you grow older – in fact, I think you are getting worse!

"This life doesn't provide enough of a challenge for you. Having come here as a child, you have no memories of the temptations which life beyond the cloister might bring for you. So unlike Brother Ignatius, for instance, you have no longings of the flesh to torment you, and which you can set yourself to overcome. And may God forgive me for saying so, but Brother Eustace is far from the scholar Brother Rhys was, and he knows you can run rings around him at every point when it comes to learning. Nor does he like the fact that the youngest novices remember your lessons more than his – even if it's merely because you're actually repeating Brother Rhys' lessons rather than your own. The only thing you are useless at is illuminating manuscripts, and we don't have enough valuable parchment for me to be setting you to spoiling sheet after sheet just to be able to improve!

"So what to do with you, eh? …Do you think you could manage outside in the world? Could you bring yourself to talk with ordinary people who do not have your learning? Because I am inclined to send you away from here for everyone's sake, including yours. Eustace and Humbert will never settle while you are here – they've made that clear by their actions if not their words over this incident – and they fear you incite rebellion into the novices. I don't think that's true, necessarily, but your restless spirit is certainly a distraction.

"Therefore I have a mind to send you to help Brother Cadfan who looks after our church at Llanbedr, just below St Issui's at Patricio, up in the mountains." Augustine shook his head wearily. "No Norman-born monk wants to go there – not stuck up in that tiny valley with only the local Welsh for company. They feel too threatened." Here Tuck felt the prior might well have been silently including himself, for Augustine never ventured into the valleys either. "So I have no choice but to have Cadfan up there, who is another of mixed breeding like yourself. And have someone we must, for there are pilgrims a plenty who wish to go to St Issui's, even if they are not highborn folk.

"Jesu, help me, but I'm not sure if even the Pope himself knows who this saintly Welshman is, so none of my own kin have any reverence for him, much less wish to tend his shrine which only gets visited by the Welsh. But it's lucrative, that I cannot argue with, and with that much coming in in the way of offerings, if we don't tend to the shrine, the Welsh bishops will be staking their claim to the place in a heartbeat. And the loss of that money my superiors will not tolerate. But Cadfan is also getting old now, for he's been there for many years and from long before my time here, or my predecessor's, and so I've a mind to give him a vigorous young helper.

"So will you go, Tuck? Will you go up into the Black Mountains and do your best for the pilgrims who come to visit this local saint? Promise you will not desert your post? If you can't promise me this, I cannot send you, for I will not have another brother vanishing off into the Welsh mist, whose absence I have to account for to the mother church in Normandy! If you force my hand in this, I will have you confined to a cell."

But already Tuck was shaking his head at the same time as a huge grin had spread across his face. Cadfan! Brother Rhys' old friend, and as good a monk as ever drew breath, and even better, a monk who had a love for the ordinary people. Oh yes, Tuck could feel a great bubble of joy welling up inside of him at the prospect of leaving the empty observances behind and joining Cadfan in doing some real good. He'd take the tiny, homely church, and ploughing the fields with the locals, over this prestigious abbey any day. And so he didn't have to force himself to answer, "No, Prior! You need have no fear of me running off into the mountains. This is what I've been praying for for months! The chance to be *useful*. The chance to help people. St Issui calls to me in my soul!" and he did, and would continue to do so for Tuck for the rest of his life.

Chapter 2

Wales & the Marches, Early Spring, the Year of Our Lord 1177

Two years on from his arrival at Llanbedr, Tuck had found his place, he believed, and a mentor in Brother Cadfan. This was where he felt needed, and he revelled in helping the people of this mountain parish in more than just spiritual guidance. He was then made a full priest, taking over from the now frail Cadfan as the main officiate for the small local flock of parishioners, plus also helping out up the road at St Issui's with the many pilgrims who came to the shrine. Not that Tuck was under any illusions as to why he had been so promoted – it was out of necessity and nothing more, and it would never have happened if he'd stayed at the abbey, of that he was certain. A mongrel brother, and of such youth, would never take an office at Ewenny these days.

Indeed his trip back down to Abergavenny to see the bishop for his ordination was hardly the stuff to bolster a lad's ego. As he'd stood outside the prior's door, waiting to be called in to see the bishop, he'd heard the two men talking.

"I hear Archdeacon Gerald of Brecknock has been stirring the pot again," he heard Prior Augustine say, and the bishop reply,

"The man's trouble! And now he's being nominated for bishop of St David's – there'll be no stopping him if he gets the post. Some say he's even mooted St David's becoming a third archdiocese! He pushes his luck with King Henry at every turn."

"Indeed, but isn't that the Welsh all over? All this nonsense about making St David's a third archdiocese, *tsk*, ridiculous! As if we don't have enough trouble finding priests to send out into that God-forsaken land. And their own monks have no respect for the Norman mother churches, that they make very clear in their attitudes, even if they know better than to say much."

"*Hmm*, speaking of that, have you a candidate for me for the vacancy, Augustine? Or are we reduced to having another Welsh hedge-priest?"

And Tuck had heard his prior heave a sigh. "Well he wouldn't be my first choice, Bishop, I'll grant you that. Not even close. But when it comes to the candidates you or I would have by choice, I've three sons of wealthy families here who would be far from pleased if I shoved them out into the wilds. One at least may yet have to return to his family if his elder brother does not recover from his wounds. And these families have been most devout in their donations, if you understand me. Neither of us would want those particular wells to run dry."

"Oh indeed not. Normandy can be a demanding master, can it not?"

"Very demanding, my lord bishop, very! Especially when it comes to the weight of the purses going back there." He sighed. "And as for the other possibilities, one is a nervous brother who would probably expire the first time he saw a Welsh raid going past, and another is distinctly frail. The brother I have in mind has the constitution of an ox, and nobody who's going to raise a commotion if the Welsh princes cut his head off. I believe it would be in all our interests if you could see your way to ordaining him."

And so when Tuck had walked in and heard the bishop murmur, "A veritable St Luke," he knew he was being insulted by the ox reference, and that neither the bishop nor his prior thought him learned enough to get the reference.

Knowing that he was so disposable had cut him to the quick more than he had expected it to, and he was glad to get away from the monastery and all its politics back to the more earthly world of the wet Welsh hillsides. Cadfan still lived, just, and so now Tuck had a free rein with what he said and did at the church for the most part. And because of that, Tuck had found a new zest for life in passing on the learning he had gained in the monastery, especially in translating the Latin into Welsh so that the ordinary people knew what was being said.

"You're a born teacher," Cadfan said to him one day, having sat and watched Tuck telling a group of children the story of Daniel in the lions' den. "What a pity you're so wasted up here with me. You should be down teaching the novices in the monastery, passing on all that love of learning you have."

Tuck, however, had shaken his head. "No, Brother, not wasted at all. These village children have a thirst for knowledge that most of the young novices do not. Don't forget that these days, most of the young boys we have come in are not like I was. They're the third or fourth sons of noblemen, brought up alongside their older siblings until their parents were sure they wouldn't need one of the spare heirs. So they're more used to the tilting yard than the scriptorium, and many of them openly resent that they've been forced into what they see as a life of going without all those things they were brought up to regard as necessities, not merely luxuries.

"The only value they see in reading and writing is that they can now understand the manorial accounts for themselves, instead of having to rely on a 'lesser' brother like me to read them out to them. They have no desire to learn more. The beauty of the language of the Bible would totally pass them by, even if they could master it sufficiently to understand the subtleties. No, I'd sooner give these poor children the joy of it. At least they come from homes where a bard is still valued, and being able to go home and tell their parents a new story is something they'll be praised for."

Cadfan shook his white-haired head as he gratefully accepted the soup Tuck brought to him, and then helped steady his palsied hands so that he could eat. "Oh Tuck, I do worry about what will become of you once I'm gone. You must promise me to tread carefully. If you don't, then sooner or later the prior will hear of what you are doing here, and then you'll be in so much trouble."

And now, a year further on again, that trouble had arrived. Cadfan had died in the winter, but that hadn't been a problem as far as Tuck had seen, for all that he mourned the loss of his elderly friend and mentor. He'd sung masses for Cadfan's soul all by himself in the tiny single cell church by the river, but with great love and fervour, and then he'd just carried on. What he hadn't bargained for was some lord going to the prior claiming that there was a rebel priest up at Llanbedr who was teaching the peasants the Bible in Welsh. Scandalous! What was the world coming to?

Had Augustine still been prior, even so that might have been the end of it, and Tuck would have merely been given a severe warning. But Augustine had been carried off in the winter by the same hacking cough which had done for Cadfan, Tuck now discovered, and horror of horrors, his old nemesis Humbert was currently acting as full prior until the new man arrived from Normandy. And to the abrasive Humbert, Tuck landing in his grasp had seemed like a gift from God himself – one which was to be relished in every detail.

So Tuck had been summoned back to Abergavenny by the brother sent to replace him – although how long that one would last was debatable since he hardly knew a word of Welsh – and he was currently standing in the prior's private room while Humbert vented his spleen.

"You're a disgrace, Tuck!" Humbert fumed, so agitated that he was even starting to froth at the mouth. "Teaching Welshies what the Bible actually says? Have you gone mad? The word of God isn't for the likes of them! It's for us to know, and them to accept what we choose to tell them! We can't have *them* knowing enough to question *us*! Where would that end?"

Privately Tuck was thinking that Humbert's attitude was precisely why the locals *should* know what the Bible said. This pompous Norman lord's son would have no conscience about distorting the Bible's words if he thought it would get him what he wanted, that Tuck was sure. And Humbert's certainty that he would always be in the right in any confrontation with someone poorer than him, was just an invitation to spiritual disaster in Tuck's mind. As a result of that, he was far from repentant for his supposed sins – for in his own mind he was sure that God was not of the same closed mind as the likes of Humbert – and the only thing he was vaguely bothered about was what was going to happen to himself, as he now knew beyond a shadow of a doubt that he could not come back to within the stifling walls of this priory. And as if reading his mind, Humbert next said,

"I was going to keep you cloistered here for a while. Some discipline would do you good, I feel! But then Brother Eustace pointed out that you might do irreparable harm to the younger brothers."

*Humph! Tuck thought. More likely that Eustace is worried what I might do if I find that my suspicions about his perversions are all too true! Because I bet he knows that I'd shove that cane of his where the sun doesn't shine if I found him at one of the younger novices! ...Oh Lord, forgive me that thought here on your sacred soil! But I would do it if it would save some poor lad from a sore arse, and I hope you would think **that** a sufficiently wicked act to forgive me my violence?*

"And then God intervened," Humbert was droning on sanctimoniously. "My lord Cadwallon of Elfael wishes his younger son to go on pilgrimage – something to do with not wanting his two sons to fight one another to the death before one of them has the chance to succeed him, I believe. And because of this, he feels that his younger son will be kept more on the path of righteousness if he has a religious companion. Personally, having seen young Lord Hywel, I think that is more than a little optimistic, but Lord Cadwallon is advancing in years and I cannot blame him for wanting a little peace in his old age.

"I have to say that I was struggling to pick one of our number, for few of our brothers would cope with what I've been told of what I might call some of Lord Hywel's men's more ...*ah-hem* ...earthly appetites! But you, Tuck? I think there is very little left in you to corrupt. So you will present yourself at the gatehouse three weeks from now, suitably attired for a long journey, and be prepared to attach yourself to Lord Hywel's retinue when they pass us."

Humbert leaned back in the leather chair, folding his pudgy white hands over his paunch, a smirk on his jowly face. "*If*, by some miracle, you come back in one piece, well, we shall have to review the situation. But don't you dare think that you can just wander off for a few weeks and then ingratiate your way back in here! I'm wise to your sly ways!"

That baffled and worried Tuck, for he had automatically assumed that any Welsh prince would want to visit the shrine of St David – the Welsh's beloved *Dewi Sant* – and that wouldn't take more than a few weeks even if the weather turned particularly foul. So where was Lord Hywel off to, then? It had to be Canterbury, and Tuck found his pulse quickening in anticipation of seeing far off places, as he thought of them, even as he stomach did a little lurch of worry at the thought of going so far from the world he knew. For a young man who had never travelled more than twenty miles from the place of his birth, going all the way across England held the exciting promise of adventure, and yet felt more than a little daunting at the same time. A trip to Brecon to pay the rents of the villagers to their lord, de Braose, had so far felt like the biggest adventure a young monk like him might expect, but this seemed like it might cap that and more.

He was even more surprised when he presented himself to the gatekeeper in the early hours of a chilly May morning, and saw who he was to be travelling with. From Humbert's words, Tuck had assumed that he would probably be one of a group of half-a-dozen to a dozen men – for surely Lord Cadwallon wouldn't send his precious son into enemy English territory without a decent escort? But what began streaming past the monastery was a vast cavalcade of noblemen and their retinues, and soldiers – so many soldiers!

Swallowing hard, Tuck watched them go past and wondered in a sudden bout of panic what on earth he was doing here? Like every other normal young man of his age, Tuck had been enthralled when stories of fighting in the Holy Land had reached the village, but he'd never thought for a heartbeat that he might associate with such fighters, much less have to travel with them. Old Martin, who'd come to live with his sister and her husband at the hill-farm by St Issui's had often come to keep Cadfan company in his last year, regaling them with what Tuck had assumed were tall tales of fighting in Normandy. But looking at these tough men, with their scuffed and battered gambesons, and dented, pot-like helmets, had the look of men who could do all that

Martin had described and more. *Lord, let me keep body and soul together for long enough to return home,* Tuck silently prayed as another wobble of nerves set in.

Towards the end, a burly sergeant detached himself from the column and trotted up to where Tuck stood, still aghast at the size of the party.

"You the brother who's coming with us?" he demanded without preamble.

The gatekeeper gave Tuck a little shove. "This is him," he replied for Tuck, and turned on his heels to close the gate firmly behind him, leaving Tuck standing in the mist.

"Come on, then," the sergeant said, but not unkindly. "I hope you can keep up, Brother, because we don't have a horse for the likes of you."

Pulling himself together, Tuck shouldered his small pack and fell into step with the sergeant. "No, I shall have no trouble keeping up," he assured the man. "I've been up in the hills near St Issui's shrine for the last three years, and I've had to work our own fields – what there were of them. The folk up there didn't have men to spare to look after an idle brother and another old one. Don't you worry, I'm not one who's spent his years sitting at the desk in the scriptorium. …I'm Brother Tuck, by the way."

The sergeant, who had instantly taken a liking to this huge young brother with the pleasant if slightly nervous smile, gave him a smile back. "Unusual name …Tuck. Where does that come from? I'm Rhodri, by the way. Sergeant to Lord Cadwallon, and for my sins, the leader of those men-at-arms we'll be carrying on with on the pilgrimage."

"My name? Oh, erm, yes …it's an oddity, isn't it? Old Brother Rhys, who taught me as a boy, thought it might be a shortening of Caradoc. I was only a toddler when I was brought to the brothers, you see, and he thought that maybe in my stumbling speech the shortened 'Doc' got twisted into 'Tock', which others then heard as Tuck. It's about the only halfway sensible explanation I've ever been given, but I've been called Tuck for as long as I can remember."

"Caradoc?" Rhodri mused. "That's more of a lord's name, isn't it?"

Tuck gave him a rueful grin, already feeling rather relieved that this Rhodri was more like the older farmers of the valleys in his mannerisms than some bloody butcher. "Much good it's ever done me. Again, I was told that I was the result of the rape of some fine lady, and her family wouldn't have me around, so maybe it was a family name? I honestly don't know."

Rhodri instantly felt rather sorry for Tuck, remembering his own happy boyhood in the rough and tumble of the extended family who still worked their hill farm. It had never sat easy with him, this thing of the nobility being able to 'pay off' their sins by dumping some poor little sod into the uncaring hands of a bunch of celibates – for while some, no doubt, were as good as they ought to be, Rhodri was enough of a man of the world to know from his years of soldiering that men had appetites, and it was one thing to abstain voluntarily, and quite another to have abstinence forced upon you, and what could happen then. He'd also been quietly fearing they might end up with some timid brother who would be looking back to the safety of the monastery for the entire trip, but the way Tuck was swinging along beside him without a single backwards glance, made Rhodri suspect that there wasn't much back at the priory that Tuck would miss. This was a man gratefully escaping a wearisome confinement, or his name wasn't Rhodri ap Thomas.

And Tuck now had questions too. "Are all of these people going on pilgrimage?" he asked Rhodri in awed tones.

"Lord bless you, no! Have you not heard? King Henry has summoned the Welsh princes and their men to Oxford for a great council. He means to make them swear fealty, and for once the princes are probably going to obey him. He's a fearsome man, this Norman king of ours, and I think all of our nobles and princes are thinking that if they don't do this, then there's a real chance of him summoning fighting men from Normandy as well as England, and picking them off one by one. He had his work cut out early on in his reign just sorting out his own territories, but he's secure enough now that he can turn his gaze our way.

"So from what I heard, when my lord Cadwallon went to visit his brother, Lord Hywel – lord of Gwrtheyrnion, and after whom our young lord is named – and then on to the brothers Lords Iorweth and Owain, of Gwynllŵg and Brychan, they all agreed that as their lands sit closest to the English border, and would therefore be the first to be overrun, that they would have to tread very carefully! If Lord Rhys of Deheubarth took it into his head to give King Henry the archer's salute, well then *he's* got more places to run and hide in out in the western wilds. But with Lord Rhys also being Iorweth and Owain's liege lord, he could equally summon them to fight by his side, and yet use them and theirs as a buffer for his other cantrefs. …And that's even before we get into the complications of what Lord Owain Cyfeiliog of Southern

Powys might get us embroiled in! He's too bloody close to our northern borders to be ignored, as well!

"So we were all holding our breath for a while, but it seems that by some miracle – and I do not blaspheme by that, Tuck, I mean it – even the warlike lords of northern Wales have decided that discretion is the better part of valour for now. Therefore we all journey to this great council at Oxford, and pray that the gifts that have been brought along for this troublesome Norman king will appease him. Do you know, we've heard he can get into such rages that he gnaws at his robes, and even at the precious carpets from the east which adorn his chambers? *Duw!* That's some temper!"

Far from being alarmed at all this, the wheels within Tuck's considerable mind were now whirling furiously. Particularly once he'd been out of the monastery, he'd heard a lot more of the world from the visiting pilgrims, some of whom had been quite highly born, and so he was far from a total innocent in the matter of politics. "You do know that it's called Normandy because it was settled by the Norsemen at the same time that they plagued our shores, don't you? Well there are some old accounts in the priory's library, and they talk of the wild Norsemen flying into such rages. Berserkers they called them, when the red mist came upon them like that in battle. I'm thinking that maybe that northern blood runs strong in King Henry's veins."

Rhodri turned to look at Tuck in amazement. "Really? Now there's a thing! I didn't know that about Normandy. But you're right, it does explain a lot."

But Tuck hadn't finished yet. "And is Lord Cadwallon just sending his son on pilgrimage to keep him from fighting his brother? That was what my prior was told."

Rhodri looked a little puzzled. "Well, yes... But there's not that much bad blood between Maelgwn, Lord Cadwallon's older son, and Lord Hywel. Why?"

"Hmmm... given all that you've just told me, don't you think it's more likely that Lord Cadwallon is playing this even more craftily than you all thought?"

"Go on." Rhodri was puzzled. What had this sharp young priest spotted that he hadn't?

"Well even up in my secluded little valley, I heard the news two years ago that Sheriff de Braose had gone on the rampage and murdered Seisyll ap Dyfnwal, and then massacred his household too. I had a lot of terrified parishioners coming to me in those days, because we all know that de Braose's acting as the king's dog of war, don't we? No way would that have been sanctioned if any English tenants had been involved. De Braose was set on Seisyll, and his own punishment little more than a wrist slapping as a token gesture.

"Now ten years before that – back when I was in the monastery and word got brought to us – we heard of how it was the *king* in person who came and took Welsh prisoners, blinding even the boys he took as some perverse gesture to show just what he could do with impunity. But in between those two events – indeed exactly five years either way by my reckoning – the king fell afoul of the pope for the murder of Archbishop Becket, didn't he? So it's not hard to think that the king at the moment is considering his immortal soul, and letting his lords do his dirty work for him."

"I'm not sure where you're going with this," Rhodri said, "but go on."

Tuck wagged a knowing finger. "Ah, but it all ties in! King Henry's making peace not war, and a very particular kind of peace with people he's not hesitated to treat with breathtaking brutality in the past. Part of it might be that at the priory we heard that his sons are now fighting amongst themselves over in Normandy and Aquitaine, spurred on no doubt by Queen Eleanor. So the king's hardly got an army to spare as Lord Cadwallon may fear – and you might want to pass on that thought to him if you have his ear.

"But that may also mean that our Welsh prince may justifiably be fearing what hostages the king might demand as the price for this peace, and what may well befall them in the king's un-tender care…"

"…God's hooks!"

"…Indeed! Yet given that the king undoubtedly knows that the Welsh princes, even so, might put up a considerable fight if he rounds up all their *direct* heirs – because I doubt he's forgotten about what he did in 1165 with the previous hostages, any more than the princes have – and that he can't afford to get into a direct fight with them just at the moment, who do you think is in more danger of getting taken to his great White Tower in London, eh?"

"*Dewi Sant!* The younger sons!"

"You begin to see it now, don't you! But what's the one situation where the king might actually hesitate to act? …Something which connects a son directly to not just the Church, but to the protection demanded by the very Pope himself – a pilgrim! Even a Welsh lord ought to be safe when he's visiting the shrine of the very bishop who brought the king to his knees, quite literally, in a massively public display of humility and penance only seven years ago. Lord Cadwallon isn't sending young Lord Hywel away because of some daft spat between brothers. He's very cunningly saving his youngest son's life, and making sure that he'll have at least one heir left at the end of it if King Henry turns treacherous again!"

Rhodri stopped in his tracks to stare at Tuck in amazement, forcing the men behind him to grumble as they had to stumble out of his way. "Tuck, that's …that's …Bless me, he *is* playing it clever, isn't he? And clever you for working all that out. You're going to be quite the asset, I can see."

Tuck smiled wanly. "Yes, well don't go spreading that around, because I reckon Lord Cadwallon's put out this rubbish about the brothers' fighting so that he doesn't seem to be outmanoeuvring the king. It's not going to work so well, though, if the rest of all the younger Welsh princes suddenly take the Cross or head for Canterbury, will it? So he won't love you if his crafty plan goes down the guarderobe because of you."

And Cadwallon's gone and ensnared me in his scheme, too, Tuck thought bitterly. *Oh yes, very clever to ask the most prestigious monastery in the area for a companion, so that if King Henry questions whether young Hywel is a genuine pilgrim, Lord Cadwallon can say hand on heart, 'ask the Prior of Ewenny.' …Blessed St Issui, I hope you're looking out for your faithful servant, because before this is over, I have a nasty feeling I'm going to need a spot of divine intervention!*

Chapter 3

England,
Spring, the Year of Our Lord, 1177

At Oxford, Tuck's predictions seemed to be coming true. Even though the king did nothing while the Welsh princes were arriving, as ever, word spread from servant to servant of the king's intention to take hostages. In the case of Tuck's companions, the word came via a handsome lad whom Rhodri sent to chat up a serving lass who had to be the sister of one of Lord Mortimer's guard, going by the unmistakable family resemblance between them – and the Mortimers, being another of King Henry's Marcher guard-dogs, were in the know!

"*Duw*, Tuck, you were right!" Rhodri said to him, having drawn him off to a quiet area by the horses so that they could speak freely. "I told Lord Cadwallon what young Idris learned, and without batting an eyelid, he tells me to get you all ready to leave in the morning. He's not hanging about until King Henry openly declares his intentions, he's getting Hywel out of here while the going's still good."

"So we make for Canterbury?" Tuck was thinking that it was a good thing he'd be accompanying some tough soldiers if they were going into the metaphorical lion's den. Harm could come to a young Welsh monk if alone on such a journey!

Rhodri gave him a measuring stare. "I'm going to trust you with the truth, because you've played fair with me so far, but if you betray me by telling anyone else of this, I won't be quick to forgive you, understand?"

"Absolutely."

Rhodri took a deep breath, but then spoke so softly Tuck could barely hear him. "Yes, we are going to Canterbury, but only until we know how the king is going to act. If he takes a mere handful of hostages, Hywel will be allowed to come home after a visit to St David's as well. But if the king does as Cadwallon has just told me he fears, and takes as many hostages as he can, then we're to carry on."

"Carry on? To where?"

"The Holy Land."

"The Ho…!" Tuck just muffled his exclamation with his hand in time. He gulped hard, then managed to ask in hushed tones, "You mean all the way to *Jerusalem*?" His insides were doing somersaults and back flips in a weird combination of terror and excitement.

Rhodri gave a thin smile. "Yes, all the way. I know I ought to feel grateful for the opportunity, but I have a wife and children who think I'll be back in a couple of months. I don't know how they're going to cope without me."

"I will pray for them," Tuck replied earnestly, and with such sincere belief, that Rhodri didn't have the heart to tell him that he thought that they would need rather more in the way of earthly help.

In contrast, Tuck himself couldn't believe that this opportunity had just fallen into his lap. The Holy Land! The most sacred place on earth, and somewhere he had only dared to dream he might deserve to go to much later on in life, when he had proven his worth to God. And yet here he was, barely into his twenties and to all intents and purposes, fresh out of his monastery, with the journey of a lifetime laid out before him, and not even having to worry about how he would get there and back. Those sorts of practicalities had been taken care of with the funds Lord Cadwallon had made available, Rhodri had told him when Tuck had finally managed to pull himself together enough to ask.

Lord, I will do my utmost to deserve this bounty you have laid before me, Tuck prayed later on that night as he lay still shivering with nerves of both kinds. *Dare I believe that this is a sign that you approve of me teaching the children in the valley, despite Humbert's bigoted words? If I've read your gift wrong, then I humbly apologise and ask you to send me a sign showing me the right path instead.* Yet far from any dreams of him being struck down, instead he dreamt most vividly of an older version of himself, seemingly standing before someone who looked suspiciously like a senior churchman, and vehemently chastising that man while just behind him, and out of his sight, an angel appeared to be hovering at his shoulder. Men clad in hoods, and with long Welsh bows slung across their shoulders, stood beside him, and somehow in that dream Tuck knew that they were his friends, and that it was because of what they had found that he was so incensed with the churchman lying in bed, and clutching his blankets fearfully. They, and not the churchman, were doing God's work, and the angel approved.

Only hours later, and with the sky in the east barely showing the first hint of light, Tuck found himself taking the road to London from Oxford with Rhodri and Lord Hywel, plus a dozen well-armed foot-soldiers. It took them the best part of ten days to get to Canterbury, for Rhodri was insistent that they avoid London itself, even though young

Lord Hywel clearly wanted to go and see one of the greatest cities in Europe for himself.

"No, my lord," Rhodri had told his young lord firmly, "your father was most specific on the matter – we must not set foot within London. Who knows what spies there might be about the place? Or what instructions the king may have left behind when he departed? We could find ourselves very swiftly being chained up in the White Tower, only beating your cousins' arrival there by the speed of our incarceration." And with that Hywel had had to be content.

Yet even Hywel stood in open-mouthed awe when they reached Canterbury and came up to the great cathedral.

"Look at the size of it!" he gasped, looking up at the huge west front, and indeed it was a sight none of them had ever imagined. Even now there were signs of stonemasons still beavering away at the place, though none of them could imagine what could possibly be left to do. And they were far from being the only pilgrims. The whole area around the cathedral seemed set up to cater to the veritable horde of faithful who had come to visit the blessed St Thomas' shrine.

Yet that was the very thing which stopped Tuck from being overwhelmed. He had expected to feel very much the poor cousin, humbled and overawed by the sanctity of the place. Yet here there was no altruistic concern for the poor and needy, who had probably walked all the way from their homes, but instead there was a very efficient business set up to fleece them of as much as could be had, and that rankled with Tuck. Where was the humility? Where the gratitude for having the chance to serve the most holy martyred archbishop?

All the old feelings he'd had to keep bottled up during the years at the priory came bubbling back up again, and with a silent sigh he felt that rebellious streak in him coming to the fore once more. So when he saw a frail old man being brutally shoved aside by one of the lay brothers to make way for a nobleman and his retinue, his Welsh blood truly began to boil. Grubby and stinking, the old man was in a pathetic state Tuck had never known anyone in the valleys get into, and that tore at his kind heart. In the close communities of home, somebody would have found this poor soul a place to stay, even if it was only in the barn. He would have been somebody's poor relative, even if they had to go back three generations to find the link, for what Welshman could not recite his lineage? And yet the farther from Wales they had got, the more verbal abuse and prejudice they had encountered. That made this the last straw for Tuck. How dare they look down on him and his when they could treat their own with such disregard?

"For the love of God, take this before I hit someone with it!" he begged, shoving his walking staff into Rhodri's hands for fear of what he might yet do. Then announced, "Follow me!" as he marched forward, scooping up the old man with one strong arm as he passed him.

At the great west door, he hardly paused before stomping up to the brother in charge and letting rip a string of very fluent Latin. He was being very polite, remembering Brother Rhys' lessons on treating strangers, yet what he wasn't expecting was for his words to not be understood. As the brother blinked disinterestedly, then found himself looking up into Tuck's flashing eyes and suddenly gulped, Tuck tried again with politeness that despite his best efforts was getting distinctly icy.

"Oh excuse me, brother. I assumed you would understand me. Let me put that into English for you. I am Brother Tuck, come from Ewenny Priory with the prior's *explicit* instruction to make *sure* that young Lord Hywel, here, gets to pray at the blessed shrine. May we enter?"

The brother took another look at Tuck towering over him and gulped convulsively. "You are a Black Monk?" he asked timorously.

Tuck snorted in exasperation, but the effect was rather more of a massive bull about to charge. He was just about hanging on to the tatters of his patience, but youth and passion weren't doing much to help that. "Of course I'm a Black Monk! Just because we're on the other side of the country doesn't make us a bunch of hedge-priests! We answer to St Vincent Abbey at Le Mans in Normandy, and we follow the rule of St Benedict just as you do."

That seemed to satisfy the brother and they were waved through the portal, but once inside they were aghast to see a scene of total devastation. Clearly there had been a fire and a massive one at that, for while the nave was only badly singed, the area beyond the crossing with its two transepts was just a vast building site.

"*Duw!*" Tuck gasped in shock. "I'd heard that they had a fire here three years ago, but I had no idea it was this disastrous!"

"It was a terrible thing, Brother," a different voice came from behind them, and an older and more welcoming monk came to join them. "The flames were twenty feet high! The whole roof came down over our choir stalls and it was weeks before it was cool enough for us to start clearing up. We started rebuilding the choir-stalls in September two years ago. As you can see, we've got eight columns up already and hope to have two more complete by the end of this year, but I fear it will be many years before we have a suitable home for our beloved saint."

Belatedly Tuck realised he was still hanging on to the elderly man, who was staring up at him as though one of God's archangels had just taken human form, and was about to start smiting the ungodly surrounding him. Handing the old man over to one of the soldiers, he turned his full attention to the local brother.

"So please tell me, Brother, where do we go to to pray to St Thomas in the meantime? Please God you got his remains out in time?"

"God be praised, yes we did," the other monk replied, "but several of our brothers got severely burned in the process of saving him and our other precious relics. As for where you can go, there are still the remains of the ambulatory and you can get to the crypt that way. But be careful, Brother! We have had several accidents already with the wooden scaffolding giving way. There's a lot of heavy stone being hauled about the place, so if the masons call to you to wait, you'd best obey them or risk getting squashed when the ropes give way."

"We'll take care," Tuck assured him and gestured Lord Hywel to come forward. "Come, my lord. Let us go and find the blessed martyr himself," and with the confidence of a man returned into his natural habitat, Tuck set off across the heat-crazed terracotta floor tiles, weaving a serpentine course which took them around the worst of the construction work, towards the square east end.

As they picked their way around the huge blocks of stone in Tuck's wake, Rhodri's friend chuckled and said to him,

"Quite the force of nature is our young brother! Did you see the expression on the face of that brother at the door? I don't think he understood one word in ten that Tuck said to him in Latin, but if he didn't have to make a rapid call to the privies afterwards, my name isn't Sulien. I don't think Tuck realises the effect he has on people when he's in this mood."

Rhodri was also smothering a grin. "And that's the first time young lord Hywel's done as he's told without arguing, as well. You know, I think if we need to get our lord shifting in a hurry, we could do worse then let Tuck loose on him. I'll admit I groaned when Lord Cadwallon said we had to have a priest with us, but Tuck's nothing like I imagined one would be."

And Tuck continued to surprise them when they got down into the confined space of the crypt. Candles flickered in holders to light the space, but it was still dim down there. Yet as if by instinct Tuck made for one spot and went down on his knees, dragging Hywel down with him. And far from making some muttered obeisance, he began praying out loud in clear ringing tones which seemed to reverberate off the walls and fill the crypt, until it almost seemed as if a whole choir of monks was down there with them. Yet what astonished all of the party even more, was the way that Tuck said his prayers in Latin, and then immediately repeated what he'd said in Welsh for their benefit, and then in English to the old man, who Tuck had drawn forward to kneel with him at the tomb.

It was only as Tuck rose and helped the old man and Lord Hywel to their feet, and said, "Come, we mustn't hog the space at this sacred spot, others are waiting to come in," that they all realised that there was a press of people behind them. What was more, although there weren't a huge number of them, they had all squeezed in closely to hear Tuck praying, and were now looking at him in awe as he led the way back out into the cramped passageway.

Purely out of instinct at seeing so many of the ragged poor, Tuck fell back into what he would have done with his old parishioners, placing a comforting hand on each shoulder as he passed them and saying, "Bless you, brother," or, "Bless you, sister," as required. Yet the effect on those he touched was positively electric, each one suddenly standing that little bit straighter, and with a smile coming on their faces. This was no ego on his part wanting their adulation, he was just reverting to his caring role that he'd only left a few weeks ago, not giving a moment's thought to how it might be misconstrued. That was until he got past the last of them and found himself confronted by a furious monk.

"Who are you? And what do you mean by such …such *preaching* in our crypt?" the brother spluttered angrily.

Tuck blinked owlishly, momentarily still so caught up in the wonder of what he'd felt in the crypt. "Preach? I preached nothing. All I did was say the usual prayers."

"No you didn't!" the monk snarled with a stamp of his sandaled foot. "I heard you! That wasn't just Latin you were speaking. You spoke in English! And in some devilish other tongue too!"

Now Tuck's hackles were rising too. "Devilish? That was Welsh! *Duw*, there's nothing devilish about that! And if you'd paid a bit more attention to your studies, you would surely have known that all I did was say the words of the Latin prayers in English so that others might understand them too. Is that not what are meant to do? Tend to the spiritual needs of others?"

The monk's jaw dropped, but not in awe at Tuck's learning. "Understand?" he echoed in dismay. "You fool! You don't just hand out the mysteries to the common herd! That's casting pearls before swine! What kind of Godforsaken country do you come from, that you would think such a thing acceptable?"

"If there's a land forsaken by God, then I don't think it's Wales," Tuck bit back, glad to see that Rhodri had already ushered all of the others out past the monk. "But don't worry, *Brother*, we're leaving. You can go back to hoarding God's bounty, and fleecing the true believers who come here, without worrying whether I'll tell anyone about your profiteering. …Not because I wouldn't, mind, but because I suspect that those above you already know and must approve, though I expected better of Archbishop Richard, given that he was a companion of St Thomas before he died."

The monk again spluttered furiously at Tuck's chastisement, but could only throw at him after Tuck had shouldered him out of the way, "If my lord Richard were here I'd have you dragged before him, you reprobate!"

Striding across the nave to catch up with the rest of his party, Tuck's initial distress at being so confronted and misunderstood gradually calmed down enough to wonder about that last statement. He'd heard that although Richard of Dover had been the one to save Thomas Becket's body, that there'd also been contention over him succeeding his friend, and that the monks had wanted their prior Odo instead. Now he wondered, was that because Odo knew what schemes and tricks were already going on here, maybe even being an instigator? Canterbury had been a major pilgrimage site because of its multiple relics even before Becket's death, which no doubt explained why the brothers had been so well set up to exploit the influx of new worshippers. But in the inn last night, Tuck had heard that Archbishop Richard was being kept busy by the king, running hither and thither on things like diplomatic missions. So maybe that was because *King Henry* was being crafty again, and not giving the archbishop enough time back in his own see to upset the apple cart with his monks?

Tuck shook himself. *Not your fight*, he told himself sternly. *You're already going to have to pray for forgiveness for speaking to those monks that way. Stop being an idiot and biting off more than you can chew.* God, or at least St Thomas, would have to deal with something this big. His job was now to get young Lord Hywel to Jerusalem and back, for at the inn word had also caught them up that King Henry had heavy-handedly scooped up many hostages, just as feared.

Yet outside he noticed that the men around him were now looking at him slightly differently.

"Is that why you're in your prior's bad books?" Rhodri asked him, as they walked back to their lodgings. "You told people what the words actually meant?"

Tuck gave a huge sigh. "I'm afraid so. I don't understand it, Rhodri, truly I don't. What is so wrong with that? Didn't Christ himself preach to the poor? Didn't he heal them? To me this withholding of grace is all about earthly power, not God's. We monks get to hear the word of God directly from the Bible, yet when I meet brethren who feel they can just pick and choose which bits they obey, it bothers me – especially when they are deliberately denying good people the chance of a little comfort in their poor lives. I don't know how they can sleep at night, much less go before God's altar and still not fear what He might do. I'd never get out of the privy if I thought I was taking the Lord's words in vain like that!"

"Oh dear, Tuck," Rhodri said sympathetically, "I'm afraid you're going to find the outside world a very disappointing place."

That didn't stop several of the men sidling up to Tuck during the next day, as they marched for Dover, and asking Tuck if he would pray with them later on. Not that anyone had time for serious prayers that night. Rhodri was determined to get them onto the next ship bound for France, because he hadn't the heart to upbraid Tuck for his actions at Canterbury – indeed he suspected that it would have no effect anyway, for Tuck would probably believe that God would watch over them – but he feared that those monks would now take a while before they forgot that a young Welsh prince had come calling.

"I haven't the heart to tell him he may have jeopardised the mission," Rhodri said to Sulien, as they shared a last beer before bed. "Not when he only acted out of kindness."

Sulien cuffed the beer-froth off his moustache. "I agree. And I wouldn't be too fast to think that he didn't help in a strange sort of way. You know me, Rhodri, I'm a practical sort of man. So it could just have been everyone breathing hard in the crypt making the candles gutter and then burn that bit faster and brighter …could have been. …But even I can't wholly dismiss that Tuck summoned up something more in there, and I tell you, I saw Hywel's face when he got up, and he definitely sees Tuck as being touched by God now!

"Back at Oxford when we said that Tuck might be the one to stop Hywel behaving like an idiot in some crisis, I don't think we knew how true those words were going to be. Because there was definitely a touch of awe in Hywel's gaze after we came out of the crypt, and I think that whatever it was that Tuck did down there, it's made Hywel take this pilgrimage seriously for its own sake – not just saving his skin from a flogging by the king."

Chapter 4

The Journey,
The Year of our Lord, 1177

They had hardly got a day beyond Paris when they ran into their first bunch of thieves. In this case they were easily run off by a bunch of experienced fighters such as Rhodri commanded, but it made Rhodri reconsider something. As they settled down for the night in a camp they had made down in a wooded hollow, which just at the moment felt safer than one of the roadside lodgings, he drew Tuck off to one side.

"I need you to do something for me, Brother."

"Me? Of course, if I can help?"

Rhodri rummaged deep inside his shirt and brought out a small bundle wrapped in oil-cloth. "These are promissory notes. Obviously I couldn't carry enough in coin to get us all the way to the Holy Land and back, or at least not without it being obvious to every ungodly outlaw we passed on the way. So Lord Cadwallon did what he assures me is the usual practice, and has had promissory notes written up with which we can go to Jewish moneylenders and draw coin upon. It's also a back-up in case we get robbed, because there's more available here than we ought to need.

"But these are on parchment, Tuck, and that makes them vulnerable. And more to the point, I don't think I should be the only one carrying our entire funds. If I'm called upon to fight, I might end up bleeding all over them and them becoming completely illegible – and that would be as bad as losing them! But you? You're a priest, and I think even the most villainous outlaw would at least have a second thought about robbing you, and certainly over killing you outright. So I want you to carry these notes.

"And there's something else, too. While the Jews might be the primary lenders, I was told that the notes would be honoured by some of the great monasteries too, should we need urgent replacement money. Yet having seen those avaricious brothers at Canterbury, I'm now not feeling so quick to trust them to be fully honest. And I can't read, so I'll have no idea whether they're giving me the whole amount we're supposed to have or not. But you would! I believe they're for different amounts, you see, and I have a fear that I'll hand over the one with the largest amount on it – which is supposed to pay for our sea journey back home – too early, and for some bright-eyed monk to think he can hand us what we're expecting, then be getting his praises from his abbot for adding to the monastery's funds with the remainder."

Tuck nodded sagely. "I wish it wasn't so, but I fear you have all too many of my fellow monks measured up accurately. They wouldn't outright refuse to give you anything, but a sleight of hand wouldn't be past many a brother I've encountered, despite their vows. So yes, I'll hold these notes for you, and when we get to somewhere where you feel secure, we'll open this bundle up and I'll read each one to you. That way you'll know what you have in reserve, and what to ask for at any given time.

"Hmmm… In fact, if we can find another bit of oil-cloth, it might even be worthwhile splitting this package up. You know, put the ones we think are going to be needed for our return together, so that when we have to open the package in front of someone, they don't see all we have with us. It sounds a bit alarmist, I know, but better to be safe than sorry. And that way I can hide the reserve under my clothing on a cord, and just keep a few at a time in my scrip. Let's face it, we know we have another sea crossing to make at least once, and who knows how wet we're going to get? So the more precautions we can take the better."

Rhodri breathed a sigh of relief. "I knew you'd understand. Thank you, Tuck, that's a weight off my mind. I trust my friend Sulien, but he can't read any more than I can, and because he's only one of the ordinary men, Lord Hywel could also command him to hand them over and he'd have to obey, whereas I don't think he'd try anything like that with you."

They did as they planned, but although the journey got harder the further they went, no disasters befell them. Beyond France they entered the Kingdom of Burgundy, and for the first time were in territory that was part of the Holy Roman Empire. Here they had to make a choice.

"We can carry on directly eastwards," Rhodri explained to them all, as they sat in a small wooden tavern in the foothills of the vast mountain range they could see rising to the east of them. "If we go that way, then we have many more days of travelling in this sort of terrain and steeper – we'll have to go up over the great St Bernard's Pass, too, and there'll be snow up there even at this time of year, but it is the famous pilgrim route, and there will be refuges where we can spend the nights. If we then carry on south on one of the pilgrim routes, the danger is that they are well-known and well-used, and it's where anyone hunting us on King Henry's orders might expect us to be. I have no idea how far outside the Papal States the Pope's worldly reach extends to, you see. If we were English, that might not matter, but who knows what King Henry has had written to him about us Welsh? There might even be senior Englishmen still within the Roman churches from Pope Adrian's days, so I'm not worrying about that without cause – and so did our master, who I heard all of this from.

"However, once over the mountains, it would still be easy enough to head for Bologna, and onwards to the eastern coast. That would mean we avoid Rome altogether. But then we run into the problem of where we would catch a boat from – and catch a boat we must if we're to get to Jerusalem. At Brindisi, I'm told you can get a boat across the narrow sea to the lands controlled by the Eastern Empire, and that's somewhere where King Henry's writ does not run! However, we ourselves may not be any too welcome there, either, for the Eastern Church may not recognise much of a difference between Englishmen and Welshmen. Remember, it's still only twenty years ago that the Pope was an Englishman, and the Popes and the Patriarchs of Constantinople are always at one another's throats, so who knows what feuds we might awaken?

"And – may God help us – there's the matter of the Holy Roman Emperor's nominated pope, Callixtus, who's right in our way on the main route south at this place called Viterbo – looks only about fifty miles north of Rome – and who knows what sort of army Emperor Frederick Barbarossa could have left protecting him? Down there we're not nearly so far from Barbarossa's home duchy of Bavaria as we are from France, and he holds the western coast running down past Genoa and Pisa – so if he and Pope Alexander get into a spat, we could get caught in the middle!"

"*Hmph*!" Tuck snorted. "The Anti-pope Callixtus! Yes we've heard of him. Abbot of Struma, he was, until he saw his way to earthly power by backing Barbarossa. He's not as powerful as the true pope, Alexander, but you're right, Rhodri, he could give us a lot of grief if we're passing as trouble breaks out again."

Rhodri sighed and gave a world-weary roll of his eyes before continuing, "Alternatively, we can gradually sweep south from here, and come down to the Mediterranean coast while we're still in the Kingdom of Burgundy. We can follow the coast from there all the way if we choose, since we're a well-armed band, but that's not the usual choice for pilgrims, I'm told. It's the slightly longer route, but it takes us off the best known pilgrim route at least as far as a bit north of Rome, which is where anyone following us might look for us. After that, the route will take us down through the Papal States, passing through Rome, to the Norman Kingdom of Sicily, where we're pretty much guaranteed to be able to get a ship to Crete. But just remember that those southern lands are held by men who may have English cousins with a loathing for us Welsh, and King Henry's word may hold more weight there if he's seeking a Welsh prince who has slipped through his fingers."

He leaned back and looked around at the others. "So… any questions? Any thoughts? Anyone think there's more of a virtue in one route than the others?"

"Will there be any significant difference in the length or cost of the sea journey?" Tuck asked, trying to quell his own excitement at the prospect of seeing Rome and the Holy See. Three sanctified places in one epic journey was a thrilling prospect!

Rhodri sighed and spread a very basic map out for Tuck to see. "Going on this? It doesn't look like there's much in it. Of course we could get there and find it's very different. I've no idea if the man who drew this map had ever seen any of these places, or was just going by what travellers told him."

"I want to see Rome!" Lord Hywel declared. "If Canterbury was that grand, what must Rome be like?"

Tuck gave him a sympathetic smile, "I think we all feel like that, my lord, but we have to consider the practicalities too." He turned to Rhodri. "What about availability of boats? This map seems to show that pilgrims will travel by sea to Crete from down in the south by Sicily. Could we find ourselves more delayed by problems in finding boats if we go by the other route to Brindisi? Or could we find ourselves having to pay a local fisherman to bring us back to these shores to get that boat to Crete anyway? I know that the Ancient Romans held their heartlands for centuries longer than they were in England, so there must be good roads throughout these lands, but that won't help us if there isn't a boat at the end.

"You see I'm thinking that if we do run into trouble near Rome, we may at least have the chance to make a run for a boat if they sail regularly from down by Sicily. We're coming towards the height of summer now, as well, so we don't have to worry about finding shelter every night. Indeed we could rest up during the worst of the heat around midday, and then walk on well into the night since it'll be light and cooler."

"I think Brother Tuck has a point," Sulien chipped in. "Walking in two stretches a day, with a good rest in between, could mean we cover a lot more ground. So if the old Roman roads are still in decent repair, we could make much better time than we have so far, should we find ourselves being hunted."

"And there's something else," a man called Anian said. "I talked to the serving man of that family who were heading back to England, who we met at the inn last night. He said that the ships which run from by Sicily to Crete, and then on from Crete to Cyprus, only do those voyages from spring until autumn – pretty much from one equinox to the other. If we take the less-travelled route and get held up, we could find ourselves stuck for the whole winter! Because there'll be fewer boats from the eastern side of this arm of sea we're looking at on the map, since they have far fewer in the way of pilgrims, and they may stop the crossings earlier in the year."

"*Duw*, Anian! Now that is something to consider!" Rhodri groaned. "And well done for thinking to ask those who've been there before us. You're right, that makes all the difference, and it forces us to go via Rome. In which case, I think we need to spend some of your father's money, Lord Hywel, and get ourselves some weapons before we get to where the dangers might lurk. We couldn't very well bring arms with us from home and convincingly say we were going on pilgrimage, but now it would be foolhardy not to take precautions."

They decided that the coastal route would at least throw any followers off for a while, and so they kept the huge mountains off to their left and marched southwards. When they found themselves coming down into the softer coastal lands near to the Mediterranean, Rhodri took Sulien, Anian and Tuck into a small but prosperous town a safe distance from Genoa itself, with the intention of getting themselves better kitted out. There was little point in purchasing swords, for men like themselves had no experience of using them. But now their stout pilgrim's staffs were supplemented by rather longer and more substantial quarterstaffs made out of seasoned wood, and Rhodri was insistent that Tuck have one too.

"You're the right build to be a dab hand with one of these, Brother. You've got the length of reach to keep anyone at bay when using it to jab at them, and the strength to deliver a mighty whack with the pole itself. You don't have to kill anyone with it – just knock them out!"

That all by itself reassured Tuck, for he now found that in his own mind he had a great aversion to spilling blood. It had never been a question he'd had to think much on before, but he realised that he would have to be very lucky indeed to get all the way to Jerusalem and back and never get into a fight of any sort. He hoped it wasn't cowardice on his part, but rather a proper aversion to harming others, yet it wasn't something he felt he could ask the soldiers about. On the other hand, while he was quite prepared to turn the other cheek in most circumstances, and would have given the genuinely needy the very shirt off his back, handing over those promissory notes – which everyone else depended on – to those who were robbing through nothing but sheer avarice was, to Tuck's mind, a very different kettle of fish. And so as they travelled on southwards, Rhodri and Sulien began putting Tuck through his paces with the quarterstaff.

"*Ouch!* Steady on, Brother!" Sulien protested, as Tuck got a bit enthusiastic and walloped him back without restraint in one of their earliest sessions. "By *Dewi Sant*, you've got a strong arm there! We're going to have to teach you how to pull your punches, as well, or you're going to be in danger of flattening some poor sod with one blow."

"I'm so sorry!" Tuck was mortified at hurting his willing teacher. "Blessed *Issui Sant*, I never thought I had such capacity to harm!"

Clapping Tuck on his muscled shoulder, and quietly thinking that it was a bit like slapping a side of beef, Rhodri knew he'd have to get Tuck past this fear of harming anyone, or he'd be cut to shreds in a proper fight. "No, no, Tuck, you simply have to get the measure of what you can do! You're a big lad, and like as to grow into a huge man in the next few years as you bulk up with age. That means that you're likely to draw the biggest opponents like flies to honey. So you have to know how to truly lay about you with this thing. It's all well and good holding back if you find yourself facing some lad who barely comes up to your shoulder – but beware, he may be the one who's expert at fighting with a knife! So don't assume the small men are always going to be defenceless. We don't want you going back to Wales ball-less, do we! And some little chap diving in low would be at the right height to rob you of your family jewels, see?"

He saw Tuck gulp and knew he'd given the right example. Just because Tuck had no intention of taking a wife and fathering children, it didn't mean that he didn't have a normal man's strong aversion to forcible castration. Good, that meant that he might not be too kindly in the face of real danger.

"I once got stabbed in the nads," Anian confessed. "Scared the crap out of me! One of bloody de Braose's men-at-arms, it was, come with his black-hearted lord to a meeting with Lord Cadwallon. The bastard couldn't hold his beer and decided to pick a fight with me. Well I just thought I'd fend him off until he fell over, or passed out, but then he goes and pulls this knife out of his boot. Not much of a thing, but you could see he kept it as sharp as a needle, and did it ever sting when he poked up at me with it from where he'd slipped in split beer and fallen to the floor. Didn't go in that deep, thanks be to God, but I've never been so grateful for a wound staying clean and not going bad! So be warned, young brother, keep your guard up whoever you're facing, and don't underestimate your opponent!"

"I won't," Tuck promised, and found that he meant it. It might have been naivety on his part, but he'd never had anyone threatening him with serious bodily harm in the past, so he'd never thought before about fighting back to save his own skin, and what that would mean to him. But the realisation that he might have to face that now was altering his perspective on life considerably. He would never get into a fight from choice – or hoped he wouldn't, for these last couple of months had turned his world on its head, and he was far from as certain of how he'd behave at times as he'd once been – but just how far he'd go defending a friend was a conundrum he was still working out in his own mind. So he paid close attention to subsequent lessons, learning how to rub a bit of dirt onto his hands in an emergency if they were sweaty, to improve his grip, but that this was why the experienced men carried a small pouch with some chalk in. And more than that, he learned why three of their number had not been upgraded to full quarterstaffs like the others. What he had taken for additional and rather spindly pilgrim's staffs which they'd had from the start, carried by straps across their shoulders in oil-cloth wraps, turned out to be something very different.

"This," a man he now knew was called Bryn said proudly, "is a Welsh bow! Best Welsh wych-elm, this is. See how it bends? Now watch this!" and with the skill that Tuck knew had to come from years of practice, he set the string first into the horn tip at one end, then flipped it over the other horn-tip as he bent the bow. And the long bags that these three carried were suddenly revealed to be quivers of arrows.

"That's why we're carrying some of their kit for them, see?" Anian explained. "You feel the weight of Bryn's quiver …no featherweight for all the feathers on those arrows, is it?"

Tuck hefted the quiver in his hand and then very reverently pulled one of the arrows out. It had to be a yard long, and unless he was much mistaken, fletched with goose feathers. "How far can this thing go?" he asked in awe. "What's the range of your shot, Bryn?"

The archer grinned at him. "Let me show you!" and he nocked the arrow in the bow, and then with a call of warning to the rest of the party, let it fly. It embedded itself in a distant tree with an audible *thunk*. "Go on then, Brother, pace that out and tell me what you count," Bryn challenged him cheerfully.

Tuck began his pacing, keeping his stride to about a yard. After he'd passed a count of one hundred, he looked back and saw he'd probably only come about half way. Jesu, how far could these things go?

The tree turned out to be two hundred and four paces away, and yet it still took all of Tuck's strength to pull the arrow out without breaking it.

"Impressive, eh?" Sulien said with a chuckle, as Tuck panted his way back to them in the heat. "You see why Lord Cadwallon wanted us to have archers with us now, don't you? And why we had to wrap the bows up so that they weren't obvious." Carrying weapons was not something any pilgrim was supposed to do, and they would have been denied access to the hostels along the way if that had been clear. Luckily nobody over here had ever heard of Welsh bows, much less been able to spot one. "They can hold men off at a distance without us ever having to engage them. Very useful if you're outnumbered in a fight! You can whittle your opponents down nicely, especially as Bryn, Madog and Llew' can pretty much guarantee to hit their target every time. Not dead on the target, not every time, mind, but then hitting a man anywhere with one of these arrows is going to take him out of the fight."

"I can see that it would," Tuck agreed in awe. "Would it help if I took my turn at carrying one of these quivers? I feel a bit guilty that I've only had my own paltry things to carry so far. You should have said earlier – I'd have been more than willing to shoulder my share."

And so that evening, as they set out as the sun began to lower and the day cooled a touch more, Tuck found himself with two of the long bags slung across his back crosswise, for as he said quite truthfully, their weight was nothing like as much to him as it was to the other men, and he could still manage his own light pack on top of them. Even better, the archers had a private chat and decided that with his strength of arm, it would be worth teaching Tuck the basics of archery.

"You'll not be in our league for accuracy, simply because you haven't had chance to practice enough," Llew' told him. "But if we run into real trouble and one of us three gets hurt, I reckon we can get you to the stage where you could at least make a decent show of helping to defend the others."

And so each morning while it was still cool, Tuck was given a short lesson with the quarterstaff, and then just before they set out again after their midday rest from the heat, the three archers began teaching him how to use the big Welsh bows. Bows which somehow found their ways into his dreams, and with those same men wearing hoods as he'd dreamt of before. They were archers and he was one of them, even though he still wore his monk's habit. Was this a product of his overactive youthful imagination, or a foretelling of a part of his life yet to come? In those dreams he was older than he was at present, but no more than ten years, he thought, and he and the people he somehow knew were his friends were in a forest the like of which he'd not encountered yet. Was it in Wales or England, or some other land he'd yet to get to?

Three hundred miles further on, they found themselves approaching Rome – heart of Christendom in the west, seat of the most Holy See, and currently home of Pope Alexander III.

"And once again, my friends, we arrive at a place of conflict," Tuck said with a despairing shake of his head. "I didn't tell you all of this earlier, but we within the monasteries have heard much of this. You see, Pope Alexander was the choice of his English predecessor, Pope Adrian, to succeed him, and our own King Henry was one of the many monarchs who recognised him as such. But Frederick Barbarossa, that most troublesome Holy Roman Emperor, backed the choice of the people of Rome – helped in no small measure by Callixtus being an ardent supporter of him in return. Two avaricious men scratching each other's backs, or so said my prior, and he'd known a few! So for years Pope Alexander couldn't even reside here, and the last I heard, a peace was having to be negotiated between the Emperor and the Pope. So even forgetting about our own king, be careful what you say in this city! If you sound as though we're too much the supporters of Pope Alexander, who knows what sort of trouble you might get us into!"

"*Dewi Sant!*" Rhodri grumbled. "What is the world coming to when you can't even mention the pope's name when in Rome? And there was me thinking that all we had to worry about was being spotted for Welsh while we're here!"

Chapter 5

Rome,
Late summer, the Year of Our Lord, 1177

They entered Rome through one of its great gateways on its northern side, all of them staring in wonder at the great expanse of terracotta-coloured stone and brick city walls which disappeared off on either side.

"It's like the whole city is a vast castle!" Llew' the archer said in hushed awe. "Look at the length of those walls and the height! *Duw*! They have to be close to thirty feet high! They don't even seem to be curving to turn back on themselves. How many people live here?"

"Strangely enough, although many more in this last century than in the ones before it," Tuck told him, never more grateful than now for Brother Rhys' wide-ranging interests and learning, "still a lot less than there were in the days of Imperial Rome, I was told." He thought hard and then said, "I'd guess a few thousand, but I'm sure that's far from accurate. Brother Rhys told me that one of the great tragedies of the time before Emperor Charlemagne, was that Rome got sacked by the heathen tribes who came looking for new lands from out of the east. We very nearly lost Rome back then, you know, just as we lost the papal seats in Alexandria and Antioch. Only Constantinople held fast in those dark days, and that's why it's still such an important place nowadays. The pope and the patriarch of the Eastern Church may be at loggerheads, but they're both as seated in antiquity as one another. As Brother Rhys said, what a terrible shame that they waste their energy in arguing with one another, when they could do so much good if they pulled together to restore the Holy Land to Christianity."

They had been marching south along the ancient Via Salaria, the salt road, and so it was no surprise when Tuck read one of the street plaques by the gate and told them that they had just entered the city through the Porta Salaria. For all of them it was a revelation that streets and gateways would actually have their names written on them; and if not every street was so named, the sheer height which the buildings rose to, even in the side alleys, was a source of amazement to men used to only seeing the Normans' great castles, and the bigger churches, rising to such heights. The realisation that all the buildings lining both sides of the stone-paved streets, and even the alleyways, were each the homes of multiple families, had them walking with their mouths open in amazement much of the time. Many seemed to rise to five or six storeys, with the upper floors being wooden ones built upon the stone ones down at street level. The smells from family cooking fires filled the air, and women were busy going about the usual domestic tasks, with children running around beside them, as if it were the most normal thing to live on top of one another like doves in a dovecot.

One pair of enterprising urchins scampered up to them, and when he'd worked out their heavily accented near-Latin, Tuck realised that they were offering to be their guides. As they had travelled towards Rome, Tuck had discovered that his Latin stood him in good stead, but that the language of the ordinary people had moved away from pure Latin by quite some way. Luckily the roots of many words were still understandable if he took a moment to think about it, and so he had become the party's official translator. It was something he was far from comfortable about, being very aware of his own limitations, but given that his worst attempts were still better than anything the others could do, he had become their reluctant spokesman.

"How much do they want?" Sulien asked suspiciously. "Are we likely to find ourselves in some dark alley being robbed by their fathers?"

His caution was understandable. With the houses rising so high, while the wide main streets remained brightly lit in the blazing summer sun, the side alleys were gloomy and blocked from the light – anything could have been lurking down there and they wouldn't have seen it.

"I am a priest and these are soldiers," Tuck told the urchins firmly. "Do not try to play any tricks on us, alright?"

"Yes, Father!" the older one said with a beaming smile.

"We wish to see the church," Tuck told them, offering them the lowest denomination coin he had.

The boys held out for three of the coins, but then set off with purpose, at which point everyone realised that they could have wandered around for hours in this warren of streets, without ever coming close to where they wanted to be.

"I suppose this is the result of having a city which has just grown and grown," Lord Hywel said to Tuck as he walked beside him. "They must have had to use every available space within the walls or risk living outside them. Still, I never thought to see people living high up like squirrels." The young lord was going to have a very stiff neck by tonight at the rate that he kept twisting and turning and looking upwards, trying to drink in every detail of this ancient place. "Do you think we're walking in the footsteps of emperors?"

Tuck smiled at him. "Oh, I don't think the emperors walked anywhere much! They probably rode or were carried. But no, I don't imagine they came down these particular streets. I was told by old Brother Timothy, who had come here on his own pilgrimage, that there are great wide streets where two large chariots or wagons can pass and not even come close to one another. That doesn't sound like these, does it?"

Yet before Hywel could answer, they turned a corner and came out into an open square, and before them stood an octagonal-built brick building.

"*San Giovanni*," the oldest lad declared with another beaming smile, and the two vanished before anything more could be said.

"This is it?" Lord Hywel asked, clearly more than a bit disappointed. "*This* is what we've come to see?" It was a reasonable sized building, and taller than most parish churches the men had known if not with as big a footprint, but with little in the way of decoration. In short, it was far from impressive on the outside.

Tuck shook his head and placed a consoling hand on the young lord's shoulder. "No, my lord, this is most certainly not St Peter's. Didn't you hear the lad? This is San Giovanni – St John's. But the good news is that there are bound to be monks here who can direct us to St Peter's, and even better, to where we might safely find lodgings. We don't want to be robbed in our beds, do we?"

He led the way around the octagon, at which point they realised that this was just the separate baptistery and there was more of the church behind it. At the church's door they encountered someone who was clearly a monk here, and once Tuck had made the introductions, the brother was only too glad to take them in to see his church.

"It was rebuilt around two hundred and fifty years ago," he told Tuck, then paused while Tuck relayed the information back to the others. "It was dedicated to St John just fifty years ago, but there's been a church on this site since the fourth century. *We* are the cathedral church of Rome! The Lateran Palace next door is where the Holy Father lives when he is in Rome."

"I thought that was St Peter's?" Hywel softly hissed back to Tuck, who could only answer,

"It seems as though there's a difference between the place of the great shrine, and the church which serves the people – but I didn't know that about the Holy Father, either. Yet I can't imagine that the brother would lie about something that important, so it must be true."

The monk was still bustling onwards, declaring, "Come! Let me show you our altar, for its workmanship is unsurpassed."

"I reckon there's a bit of jealousy between the two places," Sulien whispered to Tuck, watching the guiding monk's proud gesturing, and Tuck couldn't help but agree.

They walked up the long nave, welcoming the cool darkness after the blistering July sun, and because of that it took a while for their eyes to adjust, and to realise that the whole church was indeed beautifully decorated. High above them, a great beamed ceiling seemed to be reaching up to heaven itself, while the towering two-storey walls were covered in either frescos or mosaics, but the crowning glory was the apse at the east end. As they walked towards it, they realised that the half-domed ceiling was covered in gold and precious stones. The brilliant sunlight streaming in through the long, thin windows beneath it barely lit high enough for them to see it fully until they were close too – or as close as they were allowed – but then it was revealed to be the most astonishingly beautiful mosaic.

"*Duw*! Would you look at that!" someone behind Tuck breathed in awe.

Christ's head was haloed in gold, while Heaven was the deepest, richest blue.

"Is that lapis?" Tuck asked, stunned by the absolute luxury of the stones used. How wealthy was this church that it could use gem stones and actual gold to cover the whole ceiling of the high altar?

"Indeed it is," the brother said smugly. "Do you not have the like where you come from?"

There was something a touch too patronising in his tone for Tuck's liking, and though he remained civil and said that no, they did not, there was a part of him that was rather glad that the ordinary people of England and Wales didn't have quite such ostentatious wealth flaunted before them in their poverty. Surely that was not what the Church ought to be about? He was fully aware of the sin of pride, and therefore of thinking too much of where he had come from, but even so, he felt prickled by the other monk's assumptions that poorer must mean less godly. The great prophets of old, like Abraham, had been simple working men, shepherds like the men Tuck had known back in Wales, not priests living in monasteries decorated with precious jewels. For his own part he was only disappointed in this avarice, but on his friends' behalves he felt more than a little slighted, and that their willingness to come on pilgrimage this far should be so looked down upon.

But it made him stop and think about what he was expecting to see here. He'd been anticipating being overawed by a feeling of sanctity in such a place, possibly even from the moment he passed through the gates of the city, and yet he'd felt far more in that simpler stone crypt at Canterbury than here. Somehow this was too much about earthly wealthy and power for him. Yes, he'd known that these churches would be far grander than any he'd know before, but he'd been thinking of seeing exquisite cravings and large windows, not such lavish encrustation with actual jewels. He would have expected that of a mighty king or an emperor, but not the leaders of his faith, and that was unsettling. Had he been hopelessly naive to think like that?

However, he did his best to keep his feelings to himself, and after leading his friends in prayer, this time being very careful to not translate the Latin words for them in front of the other monk, he asked for directions to where they might stay. He was secretly very relieved when the monk didn't offer them a place to stay here. Remaining that tactful for the days they would be here might have proven too much for Tuck's own innate honesty he knew! Fortunately there were sufficient lodgings available for pilgrims that the monks didn't have to cater for large numbers of visitors within the immediate church precinct, though most of the pilgrims' lodgings did seem to be owned by the various churches, and they did have a guest house attached to their own dwelling which seemed to be reserved for other monks. So Tuck was thankful that he could say in all truth that he didn't want to be parted from the others, and they made their way to the nearest hostelry as directed.

With the bricks of the building still holding the heat of the day, none of them had a comfortable night, and they were all glad to be up early and to get out into the almost-cool of the early morning. The lodging house owner had given them directions to St Peter's in bored tones, which said that he'd done this so many times he could have recited them in his sleep. Luckily they would need no guide today, they had been informed, and sure enough, once they were outside and had turned into the street he had directed them to, they could see in the distance the highest levels of the great Coliseum towering above the ordinary dwellings.

"Can we pause and look at it?" pleaded the youngest of the men, Owain. "Was he telling the truth? Did gladiators really fight lions in there?"

"I don't know that we can get inside," Tuck warned him, "and it wasn't just lions they fought in there – many a Christian died on the sands of that arena, you know."

"Oh." Owain's enthusiasm visibly wilted, and Tuck wished he hadn't been quite so quick to burst this soap bubble of dreams. He was still learning his way with these men, trying desperately not to tread on too many toes as he tried to work out what it was politic to say, and when it was better not to flaunt his learning in their faces. Owain was only a year or so younger than him, and the rest older, going up to Sulien who might have been old enough to be his father, yet for some reason Tuck couldn't quite fathom, they often seemed to defer to him, and he still found that unnerving.

He therefore gave Rhodri an apologetic shrug before saying, "But I suppose it wouldn't do any harm for us to at least walk around the outside and see what we can find. If what our host said was right, even the ordinary people used to be able to get in and watch the fighting, so it wasn't just for the emperors. Just remember to keep a track of which road we came out of, though, as we go round, because we're supposed to go straight onwards from the road we've come out from! We don't want to be going around in circles for the rest of the day."

They all walked around the great amphitheatre, marvelling at the huge arches which rose tier upon tier, the ground-floor ones rising to three times the height of a big man like Tuck, and the others above it only reducing by a small amount as they went up tier by tier. Upon further investigation, they found that they could get inside the arena by creeping through behind the lower tiers of stone seats, and so they went to explore. The arena floor, where it was still possible to see the pits where the wild beasts had been kept, particularly fascinated Lord Hywel and a couple of the younger men, and it was all Tuck and Rhodri could do to stop them trying to find a way down into what seemed like a warren of tunnels underneath.

"We don't have torches and we don't have time!" Rhodri said firmly in the face of much pleading. "*Dewi Sant!* What would we do if some of the old ceilings fall in and you get trapped, eh? No! We are *not* going down there."

Even so, it proved impossible to prevent an exuberant mock battle between the younger men, and Rhodri and Sulien found themselves shrugging to one another in exasperation, knowing that they had no chance of moving anyone on until they had had some chance to relish the moment.

For himself, Tuck found it surprisingly emotional to be standing in the very place where he knew fellow Christians had died for not renouncing their faith. *What did it feel like for you?* he wondered, as he stepped out into the open space and looked up at row upon row of stone seating rising away from him. *Were you already so terrified it wasn't possible to be any more afraid? Or did you get out here and hear the crowd baying for your blood like young Hywel's hounds, and suddenly realise that there wouldn't be a scrap of compassion for you in this place? Those lower ranks of seats would presumably have been for the richest, so you wouldn't have seen a friendly face there, and the poor who might have had some sympathy for your plight would have been far out of your view up in the top tiers.*

Did some of you, at this very last, wonder whether you hadn't made the wrong choice, because surely some of you must have felt that God had deserted you at that point? And then after a moment's reflection, *Please Lord, let my own faith prove strong enough if I am ever put to such a test, for I'm not so arrogant to think that I wouldn't waiver under these circumstances. God bless you all, whoever you were, because your names are not recorded and revered like the saints and the great martyrs. You're all lost in the mists of time, so I truly pray that you now have your rewards in Heaven.*

"Come on, Tuck!" Sulien called, breaking his reverie. "Don't *you* go all fey on us now! It's hard enough keeping the youngsters out of mischief," and Tuck saw that he, Rhodri and Anian were shepherding the rest of them outside at speed before any more adventures could be contemplated by the aspiring gladiators. Yet he couldn't resist one last backwards glance, rather shaken that he had felt such a kinship with those early Christians who had died here, and yet had not felt anything like that reverence in San Giovanni.

"I wonder what did the damage to it?" Madog wondered when they got outside, as he stared up at the crumbling stone work on the one side. "Surely nobody would besiege a place like this?"

"I believe the ground shakes in this part of the world," Tuck replied. "I think that's what our host meant when he was telling me about the place last night, but I must admit I was tired and I may have misheard him. He does have a ferocious accent – I don't think he's local, either."

Wondering what other marvels they might be in for today, they reluctantly left the jagged-topped arena behind them, and made for the next marker on their journey, the Circus Maximus.

"You'll spot it easily," their host had said. "It's a great long open space, and there aren't that many of them in Rome!"

"So this is where they held the races?" Lord Hywel said, peering down to try and see the actual track between the crumbling remains of what must have been the stone tiered seating, where the wealthiest would have sat to watch. "I bet my father's horses would have done well here." Hywel was very fond of horses, and proud of his father's stable of beasts.

This time Tuck restrained himself from saying that the stocky Welsh ponies Hywel so prized, would probably have been no match for the steeds who had once thundered around this circuit. The big horses the Norman lords rode in England might be easily outmanoeuvred by the nippy Welsh ponies, but he had the feeling that what had run here might have had a fair dose in them of the lighter-weight, Arab horses they had seen some of as they'd come further south. At least there wasn't much to see here, though, and so he managed to keep everyone moving on to where they would cross the Tiber at the island which temporarily spilt the famous river in two, and then on to the side on which St Peter's basilica lay.

Chapter 6

St Peter's, Rome,
Late summer, the Year of our Lord 1177

The closer they got, the more pilgrims they saw, until they were in quite a press of people.

"Watch your purses, lads!" Rhodri warned. "There are more than just beggars around here, I'll be bound."

Then he jumped as Tuck suddenly pounced on two people ahead of them.

"Not so fast, my son!" he growled, giving the scruffy individual in his left hand a shake. "Give this lady her purse back!" Then repeated it more slowly in the hope that the man would understand.

The woman whose arm he was holding considerably more gently in his right had gone pale, clearly thinking that Tuck was the assailant until he shook the thief again and the rascal reluctantly held out his hand with the purse in it.

Her, "Mon Dieu!" revealed her to be a lady of some sort of French descent, but Tuck thought she might not be from anywhere in France itself, not even Normandy. Then a man nearly as huge as Tuck himself appeared, brandishing his pilgrim staff in a way that said he knew how to use it, and followed close by another younger version of himself, similarly armed. For an awful moment it looked as though the Welsh party might have to fight them off, for they looked at the grubby travellers and their scowls got even deeper. However the woman let off a rapid string of a sort of Norman French and the men relaxed, the youngest coming forward to say more clearly,

"Qui est vous?"

"Nous sommes des pèlerins d'Angleterre," Tuck replied, hoping like mad that he'd remembered the right pronunciation of the phrase he'd learned in France. "Oh heavens, what's their word for 'thief', Rhodri?"

"Voleur, I think."

Tuck hoisted the scruffy cutpurse towards them. "C'est un voleur."

The young man relayed the information back to the man and woman, who now smiled at Tuck.

"You may as well let him go," the younger man said in heavily accented English. "There are so many of them about that there is no chance of anyone doing anything about him. We are just glad that you saved our mistress from him."

"You speak, English? Thank Jesu for that! My French is next to nonexistent."

The youth laughed. "I travelled to King Henry's court as part of the contingent from our part of Sicily, and we brought an English monk back with us as a tutor for my lady's young son. He has been improving me since then."

"Well I'm very grateful for his efforts," Tuck said graciously. "We are accompanying my Lord Hywel, here, on pilgrimages. Would you like to join us? It seems like there might be safety in numbers around here."

There was a quick discussion, but then his offer was accepted with alacrity, the lady willingly moving to within the safety of the group of men. Tuck then led with the young man, whose name turned out to be Stephen, with his father Walter joining Rhodri behind them.

"My lady Agnes was widowed three years ago," Stephen explained. "My lord was one of the knights King William of Sicily took with him to fight alongside King Amalric of Jerusalem in Egypt – not that King Amalric ever turned up to that fight. My lord never came back. Then last year, King William asked for the hand of your King Henry's daughter, Joanna – which was when I went to your land as part of the levy of men as the king's escort – and she is now our queen since February."

Thank you, Lord, for once for our king's empire building! Tuck silently prayed. *It has eased our introduction with these people who are almost locals – certainly more than we are, anyway.*

"So what brings you on pilgrimage?" he asked, hoping he didn't sound like he was being too nosy, even though he was fishing for any snippets of information which might help them. If Sicily was in uproar, then they were going to be in trouble.

"Ah, well you see, my lord had a very prosperous estate. Enough that his half-brother wishes to take control of it, and part of his plan has been to wed my lady to one of his knights. Oh, he will take great care of his young nephew, for he is too young to be any sort of threat to him. But my lady? Well she is more of an obstacle, you understand? Especially as she still mourns for her husband and does not wish to take another in his place. It pains her particularly, you see, that his body was never found, so there is a part of her that still hopes that he might live as a prisoner of the Saracen force they fought against."

"Oh dear, that's a very difficult situation," Tuck sympathised. "Yes, I can see that if she feels she might not even be widowed, that she'd have a strong objection to being married off again. Even aside from any deep emotional attachments, there would still be the fear that she might be marrying bigamously."

"You have it exactly. So after much discussion with her most trusted servants, like my father, it was decided that she should make a pilgrimage. That would allow Lord Tancred to rule the estates, as he so very much desires to do, but because she is on pilgrimage it would mean that he could not seize them outright. It gives her son, young William, time to come closer to his majority when he might inherit in his own right, as well."

"Is he very close to that?" Tuck wondered, having got the impression that they'd been talking about a much younger child up until then.

"No, but this journey to Rome was rather …erm, testing the waters, you might say? Our estate is not far from Messina, so we can get word of what has happened in our absence when we travel back south again. If there has been trouble, we shall collect our young lord too, and we shall all go on pilgrimage to the Holy Land. Otherwise, my lady and ourselves will continue on there alone."

"We, too, are bound for Jerusalem," Tuck said happily. It would be good to be part of a group with people who had some legitimate link to the Norman kingdom, for he'd heard that the leading families in the Crusader states had connections with their equals all around the Mediterranean. Travelling with the widow of a knight, who had fought alongside King Amalric of Jerusalem, could turn out to be a real boon the closer they got to that king's territories.

For now, though, they were getting closer to St Peter's, and ahead of them they saw a wide flight of steps leading up to an impressive facade.

"Is that marble?" Llew' asked in amazement. "On the *steps*? How rich is this place that they can afford to do that?" None of them had ever seen marble used outside before.

Tuck relayed the question to Stephen, who seemed surprised that they hadn't seen such a thing, although he admitted, "I do not recall seeing such a thing at your King Henry's court, though, now that you mention it. Perhaps it is because of your English rain? We have it in many of our buildings in Sicily."

"It does shine beautifully in this sunshine," Madog admitted, mopping the sweat from his face and brow before replacing his floppy hat, "but just at the moment I'd give a lot for some good Welsh rain. I'm melting here!"

"We'll be inside soon," Tuck consoled him, and indeed as they passed under the huge arched doorways, they seemed to be entering into another dark, cool place. Their respite from the burning midday sun was short-lived, though. They soon emerged out into a massive colonnaded courtyard, and they found themselves scurrying for the darkest side like human rats avoiding a hunter's lantern.

"*Duw*, but it's sweltering," Bryn declared, as they all found a patch of shade to rest in for a moment. "Why is it so bloody sticky here?"

"Rome is built on seven hills," Stephen explained, "but on the western side in particular it's surrounded by marshes. The richest citizens escape to the mountains east of here for a couple of months to avoid the worst in the height of summer. We ourselves would not have travelled at this time of the year had Lord Tancred not made our mistress' position so precarious. We would have waited until closer to winter."

"Would you have got a ship to the Holy Land then?" Tuck wanted to know. Had they been wrongly informed?

"Oh well, not actually winter itself," Stephen hurried clarified. "We would have caught a ship from Sicily in late August, but do not forget, we would not have had far to go to get to the port. That would have been the start of the journey, not the end of this one, as we have to do now."

"Well let's make the best of being here," Tuck said, giving Walter a hand to lift Lady Agnes to her feet from where she had slumped gratefully against one of the huge columns of the arcade. She was actually a lot younger than he'd first thought, but he also thought that she didn't look well. Was that the toll of grief, or was there something more wrong with her? If so, then that could explain her wanting to make this pilgrimage on a whole other level.

Mercifully they were able to get into the church itself relatively swiftly, and then joined the long snake of pilgrims making their way around the various lesser shrines arrayed along the one wall. There seemed to be a one-way system in place, for coming back the other way and making their various obeisances at the many lesser shrines across the nave from them, were more pilgrims gradually making their way out again.

"There're a lot of martyrs in here, aren't there?" young Owain said softly, as he knelt beside Tuck at yet another shrine. There was a hint of despair in the young soldier's voice, clearly wondering how many more times they would be not only expected to kneel and pray, but also make a donation, before they got to the main shrine.

"Yes, there are," Tuck agreed, but that wasn't what was bothering him. Yet again he was failing to feel in any way overawed by this place, and that disturbed his soul mightily. What was wrong with him? Why could he not feel a connection to God when he was here in this holy place? This, after all, was the church of St Peter himself, founder of the Christian church as he knew it.

I've felt more at my lovely little church up in the hills than here, he thought. *Why should that be? Is it the monks here? Surely I'm not so parochial that I can't recognise the worth of a brother from another land? Please God, let it not be that!* Then he gave himself a little mental shake. *No, don't be so daft, that brother over there looks too fair-skinned to be a native of this land. He has to have come from closer to home than that, yet what is it that offends me about him? Is the fault in me, or is there something amiss here?*

Certainly this famous basilica was infinitely more ornate than his own humble church, as he still thought of St Issui's as well as Llanbedr's chapel, but somehow Tuck thought that it wasn't that which was prickling at him. He wouldn't have expected it to be anything less than magnificent, especially after seeing San Giovanni. The size all by itself was overwhelming, and the trees whose trunks had made the great beams to span the nave's roof must have been giants of their kind to get such a width. Not that they could see much of the ceiling above the shades of the huge supporting beams from here in the side aisle, for there were only small windows up at the clerestory level, but there was just enough light from those and the many candles to see how wonderfully painted even the uppermost walls were.

A line of tall marble columns ran up each side of the nave to create the side aisles along which the pilgrims processed, so they could just about see the walls rising opposite them within the nave. Above them, rising in two ranks, were frescos and mosaics depicting a veritable heavenly host of angels, saints, martyrs and Church Fathers. The floor was of shining white marble, which reflected what limited light there was, and the scent of high quality incense filled the air. Yet if it was all opulent on a scale that Tuck had never dreamed could exist, it still wasn't that which was tweaking at him that it wasn't 'right', of that he was quite sure.

It took Tuck until they got to the nearest the likes of them were going to be allowed to the sacred shrine of St Peter, before he could put his finger on what it was that was troubling him, but as he knelt and prayed with all of his might that he should be considered worthy of just the merest drop of divine blessing, it came to him. It wasn't just that the brothers shepherding the crowds looked rather too well-fed, even comparing them to the likes of sub-prior Humbert. It was that at far too many points, there were places where pilgrims could be separated from their worldly wealth. If it wasn't direct donations, it was the sale of indulgences, or the sale of pilgrim tokens – purportedly blessed by the pope himself, and therefore capable of warding off whatever ailed you – or the sale of supposed holy relics themselves for the better-off pilgrims. How many finger bones of saints were there really, that so many could be on sale? And 'sale' was the key word. Nothing here was given for free.

This is like Our Lord cleansing the moneylenders from the Temple being re-enacted all over again! he thought angrily. A figure melted stealthily out of the darker recesses and swiftly replaced a bowl that had begun to fill up with coin for one which had only a couple in it. *You thieves!* Tuck mentally growled. *You're preying on these poor folk.* Already he was offering up thanks that he and Rhodri had made sure that they had shared out a quantity of the lowest value coins amongst their party, and had warned everyone not to put more than one in any offering bowl at one time, expecting that they would be asked to donate many times today, although even they hadn't anticipated this much greed.

He saw a man who had been three back in line when the bowls had been swopped put his coin in, then look again at how little was in there, and guiltily dig back in his purse for another coin. *Grrr! That's just what you want to happen, isn't it? That's blackmail, pure and simple. And what happens when someone comes who can't drop another coin?*

His answer came soon enough. A lad who seemed to have some sort of wasting disease and was likely of an age with Stephen, and therefore just a little younger than Tuck, came up alongside the brother who was filtering the pilgrims to the main shrine, but put no coin in the bowl strategically placed there. Immediately the brother's arm came out and barred his way, shooing him off to join the line of people heading back out.

Furious, Tuck turned back and, dumping another coin in the bowl, reached out and snatched at the young man's sleeve as he began to beg the brother to be allowed up to the shrine. The clatter of his coin caught the attention of both the brother and the young man.

"He is with me!" snapped Tuck in Latin, tugging the young man to him.

The brother's angry expression told Tuck everything he needed to know, for as he pulled the young man past one of the tall candles, he could see that the lad was covered in fleas.

"Stephen, would you tell him that it's alright?" Tuck asked. "Tell him he's not in trouble with me, and he can pray with the rest of us."

After a couple of false starts, Stephen seemed to find the right language and the young man's terrified expression lessened. "He's from the far south of Sicily," Stephen whispered to Tuck. "Even I can barely understand him! He speaks more Arab words than Norman-Sicilian."

Yet as they came up on the shrine, it was clear that nobody except the most highly favoured was going to get to touch even as much as the carved and gilded surround. Another haughty monk this time gestured them to one of the bowls which purportedly contained holy water, but by this time in the day, it was already seriously grubby from the multitude of fingers that had been dipped into it before each pilgrim crossed themselves.

Blessed St Peter, show me the way, Tuck prayed desperately, as he knelt at the appropriate point and frantically tried to quash his rising anger. *If I am filled with an ungodly pride and knowing, then lead me to humility, for I do not feel your presence here. Enlighten me, please! Is it me who is out of step with your Church, or has it and the men who lead it gone astray? This is not how I expected to feel, and it troubles my soul tremendously.*

The others also said their prayers at the shrine, and then they all made their way out again, but this time lingering less on the way out, despite the black looks they got from the warder-monks, who clearly thought they should have been making further offerings along the way.

To everyone's relief it was now late in the afternoon and the heat had slacked a little.

"Let's get down by the river where we can sit in peace, and then I'll find out what ails this young man," Tuck said firmly, and set off in the lead again.

"Does he always do this?" Stephen asked Rhodri, looking at Tuck's retreating broad back and the young man still held firmly in his grasp.

"Pick up waifs and strays? Err…let's just say he does seem to be making a habit of it!"

"And do all the priests in this Wales of yours do that?"

Rhodri gave a wan smile. "No, I think we can say that Tuck is unique in that."

Chapter 7

Rome,
Late summer, the Year of Our Lord 1177

Down by the Tiber, Tuck made the lad strip to his undergarments and then examined him. He swiftly decided that there was nothing that a few square meals and a good bath wouldn't do a lot to improve, and so the lad was sent into the river to scrub himself with one of the small balls of pungent herbal soap Tuck had in his pack. Hopefully, deprived of his multitude of tiny passengers, the lad might improve – especially, as Tuck impressed upon him, if he spent what little he had upon bread and fruit instead of wine! Drowning his sorrows was doing little to help his situation, although what that was in detail even Stephen couldn't quite grasp. Helping his running sores and calluses to heal was all Tuck could offer, out here with no herbarium to hand, and then pray that it would be enough.

In the meantime, the rest of them were deciding what to do. Luckily all of the Welshmen had their packs and staffs with them, not having thought much of the chances of anything being still there if they'd have left them in their lodgings. They had also only paid for the one night so far, and so they were free to join Lady Agnes and her servants.

"I want to have a look at her, too," Tuck confided in Rhodri. "There's something more going on there than they're telling us, because she's not well unless I've lost my touch at reading people."

They shared their food, bought at one of the street stalls, with the lad, but then he expressed himself most grateful for the lineament that Tuck gave him to rub on his sore spots, and then melted away into the evening glow, clutching the extra few coins they had also given him for more food the next day. Walter said that they were stopping at an inn in the area he said was called Trastevere, which was on the same side of the Tiber as St Peter's, and so they all made their way back there for the night. Most of them immediately went to their beds, worn out by the excitement of the day, but Tuck went to sit under the ancient, gnarled olive tree in the courtyard, which was where Rhodri found him.

"Alright, Tuck. Come on, tell me what's got you so bothered," he said companionably, plonking himself down on the stone bench beside this young monk whom he was starting to feel an almost fatherly affection for. "Something's got you riled, so what is it?"

"Avarice," Tuck replied darkly. "What we saw today. Pure bloody avarice! ...Ah, Rhodri, I fear for my soul, I really do. There I was, in the holiest place this side of Jerusalem, and I could find no goodness there. Is that some fault in me? Am I guilty of the sin of pride that I think I know better than these monks who serve every day at the shrine of blessed St Peter himself?"

He harrumphed darkly. "Yet all I saw were men stocking up earthly wealth. As God is my witness – and I do most devoutly believe in Him – I tried to see the good, I really did. But all I could keep thinking about was Our Lord going into the temple and casting out the money-lenders, and wishing most fervently that he would come down and do the same in that church. A church that is supposed to be upholding all that he preached and held dear, and providing the example the rest of us should be aspiring to, and yet in my eyes is failing most miserably to do. ...But is the fault mine?"

Rhodri felt deeply sorry for Tuck. This was when the young monk's lack of worldly experience really showed.

"Tuck, for what it's worth, I admire you more for seeing the flaws than if you had blithely accepted everything without question. You weren't the only one who noticed those sleights of hand going on – Sulien and I did, too. We've been in armies for long enough, and been fleeced of our wages enough times when we were young and innocent, to spot someone working a fast one; and that's exactly what those monks were doing! ...Ah, me. It's a grim thing, my young friend, but the brothers in that holy church are just as human as you or I, and sadly they seem to be just as subject to temptation. So please don't beat yourself up for spotting them for what they were."

Tuck gave Rhodri a watery smile. "Thank you for that. It does at least make me feel better that you spotted them using the kinds of trickery you've seen in the army. I can't explain why, but it makes it seem less... well, 'sanctified', for want of a better word. You know, less as though I'm the wicked one for spotting it in the first place, and lacking in faith."

Rhodri snorted. "It's not your faith that's at fault, Tuck – nor your eyes! I may not be a priest like you, but I would still say that those brothers back there have been seduced by the soft living – forgotten who and what they're supposed to be serving. For all their piety, they're flesh and blood men, and just as susceptible to corruption as the rest of us."

Tuck had visibly perked up, and now was able to joke, "Well at least if I'm destined for Hell for my doubts, I'll have you for company."

"That you will, Brother," Rhodri said with a chuckle. "Come on. Time for bed!"

Yet before they could rise, Stephen and Walter came quietly out into the courtyard, looked around, and immediately made for them.

"I'm glad we caught you, Brother," Stephen opened with. "May I ask you, are you a proper priest, fully ordained, not just a monk?"

"I am," Tuck confirmed, although not wanting to reveal that he was purely because he'd been the only one Prior Augustine had been willing to sacrifice to the Welsh 'wolves'. "But if it's about you or your lady, then I will vouch for Rhodri, here, as an honest man and one who would keep your confidences. May I hazard a guess that you need to speak to us about your lady?"

Stephen blinked in shock, then said something swiftly to his father before turning to Tuck once more. "Nothing gets past you, Brother, does it? Yes, it is to do with our lady." He paused and looked back at his father and then at Rhodri, as if confirming that he was doing the right thing by speaking up. "You see, we fear we may have to ask you for your protection when we get further south – if you are still willing to travel with us, that is."

"And why would that be?" Tuck asked, careful to keep any suspicion out of his voice. He didn't want the pair to wonder whether he was already thinking the worst.

Stephen took a deep breath, and it didn't take much imagination to think that he was furtively crossing himself in the hope that he'd read Tuck and Rhodri correctly. "You see, it's our mistress. She's with child."

As Rhodri was about to say, '*humph*, not much of the grieving widow!' he felt Tuck's hand clamp on his knee in warning, as Tuck cut across his grunt with,

"Would this be a matter of rape, then?"

Stephen jumped as if he'd been pricked with a knife. "By Our Lady! How could you have known that?"

"Easy, my friend," Tuck said, releasing Rhodri to lean over and put a reassuring hand on the lad's shoulder. "I'd already said to Rhodri that I thought your mistress looked far from well. For you to say that she is with child, and yet for her to look so distraught, particularly when she's clearly a good mother to her existing son, it wasn't such a huge leap to guess that she was hardly a willing mother this time."

There was another swift exchange between father and son in their own language before Stephen turned back to Tuck and Rhodri again. "If you've guessed that much, then my father agrees that you may as well know everything. Lady Agnes has been holding out against being remarried just as we told you. But it wasn't another Lord Tancred was planning to hand her on to but himself, and he isn't a patient man. So he took her to bed – and more than once, may God rot his miserable soul – saying that once she was with child she would have a stark choice: marry him, at which point he would get the lands he so badly wanted, or be branded a whore."

He sighed heavily. "If Lady Agnes was another high-born Norman lady, she would have had other family to turn to. Unfortunately, though, she is one of the many in Sicily who are of mixed blood. Her mother's family go back to when the Byzantine emperors ruled our island and there were many families from across the sea living there, from what was once called Carthage. And as you know, that land has now fallen to the infidels, so her family are not the great lords they once were. Yet even so, most of the rest of her family have fled back to their ancient homelands as the lesser of two evils. But my lord and lady married for love, and while he lived, she was safe."

"But now he's gone her position is precarious to say the least," Tuck sympathised. "And I can also see that you'd want to be sure that their son would not be harmed by his uncle, even if the chances of the lad actually inheriting his father's lands have become very slim."

Stephen's sigh of relief said it all. "I'm so glad that you can see it. My lady was already planning something like this journey, but then when she guessed that she was with child it became most pressing. She had to get away before anyone around her guessed."

"Oh, I can quite see that!" Tuck agreed, privately relieved that there might not be anything more amiss with Lady Agnes than bad morning sickness, for she had to be only early on in her pregnancy since she was showing no other signs yet – or at least none Tuck could see through her flowing gowns. "Any hint to this Tancred that the child was his would mean she'd be trapped with him. She must have been frantic to get away before her waiting women suspected anything."

"She was. There's an old woman whom she trusts, but the others of her former household have gradually been frightened off by Lord Tancred in the last year or so, and the ones who have come in their place have been his spies. My father and I are amongst the last left who are faithful to her, and that's why she took us into her confidence and asked her to help her to escape."

"Might I also guess that this is the reason why you didn't initially head for Jerusalem?" Tuck wondered. "If she's suspected of being a Saracen sympathiser, then going east would be an obvious way, and where Lord Tancred might first hunt for her? And that would give him an excuse he could use to seize her lands. Whereas coming north to Rome isn't such an obvious step, but it also takes her further away from where he has any influence."

Stephen shook his head in amazement. "You really are quite a remarkable priest, Brother Tuck."

"No, my son, I just use the brains God gave me."

"And they're considerable," Rhodri said affectionately. "If anyone was going to see through things it was Tuck. As for myself, don't worry, I'll prime my men just with what bits they need to know, and keep your confidences. I have no problem with us escorting a lady in such a position as hers, even if it's all the way to Jerusalem."

"Thank you!" Stephen said with relief, but adding, "It relieves both my father and me that we will be able to leave Lady Agnes with you while we go and check on young master William. We did not want to leave her alone in Messina in case Lord Tancred has men there, but equally, we did not want to take her to the villa in case he was waiting for her return. Making a run for it is something she could not hope to do at the moment."

"No, I can quite see that," Tuck agreed. "In fact it might not be a bad idea if some of us come with you to the villa."

That idea gradually solidified into a plan as they lingered in Rome for one more day. They rested during the morning, everyone glad to be able to do nothing as the temperature rose to sweltering heights yet again. But in the late afternoon, Tuck, Stephen and Rhodri, with a couple of the younger soldiers, decided to go out and explore this cluster of buildings known as Trastevere, for their host declared that there was a church nearby which could rival San Giovanni, if not St Peter's.

"Our host says that the church of Santa Maria has had much work done on it in the last few decades," Stephen told them, as he led the way through a wandering warren of narrow streets. "He told me that it goes back to when Christians were only a few in number in Rome, but that the work on the inside is still in progress. They have even just built a bell tower!"

They came around into the open square before the church, and were immediately glad that they hadn't come in the morning, for the western front had the most wonderful mosaics of the Virgin on it. In the lowering afternoon sunlight the mosaics positively gleamed, and they could see the detail of the Virgin holding her infant son quite clearly.

"Now isn't that something!" Tuck heard Owain say in awe, and suddenly he felt that certain something he'd been searching for ever since they had arrived in Rome. In this quieter place, surrounded by ordinary houses, he felt the return of the feelings he usually had in his own little church in the hills.

"Now this is better!" he said out loud without realising he'd done it, and then hearing Rhodri's chuckle from beside him.

"Hits the spot a bit more, does it, Tuck?"

"Oh yes! Although I couldn't tell you why as yet. It's just the feel of the place."

Inside it was laid out very much the same as the other two great churches they had visited – a long nave was spanned by a huge timber roof, and was also flanked by two side aisles, which ran the full length of the nave up to the point of the east end's apse. What was immediately different in here, though, were the huge columns which supported the clerestory and the roof.

"These must have come from ancient Rome!" Stephen gasped. "They're the same as the ones we see in many of the Roman ruins on Sicily! Look! The tops are so Roman – you don't see them carved like that anymore. Nothing like as graceful."

"And they're marble, not just any old stone! Look at the colours! I didn't know that marble came in anything but white," Owain gasped. "*Duw*! I've never seen anything like them!"

The tapping of tools on something alerted them to the craftsmen working away high above them on a wooden scaffold, not doing structural work here as at Canterbury, but delicate decorations to finish the building. Whoever it was up there was out of sight, but any curiosity they might have had vanished as their eyes adapted to the dim light, and they saw the apse above the high altar at the east end. And this time they got to appreciate it in all its glory, since they were able to walk up the centre of the nave and see it emerging before their eyes. In a heaven made up of golden tesserae, the Virgin sat clothed in radiant white at

Christ's right hand, crown upon her head, and with a hand above them symbolising God reaching down from even higher.

All of them stood in silence for a moment, totally overawed by the sight. It was the bell in the connected tower ringing the Nones call to prayer that woke them from their individual reveries.

"Would you mind if I stayed here and observed Nones with the other monks?" Tuck asked Rhodri. "It seems such a long time since I was with any of my brothers."

"Not at all," Rhodri said happily. "There was a tavern just around the corner. The lads and I will go and wait for you there. Come on, Stephen, you can come with us and make sure we don't get served with the local rot-gut instead of the good stuff."

Left on his own, Tuck melted into the shadows and awaited the other monks. When someone finally spotted him, he managed to speak to them in Latin and convey who he was and what he wished for. There was some surprise — clearly they weren't yet on the main pilgrim route enough to have regular visitors from overseas churches, but at least a space was found for Tuck at the end of the choir stalls, and for a while he lost himself in the pleasure of making the responses which were second nature to him by now. But what he wasn't expecting was the feeling of complete and utter peace which came over him in the process. Far from the mental itch which had plagued him in St Peter's, here he felt everything he'd expected to feel there, and it was a soothing balm to his troubled soul.

I have not lost my way, he thought gratefully as he got up from his knees. *Thank you, Lord, or St Peter, or Our Lady, or whoever has answered my prayers. I needed this.* And it was all the more apparent in the behaviour of the monks, who all seemed to be much more the kind of reverent and goodly sort he had expected to find in Rome, praying as if they truly believed, and not simply placing offering bowls at every point. Then as the monks processed back out, he was about to follow them when something pricked him to turn back to the main altar. Going down on his knees right before it, he looked up to the glowing image of the Virgin and asked her directly,

"What am I supposed to do about Lady Agnes? I suddenly feel I have to pray for guidance on this, and I'm taking it that this your hand I'm feeling, Lady? Are you watching over this poor woman who's with child and alone in the world? Are we doing the right thing in offering to take her to Jerusalem with us?"

No spectral voice answered him, and yet for a moment he was sure that the light up in the apse grew brighter in answer.

"Thank you, Lady," he said reverently. "I promise I will do everything in my power to protect this poor soul who has found her way to me, and her son, too." And feeling lighter in spirit than he had for days, Tuck made his way back outside to rejoin his friends – God was in His Heaven and, for today at least, all was right with the world.

Chapter 8

Messina,
Late summer, the Year of our Lord, 1177

When they all set out from Rome the following morning, having risen early enough to have several hours before the heat became intolerable, the first thing they found was that they were going to have to hire a donkey or mule for Lady Agnes. She really wasn't well at all, and Tuck became even more worried when they stopped just before midday in the shade of an olive grove.

"I fear she may be bleeding," he told Rhodri, Walter and Stephen. "I'm so sorry my friends, but I think we need to find some nuns to leave her with. Even getting back to the south could prove impossible in her condition. I honestly think we could be endangering her life if we continue on with her. Rhodri, do you think you could scout on ahead with Stephen and a couple of others and see if you can find anywhere, while we bring her on at a slower pace? We'll go to that farm up on the hill first, and see if they have a mule we could borrow for a short while."

Yet trying to get Lady Agnes up onto the mule only confirmed what Tuck had feared – her gown showed a growing bloodstain where she had been sitting down.

"Forget finding any nuns," Tuck sighed. "It's back up that farm for her. At least there were a couple of women up there who might be able to help her."

It took Tuck and Llew's strong arms to hold her up on the mule even that short a distance, and when they brought her into the farm yard, the farmer's wife took one look at her and crossed herself. Clearly the prognosis wasn't good. They sat around like a bunch of expectant fathers all evening, allowing Tuck to lead them in prayers for Lady Agnes, but the wife came out and said that the child had miscarried just as dusk was coming on.

"Poor little mite," Sulien said sorrowfully, "but given the way it was conceived, maybe it's a blessing that it's gone back to God sooner rather than later."

"Amen," Tuck sighed. "If it had proved to be the double of its father, it would have been a constant reminder of what Lady Agnes has been through, and she doesn't deserve that." He couldn't add that this was dredging up some sad feelings about his own childhood, too. Had his own mother looked as frightened and distressed as Lady Agnes when she'd realised she was pregnant with him? He desperately hoped not for her sake. What was the matter with these Norman lords that they felt they had a right to just take – in every sense of the word – whatever or whoever their greedy eyes fell upon? With every passing day out in the wider world, Tuck was feeling more and more repelled by his heritage from a parent he had never known, and ever more kinship with his Welsh companions.

However it was only a few hours later that the wife came and tugged on Tuck's sleeve, gesturing him to come with her, and once by the simple bed he understood why. Lady Agnes' was barely drawing breath now, and she was so terribly white she seemed to be a flesh-and-blood replica of the image he had seen in the church.

"Oh Lady, you are fetching her to your side, I hope," Tuck sighed. He got on his knees and began administering the Last Rites, and by the time he finished, she had slipped away. He stayed and prayed a little longer, but then went and broke the bad news to Stephen and Walter.

"She's gone, I'm afraid," he told them. "At least she made it to Rome and I've done what I could for her in those last moments. But in the morning you have to decide what you wish to do now."

It took Stephen only as long as it took to relay Tuck's words to his father before Walter was saying something in response.

"He says we must go and find young master William," Stephen translated back. "We have to do it before Lord Tancred hears of my lady's death. One small boy isn't going to stand in that man's way now."

"You think this Tancred is capable of murdering his nephew?" Tuck was shocked.

Stephen's harrumph of disgust was a reply all in itself. "Given that Tancred was his father's son by his second wife, and therefore our lord's younger half-brother, yes, I do. There's no family love lost there." Then added, "Quite what we'll do with Master William is another matter, but at least he'll survive if he's with us, and that has to be a good start."

It was in sombre mood that they set out again a day later, all of the Welshmen affected by the death of this lady whom they barely knew.

"Poor soul," Madog said with a sad shake of his head, as they walked past the simple graveyard where they had buried her yesterday. "To lose a husband who she loved and then be put through all of that.

Sometimes, Brother Tuck, I wonder about God. Who would think it fair to laden one poor soul with such terrible trials, eh?"

However Tuck had had chance to think on this and he replied with certainty, "I believe Our Lady called her to Her, Madog. I think She was being merciful. I prayed for Lady Agnes in that church dedicated to the Virgin, you know, and when I mentioned her by name, I'm sure my prayers were heard. Sad though we all are to have lost that poor lady, don't you think it a kindness that she hasn't had to go through years and years bringing up a child who, although innocent of any crime itself, would have been a daily reminder of the cruelty of her brother-in-law?

"Do you see what I mean? Lady Agnes had her chance to pray at the tomb of St Peter, and that all by itself would bless her. But more than that, I honestly believe that Our Lady was reducing our own burden down to what it's possible for us to fulfil, as well as interceding for Lady Agnes herself. Going back to Messina with Lady Agnes could have led to a catastrophic series of events, whereas you, Stephen, and your father going back without her, are far less visible to the likes of this Tancred you've spoken of.

"To men like him you're just one of the common herd. You're barely worth a second glance, and that immediately increases our chances of getting your young master William out considerably; whereas Lady Agnes was probably a known person in Messina, even if she had few actual friends there. So if she turned up, there was bound to be some busybody who would think to feather their own nest by running off to Lord Tancred with that information the moment she was spotted."

For all of his own devotion to God, Stephen was looking slightly askance at Tuck's absolute belief, but replied, "Well for Lady Agnes and our young lord's sake, Brother, I hope you are right."

Yet at Messina, Tuck's words came unexpectedly true. Hardly had they crossed over from the mainland to Sicily, when Walter caught Stephen's arm and gestured to someone whom the others saw suddenly scurrying off away from them.

"By Our Lady, Brother! Does your kind have the second sight or something?" Stephen exclaimed.

Sulien chuckled. "It goes with being Welsh, my friend, but I think Tuck has more of it than most. We can all get a bit fey when the mood takes us, but he seems to have the ear of a couple of our Welsh saints …but why do you say that?"

"That man who went running off? He lives on the next manorial estate to us. He knows us by sight."

Tuck patted Stephen on the shoulder. "Ah, but what is he going to say, *hmmm*? Even if his own master wants to keep in with this new nightmare that's landed on his doorstep, all he can say is that the men who went off with Lady Agnes have come back without her. And that's sure to please this Tancred. After all, it effectively means that she won't be around to challenge his claim to the manor he so desperately wants. All that cunning spy will reveal, therefore, is what Tancred wants to hear – which is that he's got his heart's desire. From all you've told us, there's nothing about you that would lead him to believe that we're about to sneak in and take his young nephew out from under his nose, is there?"

And the following evening, as they all crept up to the manor house in the deepening dusk, Tuck's words rang true. Nobody was on alert. Not a soul was out on guard duty or patrolling the grounds. There wasn't even a dog wandering around sniffing at which olive tree to pee up against.

"*Uffern gwaedlyd!*" Sulien swore in his own language. "These men wouldn't last the week where we come from! Their cattle would be gone and they'd be dead in their beds."

Stephen's eyes showed whiter in the dim light as he looked across at Sulien in shock. "Is yours such a lawless land?"

"Not lawless, exactly," Tuck chuckled softly from Stephen's other side. "Let's just say that the Norman yoke doesn't sit so hard in our homeland, so old family feuds continue with less restraint. And cattle reiving – that's what they call themselves, by the way, reivers – is regarded almost as a sport. You steal your neighbour's cattle one week, and he comes and takes them back the next! It even goes on across the border between England and Wales, much to our Norman lords' disgust. But that means my friends, here, have had rather more experience of this sort of raid than you might expect. I'd let them take the lead if I were you."

Stephen turned around to say something to that effect to Sulien, only to find the Welshman had already melted away into the shadows.

"God's hooks, they are good!" he replied in an awed whisper, then found himself being hoisted to his feet by Tuck and tugged forward to where Sulien and Bryn waited. The look on his face when he saw Bryn's big Welsh bow strung and ready to use was priceless. He'd obviously not realised quite how dangerous his new friends could be when roused, and this new weapon was nothing like he'd ever seen. Compared to the Saracens' smaller recurve bows, which they had already seen some of down here in Sicily, or the Norman crossbows, it was enormous, and the arrows looked like something the wild northern gods he'd once heard the tutor talk about would use – huge, dark and deadly.

"All clear," Llew's voice came softly in Welsh, all of them falling back into raiding mode despite the foreign landscape they now found themselves in.

With the Welshmen's shirts now filthy with the dust of Sicily, they blended into the burnt earth just as easily as their woollen jerkins had once merged with the rain-soaked hillsides of home, and they slid like ochre-tinted ghosts right up to the walls of the big stone house that stood in the middle of well-tended fields. Vines heavy with grapes, and olive trees with trunks made fat with age, helped mask their progress, and to Stephen's amazement they were up to the door and not so much as a moth disturbed.

"Right… Tuck, Stephen, Sulien and Gryff, you four go in and get the lad," Rhodri ordered. "I'll stay by the door with the rest of the lads except the archers. You three go back to that dry-stone wall and be prepared to cover our escape."

"Righty-oh," Bryn said, as if it was nothing more than a walk in the orchard, and the three archers vanished once more into the growing gloom.

"You lead," Tuck said softly to Stephen. "You know the sort of layout a house like this will have," with Sulien adding,

"Let's see if we can avoid the servant's quarters. Don't want any of them joining in unless it's unavoidable. We're going straight for the boy, never mind your evil master."

Stephen led them around the corner of the building to where a flight of stone steps ascended. "The undercroft is all storage and where the servants sleep," he whispered to them. "The family live upstairs, where it's easier to open shutters to let a breeze in during the summer. But the front door will be locked, I can tell you that, and it'll probably be bolted too."

"Is there no other way in?" Sulien asked. "What about a stair from down below?"

"No, why would there be?" Stephen seemed puzzled that he would even ask.

"Well don't they fear their stores and things being stolen?" Gryff asked, just as bemused. "Don't they go down to check on things?"

Stephen shook his head. "No, the servants bolt the door from the inside down there too. They've no desire to have their throats cut by marauding thieves any more than the family do," then seemed to realise that more of an explanation was needed. "But that's why they sleep down below, you see, because the few windows have to be shuttered up and barred at night, even in the hottest weather, whereas upstairs the family can afford to have at least the inner windows open."

That still didn't make a lot of sense to the Welshmen — what were inner windows? Their own turf-built and thatch-roofed long-houses barely had any window openings anyway, for who would want to let the rain and wind in? But Sulien slunk up the steps and tried probing around the door with a knife.

"*Pfaah!*" he grunted in disgust when he came back down. "It's like the lad said. I can feel the latch lifting when I slide my knife in, but the door's not shifting. It has to be barred or bolted, top and bottom."

Stephen looked glum. "I didn't want to dash your hopes, but I thought it might come to this. We'll have to wait until morning and then hope to try and grab the young master then."

Sulien snorted. "We're not done yet, boyo! *Duw!* Nobody gives up this easy where we come from! Come on, lads — we need the archers after all!"

Before long the three archers were back, and while Tuck kept Stephen to one side, the soldiers had a hurried discussion. Within moments Bryn had pulled back on his huge bow and sent an arrow flying over the roof, a fine line attached to it. Gentle tugging on it brought it back enough so that it caught on something, and then they pulled the line more until it fed a rope up to an eyelet in the arrow and back down to them.

"Right then, Owain," Rhodri said as cheerfully as he could in a whisper. "We'll give you a leg up to start you off. Up you go!"

Hoisted up on Madog and Llew's massive archers' shoulders, Owain was already high up the wall, and it didn't take him much effort to pull himself up to the terracotta-tiled roof. At that point he took off, nimble as a cat, and only holding on to the rope for added security since a loose tile could cause him to slide. Not that the roof was steeply sloped, and compared to the slippery rain-soaked, reed-thatch of houses at home, it was easy. In no time he was lying peering over the ridge, and then turned to give a cheeky thumbs-up to those below before crabbing sideways along the roof, taking the rope with him. He stopped when a soft owl-hoot from below told him that he was now in line with the door, and then he reversed the anchoring arrow to now latch under the corbel stones of the roof on the outside, and vanished over the ridge.

Tuck realised that they had deliberately picked a spot by the door both for speed, but also because it was unlikely that the bedrooms would be right by the main door, and it was therefore less likely that they would disturb any sleepers. Rhodri and Sulien were already leading the way back up the outside steps, and as Tuck hurried to catch up with them, he heard sounds from behind the door. With a snick of the latch, the door opened to reveal Owain's grinning face.

"Not even a proper bolt," he whispered gleefully, "just a bar!"

"Right, you keep watch on the inside but with this door closed," Rhodri instructed. "Don't want anyone getting up for a piss and while they're using the pot wondering why the door is wide open! Archers, back to your spot, and you four who were going in ...get going! The rest of us will wait on these steps."

Once on the inside they could see that there was a small central courtyard, and Stephen's comment about the windows on the inside became clearer. While the residents wouldn't risk leaving a window open to the outside world in the outer walls, evidently they had never thought of anyone coming over the roof, and so there were windows open facing onto the courtyard, which all by itself was as large as many houses the Welshmen knew. And the layout of the house was also clearer, for above the ground floor and presumably resting on that storey's stone-vaulted roof, what Tuck thought of as a cloister ran around the courtyard on the first floor. Delicately arched in what he by now had learned was the Arab style, this covered walkway gave onto the upstairs rooms, whose doors and windows led off it. No wonder that Owain had got in so easily. He had just had to swing himself down and in through one of the arches, and he could walk past the rooms to the front door unimpeded.

Yet now they also realised that this 'cloister' presented the greatest danger. Anyone across on the other side of the building would be able to see them with ease, especially as the whole place wasn't that huge. The far side was only twenty feet away from cloister to cloister. And someone was definitely still awake! Across in one of the corners a door was closed, but through the room's open window, the flickering light of an oil lantern was throwing shadows onto the wall outside. And hidden within the room, two voices were arguing – or rather one was being very forceful and the other sounded as though it was pleading.

Keeping close to the inner wall and what shadow it offered, Sulien led them around the slightly longer circuit of the rectangular courtyard, taking that route so that they didn't have to pass the lit window in order to reach the room's door. Once there, he tugged Stephen forwards so that he could hear what was being said, and it didn't take long for Stephen to hurriedly gesture them backwards so that he could speak.

"It's the tutor priest, Brother Asser! He's begging Lord Tancred to change his mind."

"Over what?" Tuck asked, already getting a sinking feeling over this.

"I think Tancred has already sent young William somewhere. Asser kept saying, 'but you have to fetch him back, it's no journey for a child of his age!' But Tancred just kept on about it was his decision to make, and that Asser has to go back home."

Before Sulien could send Stephen back to listen more, there was an angry retort from the room, a loud slap, and then Brother Asser shot out of the door, almost being catapulted over the balustrade by the boot the others caught a glimpse of as it hit Asser's arse. The door was slammed shut again, and Asser folded up in a heap, weeping. No translation was needed for the shouted words which then followed out of the window. Asser was being told to shut up and go away.

The distraught monk hauled himself to his feet and groped his way along the balustrade towards the hidden men, weeping too hard to see them until Sulien's hand shot out of the darkness and clamped over his mouth, and he and Gryff hauled the monk to them.

"*Shhhhh!*" Sulien hissed in Asser's ear. "Tell him, Stephen! Don't just stand there gawping! Tell him we're here to help him!"

Stephen let fly a string of what sounded far more like proper French, but before he'd said much of anything, Asser was turning in their grasp, having obviously understood every word.

"Of course," Tuck whispered in relief, "you're an English monk, aren't you!" Asser nodded. "Then when Sulien lets you go, you must keep quiet, alright? Come with us, and once we're outside we'll explain what we're doing here."

In no time, they had hustled Asser back around the upper floor and through the short corridor between rooms to the main door.

"Right, before we go, can you just confirm to us that young master William isn't here in this building?" Sulien asked firmly.

"No he isn't!" Asser almost wailed, although doing his best to control his voice. Then managed to whisper, "That monster has sent the boy off to get the next ship to the Holy Land! Some crusaders were in the port a few days ago, and that wicked bastard paid them to take Master William with them. He's given him to their order!"

"God's hooks!" Rhodri swore from outside. "Poor little lad! ...Right, come on then, everyone. Let's get moving."

"I'll go back the way I came," Owain offered. "That way I can remove the arrow and the rope. We won't need to bolt the door – we can just make it seem like the brother, here, walked out – and as long as there's nothing else suspicious left behind, there'll be no reason for that pig in there to think anything happened but his distraught monk up and left of his own accord. I doubt he'll come looking for you when he told you to go?"

Asser shook his head. "I was going to leave tonight, anyway. He's such an ungodly man, I was starting to fear that he might slit my throat if I stayed any longer. I've only waited this long to find out where he sent my young pupil."

"Well we're heading for the Holy Land, too," Tuck told him, keeping a firm hold on Asser's arm as he bustled him down the outside steps. "Looks like we've added another sacred duty to our journey, though – to find and save young master William!"

Chapter 9

The Sea Voyage,
Late summer, the Year of Our Lord, 1177

Back in the port of Messina, the men began enquiring about ships to the Holy Land, and immediately found that they had just missed one.

"It sailed early this morning," Stephen told them, after a rapid exchange with a sailor. "Knights of the Order of St John were on board. The man remembered that because they all wished to travel together, and so several pilgrims got taken off the boat to wait for the next one, which they weren't happy about!"

"No, I bet not," Rhodri said sympathetically. "Like us they'll either have to try and find somewhere to camp outside the port, or pay for more lodgings. When's the next boat leaving?"

"Not for a week," Stephen said miserably.

"A week?" Asser almost wailed. "But then there's no chance of us catching up with dear William!"

Rhodri clamped a hand firmly on the willowy monk's shoulder. "*Shhh*, you fool! Stop making that racket! Everyone's looking at you, and we don't want that, do we? And it's a pain in the arse that we've missed the ship, but I wasn't expecting them to run more than one a week unless someone very important was making the crossing – and I bet under that situation, all the returning ships get told to wait so that it's a whole flotilla of ships going, which would mean the ordinary pilgrims getting shoved to the back of the line, just as has happened now.
"But it's not the disaster you're thinking, either. Don't forget, these ships from here will only go as far as Crete. They won't be going all the way. So if the ship going onwards to Cyprus isn't in port when it arrives, there's always a chance we can catch them there before they move on, or even on Cyprus before we get to the Holy Land. It's not going to be like tracking someone on land, where there'd be several different ways to go. The lad's on a ship heading for one spot and one spot only, and with no way to get off and disappear – as long as the ship doesn't hit a storm, God willing. And if it does, well we're all in the Lord's hands out

there on the water, so the best people to keep him safe are you and Tuck saying your prayers, and hoping they get listened to."

With Asser now bringing their number up to sixteen, Tuck had privately wondered whether they would prove too large a party to go all on one boat, but it seemed that they were one of the smaller pilgrim bands who were travelling east this summer. And Tuck felt his prayers had been answered when they successfully secured their passage just a day before one of the larger groups of pilgrims came in. Much haggling and downright bullying went on, for one of that number was an important lord from somewhere, but the ships' agents in Messina were not to be shoved around. The next boat was already full, they declared, and anyway, the lord's party would need two ships to carry them, so they would have to wait until two were in harbour or accept being split up. What the outcome of that was, Tuck didn't hear and wasn't bothered about. As long as their voyage went ahead as planned, that was all that mattered.

Sure enough, four days later a ship came in and spent two days getting cleaned up and restocked, and then on the final day they were allowed on board to stow their stuff away, not that they had much.

Anian gave Tuck a nudge and a wink. "I think the captain approves of us travelling light. I might not know this language they speak, but if you know people, you could tell that our captain was glad he didn't have that lord's group going on his ship with all their horses, too. God's hooks, can you imagine the mess if the horses start shitting themselves in fright if it gets a bit rough? You can imagine him upping the cost to compensate, and at the same time wondering whether even then it would be worth it, can't you?"

Tuck grinned back at him. "Bless me, yes, you can! Whereas a well-behaved bunch of travellers like ourselves might not make him as big a profit, but does guarantee a quieter voyage."

And the captain was soon grateful for the Welsh soldiers. One of the small groups of pilgrims booted off the previous ship, and now travelling on theirs, turned out to have a couple amongst them who had smuggled skins of wine on board. Two days out of port, the pair got roaring drunk and began trying to pick fights with the sailors. In no time, the Welshmen had piled onto them and had them trussed up like chickens for the pot, which was how the two remained for the rest of the voyage and under guard.

It certainly meant that when they landed in Candia on Crete, their captain was quick to sing their praises to his fellow mariners, and they had no trouble finding a swift onwards passage.

"This is all good," Tuck reassured the ever-anxious Asser. "Our captain has put in several good words for us, and once Stephen explained that we were chasing after a little boy who had been taken unwillingly, this new captain of ours is going to set off two days earlier than he might." He didn't bother adding that the decision had probably been helped by the pair of drunks heading off into the town to get well and truly soused, and ending up in the local gaol for three nights. Clearly the captain wanted to be well gone by the time they got released, and Tuck wasn't so naive as to not see how much of an incentive that was too. Already on this journey he had had his eyes opened to the world, and he had the sense to be counting his blessings that he was travelling with worldly men like Rhodri, Anian and Sulien, who saved him from making a complete idiot of himself, or worse getting himself killed.

For his own part, he was also glad that the journey was going faster than it could have done, for Asser was proving a trial of a different kind. Tuck could understand why the soldiers had shoved the other monk into his care – it would seem the natural thing for them – but Asser was everything Tuck was not. It was as if their physical attributes echoed the internal differences, for while Tuck was built like one of the Welsh churches' fortified bell-towers, able to withstand fire and flood, Asser was as thin and pale as a willow wand and just as likely to bend, or even snap, in the first breeze. And for all that Tuck had been shoved into the Church long before he had been capable of making such a decision for himself, his faith was as strong as the stones his little church had been built of. Asser, on the other hand, seemed to have gone into the monastery at Canterbury thinking that this was what he desired most deeply, only to find that whatever it was that was plaguing him had simply followed him there; and worse, the monastic life had given him far too many hours to fret and niggle at it, until he seemed to be bowed under the worries of a world only he knew about.

So Asser's habit of immediately assuming the worst in every situation soon began to irritate Tuck mightily.

"Bless me! Have a little faith, Brother!" he found himself exclaiming in frustration, as Asser stood by the ship's side and bemoaned that fact that the wind had dropped, and their progress had slowed to a snail's pace. "If we have no wind, neither do those we pursue. And in the meantime, trust that Our Lady will watch over that innocent child for us."

And St Issui stay my hand, please! he silently prayed. *I know I'm far from perfect, but I do believe implicitly in You and the other saints, as well as Our Lord, and that you will do what is best for us, even if it doesn't seem that way to me at the time. Restrain me from tipping this faithless monk over the side and putting us all out of our misery! If this is what it means to be a monk at the greatest shrine in England, then I'm profoundly glad to have served You up in Your quiet church in the hills. All I ask is that we find young William safe and in one piece – both for the lad's sake, and because I don't know what this idiot will do, or what accusations he might make of us, if the lad isn't there when we land in Our Lord's kingdom on earth.*

Whether St Issui heard him, or another saint was watching over them, it worked out that they actually made an unusually swift passage to Cyprus, and having landed at Limasol, found that they could then take passage directly from there to Acre.

"And there, Brother," Tuck told Asser firmly, "we shall soon be in the Kingdom of Jerusalem – the same destination as the knights whom we follow. So let's have no more of this gloom and doom, for pity's sake!" Only one day had been lost due to the lack of wind at sea, and another now in port while they arranged passage, meaning that they were still no further behind their quarry than they had been when they left Sicily. "And that is surely a blessing, is it not?" Tuck remonstrated with the gloomy Asser. "To have travelled hundreds of miles by sea and still not have lost them is no mean feat, and it *is* them who caught the boat before ours, because the descriptions of the men match up. We're not just trailing along in the wake of random men who may or may not have young William – it's definitely them."

Asser had nodded mournfully at Tuck's proclamations, but seemed finally to realise that he was well on the way to seriously annoying his companions, and said nothing more on the subject for several days.

Acre was a revelation when they disembarked. Tuck had never seen quite such a mass of exotic humanity and beasts as seethed around in the town behind the quays. Indeed he was close to feeling utterly overwhelmed by the strangeness of it, never having dreamed such a place could exist even in his wildest imaginings. He'd seen drawings of camels in manuscripts, but the real beast was something again. For a start off, he hadn't expected them to be bigger than any horse he'd seen aside from a knight's war-horse, and he certainly hadn't anticipated that he might actually have to ride one. And the first time he saw a sailor with a monkey he was shocked to his core by how human the little creature looked, right down to its tiny fingernails and mannerisms. That the monkey flinched away from one person only to fling its arms around another had him wondering if such creatures had been God's practice pieces before moving on to mankind. Then remonstrated with himself for such a thought – God would not need to practice, he chided himself! Therefore the Almighty must have intended them to be just as they were, but this was only one of many such mental conversations he had with himself to try and cope with this alien world he had arrived in, with some only leading to deeper confusion and less peace for his soul.

The knights they pursued had paused at Acre to visit their large *hôpital* there, and so the Welshmen found themselves becoming part of the same great camel train which would take them on to Jerusalem. Not that they spotted William straight away in the milling crowd of pilgrims and natives, but once everyone was mounted up it was clear who the knights were, since they had horses from their own order to ride on, unlike the rest of the travellers. From his perch high on a camel, Tuck found that with it adding to his own considerable height, he had an unrivalled view across the heads of the other travellers, and he was sure he saw a small figure clinging on in front of one of the knights. He told Sulien and Rhodri the next time he stopped, but given that he couldn't identify the knight from any other, they all agreed that there was no point in telling Asser, nor Stephen and Walter.

"It'll only raise their hopes up," Sulien said practically, "and it's not as if we can break the lad out while we're all travelling together, is it? He's as safe as anywhere in this …what did Stephen call it?"

"A caravan," Tuck supplied. "*Dewi Sant!* I never dreamed it would be like this."

And he was very glad that he had long ago abandoned his monk's habit for simple trews such as the soldiers wore, and also wore proper boots, for Asser's habit rode up as he straddled the camel, and before the first day was out he had badly burned legs. They managed to find a pair of old woollen hosen in one of the lad's packs which would just about fit and protect Asser from further burning, but when the skinny monk began moaning that they itched, everyone found themselves wishing he would just burn to a crisp, so that they could bury him by the wayside and have done with him. His only saving grace was his genuine concern for William, and that meant that the others just about found it in them to tolerate his miserable company.

"Please God there'll be some monastery we can leave him at when we get to Jerusalem, though," Lord Hywel said to Tuck after one of Asser's evening griping sessions. "It might be unchristian, but I honestly don't want him travelling all the way back to England with us! I might undo all the good this pilgrimage is supposed to be doing me, and kill him before we even see Sicily again."

Yet the deeper they got into the barren desert landscape, the more the blazing sun seemed to desiccate Asser, and he got increasingly withdrawn and silent.

It had to be at least a hundred miles between Acre and Jerusalem, and although they stopped at various settlements along the way, what struck Tuck the most was the way that you couldn't see any great distance once you were out in the desert. He'd assumed that without much in the way of woods or mountains to block your view, that you'd be able to see for miles, but the air was so full of dust that the horizon was always a blur. Even at night, the air could be so full of dust at times that the stars themselves were blotted out except for the very brightest ones.

"They must know this route like the back of their hands," he confessed to Anian, when they'd been on the road a week. "I used to be able to navigate my way around at home with ease by the stars when the clouds permitted. I could get to my lord de Braose's castle at Brecon and back with no difficulty, but this? This is like travelling through a weird dry fog."

"Too true," Anian agreed. "You can see how men get lost in the desert, can't you? Not a landmark for miles that I would recognise, yet these men go straight for a point like one of Madog's arrows, and I'm blessed if I can tell how."

Great rock formations appeared off to one side or another every so often, their surfaces sculpted by the blasting sand and winds into towering, soft, pillow folds. At one stop, Tuck went off to relieve himself and found some primitive carvings in one of the rocks where it had been sheltered. How old they were he couldn't even hazard a guess at, but it brought it home to him that people had been travelling these lands since the Old Testament times, thousands of years in the past.

"Did you travel this way, Lord?" he found himself asking the air, his voice muffled by the scarf he'd learned to wrap over his face to keep the worst of the sand out of his mouth and nose. "Where's Nazareth from here, or Bethlehem?"

"They are far behind us, back up to the north nearer Acre," a soft voice answered, and one of the native men melted out of the darkness to come and stand beside him.

"You speak our language?"

"I am with the Hospitallers – the Knights of St John, as you may know them. Many of us ordinary fighting men are local Christians, though we follow a different church to you from the west."

"And are you such a one?"

"I am."

"Then I'm pleased to meet you. My name is Brother Tuck. I'm a priest travelling with Lord Hywel's party."

"I am Nasir, a turcopole with the Hospitallers," and he gave a strange half bow with one hand over his heart.

Not knowing whether offering his hand would offend this new and welcome friend, Tuck simply said, "I'm very pleased to meet you."

"Have you come here to see the holy places?"

"Well that's what we started out to do," Tuck admitted, suddenly realising that here was someone who might be able to get closer to William, if he was willing to help. "Unfortunately we had got as far as Rome when we met a lady from Messina with a tragic tale. She, poor soul, is now dead – she lost the child she was carrying and something went very wrong with her too. But we learned from her servants that her young son was now in danger from her late husband's half-brother, and that proved all too true when we got to the family manor near Messina. He'd already shipped the boy off with some Hospitaller knights, indeed the same ones we travel with now, but we've yet to spot the lad. We're all very worried about him because he's far too young to be gifted to a fighting order."

Nasir had begun to frown as Tuck's tale progressed, but now smiled. "Ah! Then let me reassure you, my friend. Had it been the Templars the boy's uncle tried to hand him on to, he would have been refused outright. The Templars only want fighting men. They would have no interest in a child at all. But my Hospitaller masters are a very different matter. You see they not only fight, they care for pilgrims too, and that includes children orphaned out here. The brothers who encountered the boy may well have thought that his best interests were to be brought to join the other children – especially if they feared what would happen to him if left with his uncle. In their care, a child would always be given the option of joining the order once they come of age, but it would never be compulsory. The boy you seek is well cared for, and will be given schooling when he gets to Jerusalem and joins the other children. You need have no fears for his safety."

Tuck beamed at Nasir. "You have no idea how much your explanation has comforted me! Thank you. Would you come with me and tell my friends that? I believe they may be very grateful to you if you do."

He led Nasir over to their party and made the introductions, then explaining why he had brought Nasir over. As the local man explained how the Hospitallers cared for orphaned pilgrim children, it was easy to see the relief spreading over Stephen and Walter's faces, as well as those of the Welshmen who had never known the lad, but who had taken his fate to their hearts.

"*Dewi Sant*, that's a relief!" Madog said for all of them. "That sounds like the best possible outcome."

"It does, doesn't it?" Lord Hywel said cheerfully. "He'll be with other children, get the education you couldn't have hoped to offer him, Stephen and Walter, and then when he's old enough, he'll be able to make his own choice about what he does. There's many a lord's son who doesn't get those kinds of offers," and Tuck thought he was probably speaking from the heart there. Being the son of a minor Welsh prince like Lord Cadwallon possibly hadn't made for the easiest of childhoods.

Yet worryingly, Asser still didn't seem content.

"What's wrong with you?" Tuck demanded in exasperation after Nasir had left them. "Surely all of your fears have been allayed? Nasir had no reason to lie to us, and he certainly didn't need to give us all that information. He could have said nothing to me and then made sure we were kept well away from the boy. For the love of God, Asser, buck up! You can spend as long as you like in Jerusalem – for there surely have to be some of our own monks in the holy city whom you can join – visiting William and making sure he's properly settled. And then you can return to Canterbury with a clear conscience," yet all he got in response were baleful looks.

The following night, however, things became rather clearer. As the party camped for the night at yet another watering hole, Nasir appeared out of the dusty gloom with a man of about the same slim build, but who was clearly not a native, and with them was the small figure of a boy.

"This is Frère Pascal, one of our knights," Nasir introduced, "and I think this is someone you already know."

Walter and Stephen ran forwards, and William was swept up into hugs which he returned with joy, and they began a conversation in rapid French with Frère Pascal, which none of the others could hope to follow, but which was clearly amicable. Anian and Bryn invited Nasir to come and join the others for some of the hot drink which was brewing over the camp fire, but Tuck held back as he saw Asser lurking in the gloom.

"Now what's the matter with him?" he muttered to himself, but then felt Rhodri and Sulien coming up on either side of him and grunting their agreement.

"Why doesn't he go to the lad?" Sulien said softly. "Young William's obviously glad enough to see Walter and Stephen."

Then in the flickering firelight, they saw William start to look around him from where he was still swung up in Walter's arms, and there was no mistaking the horror on the young lad's face when the light picked up Asser. There was also no mistaking the way Asser's eyes lit up as he met William's – it was love, but not, Tuck thought, of the spiritual kind.

"Judas' balls!" Rhodri swore. "I didn't see that one coming!"

Sulien snorted his agreement. "But at least we know what crept up Asser's arse and was biting him – damn, I didn't intend that double meaning, Tuck …sorry!"

Tuck gave a bitter chuckle. "No offence taken, my friend. You only said more or less what I was thinking. Oh dear. What are we to do with Asser now?"

"He's not our responsibility!" Rhodri protested, but Tuck shook his head.

"But I'm afraid he is. After all, he would never have found his way even out of Messina left to his own devices, would he? He's so useless out in the world, he'd probably have ended up with his throat cut in some Sicilian ditch before the week was out, after saying the wrong thing to someone. Bless me, I know I can be a liability at times, but he's in a whole other league! Yet we scooped him up and brought him here, even if it was with the best of intentions – and that makes him rather our problem to deal with, don't you see?"

Luckily, as Walter, Stephen and Frère Pascal had turned to come towards them, Asser scuttled off into the night like one of the camp rats which flitted through the gloom, attracted by the rich pickings of so many people – a human pest echoing the rodent ones.

"We have made a decision!" Stephen announced happily to them. "My father and I are going to join the Hospitallers as lay brothers. Frère Pascal says we will not need to be part of the fighting force, but can stay helping to look after the pilgrims. That way we can stay close to William as he grows up and he can still see us, and it's not as if we have anywhere else to go to. We would have to find some other lord to take us in, and he might not look so kindly on three new tenants when one is an older man and one only a boy."

"I think that's wonderful," Tuck said, coming to clasp Stephen's hand. "This has turned into a blessing all round, with all three of you finding somewhere safe."

For the first time Frère Pascal spoke up in heavily-accented English. "I would not call Jerusalem altogether safe," he said with a smile. "We do face the might of Salah-al-Din's force on a regular basis, but yes, within the city walls they will be as safe as anywhere, and possibly safer than in many places back in France or England."

"We'll stay with you tonight," Stephen added, "but tomorrow, when we have packed our things up again, we shall go and travel with Frère Pascal and his brothers."

Rhodri held out his hand and took Stephen's. "We'll miss you! But I agree with Tuck, this is just what you need," but as they turned and walked away again, he added softly to Tuck, "but how Asser takes that news is going to be way more of a problem, I'm thinking."

Tuck sighed. "Indeed it will. By *Dewi Sant*, why did it have to be that perversion that was what was gnawing at Asser's soul? And why did some idiot prior think that it was therefore a good idea to send him into this situation?" His impressions of senior monks in his order had not been improved by this journey, even if he thought well of most of his ordinary brethren still. "Lone tutor to a small boy? *Tsk!* Stupidity at best, and cruelty at worst, for someone surely had heard his confession enough times by then?"

Sulien patted Tuck's beefy forearm. "I think you're over-thinking it, Tuck. I suspect it was something far more down to earth, and their prime thought was just to get shot of the miserable sod and as far away as possible! It's just our bad luck that it sent him straight into our path."

Chapter 10

Jerusalem,
Autumn, the Year of our Lord, 1177

Arriving at Jerusalem was an experience all by itself. As they got close to the city, the increasing number of pilgrims was something they had expected, but not the exotic collection of other people who obviously lived there. Fair-haired western women rode by, clearly ladies of some standing, and yet dressed in flowing, clinging silks which left little to the imagination. And swarthy men carrying swords, or at least armed with long daggers, were all over the place, and yet had to be on the side of the defenders of the holy city.

"How on earth do they tell friend from foe?" Lord Hywel wondered.

Rhodri chuckled. "Probably just as easily as we can tell who's Welsh and who's English, my lord. It's the subtle differences that we can't even see that would scream the answer to a local."

Hywel shook his head in bemusement. "Well I'm just grateful that I won't have to draw my sword while I'm here, because I might just end up skewering the wrong person if I did."

"Indeed!" Tuck agreed with a laugh. "Pilgrimage and skewering definitely don't mix!"

Their friendship with Frère Pascal and Nasir now helped them greatly, for rather than wandering aimlessly around the city trying to find somewhere to stay, they were taken to the great hospice run by the Knights of St John, and found beds. The only thing Frère Pascal asked of them was if they would spend some time helping out with the sick and wounded, and Tuck for one was only too glad to do that. This was something comfortingly familiar to him from his days at Ewenny, when he would gladly have joined the brothers working in the infirmary permanently and in the surrounding villages, had Humbert not taken a perverse delight in denying him that option. Within days he had struck up a friendship with one of the infirmarers, and he was happily comparing the recipes he'd learned from Brother Ioan for soothing balms, pain relievers, and remedies for sickness, as he and the brother rejoined his friends in the refectory for an evening meal.

"We have to have willow bark brought in," said Frère Johan, a blonde-haired chunky Hollander nearly as big as Tuck, as they sat down at the end of the long bench beside Rhodri and Llew'. "On the other hand, we have ample supplies of poppy seeds, which given some of the wounds we have coming in, is a blessing of no small proportions."

"Hey, you two, no gory stuff!" Anian teased. "We're trying to eat here."

Frère Johan beamed his huge smile. "No worries, little brother, I shall not disturb your meal."

"Little?" Anian spluttered, only partly faking indignation – he was the shortest man of the Welsh party, but didn't like to be reminded of it even if he wasn't the sort to take umbrage. "I'll have you know I'm a giant amongst my own people!"

"And are they the little folk who live under the hills?" Johan quipped back, making everyone hoot with laughter.

With the rest of the meal passing with similar jocularity, it wasn't until everyone was filing out, with the lay brothers and knights heading for the chapel for one of their observances, while the rest sought their beds, that Tuck realised that Lord Hywel was hanging back and giving him pleading glances. Resigning himself to missing the evening prayers, Tuck gestured to the courtyard, saying,

"If you want to talk to me, we'd better do it out here. The lay brothers who were serving tonight will want to be clearing up in there."

He led the way to a simple stone bench beneath one of the many olive trees which provided much-needed shade during the day, thinking that by the time he got back home, he would forever associate olives with these soul-searching conversations. But it was as the last of the light played on Hywel's face that Tuck realised that he'd made a seriously wrong assumption. While they were with the men-at-arms, and in situations which he was familiar with, Hywel had the confidence of a young man well into his twenties, but seeing him now, it suddenly dawned on Tuck that he probably wasn't even out of his teens yet. And just at the moment Hywel looked every inch the rather scared young lad, all of the bravado gone and his face a picture of youthful misery.

"Whatever's wrong?" Tuck asked, forgetting to 'my lord' him when he looked more like his memory of a particular young lad from up by St Issui's, who used to get a beating from his father far too often. "Has something happened today?"

Hywel flopped down on the bench, his chin dropped onto his chest in a picture of total dejection, and his voice was so low that Tuck only just caught his words. "I want to go home. I don't like it here – though I know it's probably wicked of me to say so."

Tuck couldn't help but put his arm around Hywel's shoulders and pull him to him in a hug. Lord's son or not, Hywel had had a home where he'd been loved and wanted, and the loss of it – however temporary – was something he was feeling keenly. Never mind that Tuck himself was only a handful of years older than him; just at the moment he felt positively ancient by comparison. And it struck him that quite possibly he was the spiritually poorer of the two for never having had the kinds of bonds with people where such a separation would be so very painful.

"I don't think you're wicked for loving your home and the people in it. I don't think you're wicked at all," Tuck consoled him. "This is no small journey we've come on, and you're not the only one to be unsettled, you know? Rhodri is worried stiff over his wife and children, and whether they're coping without him. Anian is fretting that the widow he was courting might have forgotten him by the time he gets back. And Owain is worried that his elderly father won't cope with shearing the sheep all by himself. Everyone is feeling the distance – you're not alone in that."

"You're not," Hywel said, trying to sniff back the tears. "You seem to be positively enjoying yourself! Is that how I'm supposed to be feeling …coming to this holy place, I mean?"

Tuck sighed, feeling his own heart sinking as he tried to explain, "I have my qualms too, you know? It's just as strange for me here. But it's not just the holiness of Jerusalem that helps me, Hywel, although it is a consolation when I feel most lost. I was given to the Church when I wasn't even old enough to remember my own mother, but I didn't fit in there – into the enclosed world of the monastery.

"Yes, I do have a deep and devout faith, but that doesn't always help me as much as you might think. I got into terrible trouble with my prior for telling the local people what the Latin words meant, and you may not believe it, but coming with you was meant to be a punishment for me. It's my perverse nature that has discovered that I love being out in the world with ordinary people far more than I ever did being in the monastery. So of all of you, I have no home to miss, no people who I long to see.

"The old priest I shared a cottage with up by St Issui's is dead, as is Brother Rhys who first taught me, and the one lad amongst the other novices who I was friends with ran away years ago. So you see, there's nobody back in Wales for me to miss. The thing that I miss most is the land itself: the rolling hills, the soft rain and mists, the green trees and hedgerows, and the rivers and the streams tumbling down the hillsides. I'm not gifted with some magical power which takes all my sorrows away, it's rather that I have way less to miss than the rest of you."

"Oh." Hywel was clearly taken aback by Tuck's admission. "But there are things you want to do …aren't there?"

"Yes there are. I want to go and pray at the site of the Crucifixion. I want to pray at all of the sacred spots in this special place."

"And should I do that too?"

"If you want to." Tuck was struggling here, and was alert enough to know that his own inexperience lay at the root of that. An older priest would no doubt have known what to say, but he could only speak from the heart and hope for the best. He didn't want to make Hywel feel any worse if the lad genuinely wasn't soaking up the atmosphere here – and he was a lot more sympathetic to that feeling after his own experience inside St Peter's in Rome. "But it would be a shame to have come all of this way and not to get the most out of it, don't you think?"

"Suppose so." There was a long pause and then Hywel added very softly. "But could we do it quickly and then go? This place …it frightens me. It's so strange. I… I don't know what to do or say around these people. I can't work out who are the lords and ladies, and who are… are… well, something else!"

Tuck felt some small relief at that. For a lad who had spent his whole life being the big fish in a very small and parochial pool, it was understandable that the discovery that the world was a far bigger and more complicated place than he'd ever dreamed of would be deeply unsettling, especially when he couldn't work out where he stood in this much larger and alien hierarchy.

"Well I can't promise that we can just turn around and go back," he said soothingly. "You have to understand that we have to wait until there's another caravan of pilgrims going back to Acre, for a start off. But I don't think Rhodri or any of the others are going to be keen to linger longer than they have to. Would you like me to have a word with Rhodri and see if we can maybe get back to the coast in time to get one of the last ships of the autumn back to Sicily? It'll mean travelling in the winter once we get back as far as France, though, so you'll have to accept that it'll take longer as the days get shorter."

"Would you?" Just that offer seemed to lift a weight off Hywel's shoulders, and so once the lad had staggered off to his own bed, Tuck went in search of Rhodri, finding him playing at dice with some of the others.

"Just wagering in dried beans, Brother," Madog said with a wink. "Nary a coin has changed hands. It's just a bit if fun."

Sitting down with them, Tuck gave them an edited version of his conversation, thinking to ask at the end, "Did any of you spend any time with him today? Did anything in particular happen that would have brought this bout of longing for home on so suddenly?"

The spreading grins on the faces of Madog, plus Dai, Will, and Hugh – three of the men-at-arms Tuck had had less to do with so far – alerted him that the answer was probably yes.

Dai gave a little snort of amusement. "He had his first encounter with a courtesan in the market."

"A real looker, she was," Hugh added with a chuckle. "Very much the fine lady with her man-servant, so when our young lord 'my lady'd her, he got laughed at. He didn't like that much, but then when he found out *what* she was from her servant, he made the mistake of asking what it would cost to spend some time with her."

"Ouch!" Tuck breathed. He might not have been out in the world that long, either, but he'd heard from Rhodri and Sulien about these high-class courtesans of the east. Many were the kept mistresses of great noblemen, and even if they weren't, they were as far above the common whores the soldiers frequented as those soldiers were from their lordly commanders. So Hywel had offered offence twice over, and had undoubtedly been slapped down at least verbally and possibly physically too. That wasn't going to do a lad like him any lasting harm, but for the moment the wound to his youthful pride would feel like it was mortal.

Taking a deep breath, and silently offering up a prayer for forgiveness for suggesting such a thing, he said, "Then would you maybe find him some sort of suitable female companion?"

"Tuck?" Rhodri spluttered in amazement. "Are *you* asking us to find a way to get our young lord laid?"

Tuck grimaced. "I know. Not exactly the holy thing, I know. But think on this: he's probably never had to want for female company before. Would any local girl on his father's lands dare refuse him? So I can't imagine he's still a virgin? And in that case, he's been suffering a forced abstinence for months – unless you lot sneaked off somewhere while we were in Rome?"

The rueful shakes of the head told him that they hadn't, giving him the courage to go on. Talking about such earthly desires wasn't something he'd had any practice at at all. "So, that encounter with the courtesan is going to have hit him hard in more than one way, isn't it? And either I'm even more of an oddity than I thought, or this heat isn't making things any easier for any of us. My head and my soul may not desire women, but just at the moment my body seems to have a mind of its own."

The hoots of laughter and back-slapping which greeted this confession told him that he wasn't alone in finding the presence of so many women a trial he had never expected. Their exotic perfumes were the worst part, he'd discovered. Lingering whiffs of rose and jasmine, combined with exotic scents such as frankincense and warmed by a body which added something else to them, had the ability to drive him to distraction. And smell them he could. He'd been expecting the bodily stench of so many people to be far worse and more overwhelming here in this heat, and yet it wasn't. With it being so incredibly hot that sweat evaporated and didn't linger, in some ways the press of people was less obtrusive than at home on a hot day, for there the humidity usually meant that people sweated buckets which then clung to their clothes. Moreover, the people of the east seemed to take cleanliness far more to heart, and there were public bath-houses which got regularly used, and they were a delight Tuck soon found himself wishing they had at home.

Nor had Tuck ever been close enough to fine ladies before to even tell whether or not they wore perfume. So to pass one of those courtesans, or one of the ladies high enough in rank that they could ride through the city, and in the crush of people to be close enough to them for more than just a fleeting moment as everyone's progress slowed to a snail's pace, had resulted in a wholly unexpected assault on his senses. And while he could resist what his eyes were seeing, his nose and other parts of his body seemed to have joined together in rebelling against all of his vows, and his until now unquestioned belief that he would be happy with the celibate life.

"Are you sure you don't want us to find *you* a nice lass?" Anian teased him with a wink. "Come on, Tuck! Who's going to know when you get home, eh?"

Yet Tuck shook his head and with a rueful smile replied, "But God would see. And if I took up with some nice local woman instead, I'd always be worried that I'd left a child of mine behind in this place – and that would be a torment for me. I know what it is to grow up without a father."

That sobered them up, making Rhodri put a hand on Tuck's shoulder and give him a sympathetic squeeze. "You're a good man, Tuck. ...But doesn't all of that apply to young Hywel as well?"

"Well, yes it does. But all I can say in answer to that is, I can't imagine the lad abstaining any more here than he has in the valleys. As for his illegitimate offspring, I have to trust to Our Lord to oversee that matter, because again, I reckon the chances are that there's already some poor little mite running around in Wales, who was got on a pretty maid by Lord Hywel when she felt she couldn't say no, or risk having her mam and da thrown out of their cottage." Tuck had become very Welsh at this last, recollecting another young girl who had come to him distraught at finding herself with child through no fault of her own. This treating of the poor as mere playthings was something which really stuck in Tuck's craw.

He obviously struck a chord with the others, too, who all now nodded sagely and muttered darkly about high-handed lords.

"I see your point," Rhodri sighed, "so there's a job for you in the morning, Madog. Go and find some whore who's both pretty and clean for young Hywel to plough his field with. Because I think Tuck's right on this one – we'd better brighten the daft sod's life or he'll make ours a misery for as long as we're here."

Tuck gave him a grateful smile, but also thought to ask, "But he has made me think about the return. Have you made any enquiries? Do any of you have a clue about what our times might be?"

Sulien sighed. "Well we have had a talk about it. We're all missing home too. And you were right to warn young Hywel about the winter, Tuck. Yes, we could catch one of the late boats back and get as far as Sicily again, but think on how long it took us to get here. If we leave in late August, it's going to be October before we start tramping up towards Rome again, and then we're also going to start losing the daylight. I don't know about you, but we don't fancy trying to cross those bloody mountains on a freezing cold November or December day! And that's *if* the passes are still open – they could get well and truly snowed up."

"And there's another thing," Rhodri added. "If we move on within the next month or so but can't get all the way, then that means we have to find some way of wintering part way home, and that's either going to cost us dearly, or we'll have to find work. And that brings the danger of us getting into a position where one or more of us then finds it almost impossible to get away from whoever buys our services – because the one thing we're likely to find work as is as guards, but that means we'll be watched too. I don't want to leave anyone behind on Cyprus or Sicily!"

"By Our Lady!" Tuck gulped. "I hadn't thought of that particular twist! Oh dear."

"But," Rhodri added, raising a finger to halt any further words from Tuck until he'd finished, "we've been staying here with the Hospitallers for free, except for doing some helping out. And I think as long as we make ourselves useful, things will stay that way – to which end, by the way, we've started helping out in the stables on top of the other tasks we've been asked to do. That could make a huge difference to how we go home, Tuck, because we'll still have relatively full purses. Once we start on that journey, we'll then be able to afford to take fast ships and do as we did on the way out here, and go from ship to ship – not have to stop each time in the next port until we've topped up our funds somehow."

Tuck sat back and regarded Rhodri with a new respect. Unlearned he might be, but there was a considerable mind at work there, and he now appreciated why Lord Cadwallon had chosen Rhodri to lead this party, for Rhodri would never act without thought as to the consequences. Quite aside from being a natural leader, Rhodri had a maturity and depth which made him stand out even from experienced men like Sulien.

"I think you've made a very convincing case for us wintering here," Tuck agreed. "*Issui Sant* help me, I'd better break the bad news to Hywel tomorrow," and he sighed mournfully, already visualising the tears and possible tantrums that would bring on.

"*Naaa*, don't do it tomorrow," Sulien said with a cheerful wink. "Let Madog find him this whore first. He'll be in a far better frame of mind once he's played hunt the sausage a few times! He might even decide he likes it here after all," and there were guffaws of agreement from the other men.

Smiling with them, Tuck got up and went to find his bed. *Hunt the sausage*, he thought, *I've never heard it called that before. That's probably what Humbert meant when he said most of the monks wouldn't cope with men like these. But I think he was hopelessly wrong to think them ungodly. They just see the day-to-day realities of life, and may God forgive me, but I am starting to see why men like them think that monks are clueless and hopelessly naive, shut away from the world. If someone like Asser can grate on my nerves, despite all my prayers to the contrary, how badly must monks like him infuriate soldiers like these? We don't see the half of it, and yet when we do go outside, we dare to start laying down the law over how to live lives we know nothing about. Blessed Issui Sant, I don't know if I'm going to be able to go back to the cloisters ever again! Humbert was right about that – I've been far too 'corrupted', as he would see it. Dear Lord, if you can hear me, show me the path you want me to go down, because shutting myself up in Ewenny Priory after this surely isn't it.*

Chapter 11

Jerusalem,
Late autumn, the Year of Our Lord, 1177

By the time the days started really drawing in, Tuck's life had fallen into an enjoyable routine. In the mornings he and his friends joined the few regular soldiers of the Hospitallers left in Jerusalem in their exercises, for Rhodri had decided that it was too good an opportunity to miss not to take advantage of the know-how of these expert fighters. Including Tuck had been a different decision, for Rhodri was smart enough to have seen how Tuck was blossoming out in the world, and had he known it, was thinking much the same as Tuck himself about his inability to fit back into a cloistered life. Therefore Tuck needed to know how to defend himself and anyone under his protection. And he and Tuck had managed to talk Hywel into learning from the remaining knights, too, primarily by pointing out to him that, if nothing else, he would be taking back an awful lot of knowledge to his father of how to combat the Norman Marcher lords. In doing that they had managed to draw Hywel out of his gloom at not heading for home until spring, and once the young lord had worked out where he stood in this strange world, he almost seemed to be enjoying himself, which was a blessing not lost on his companions.

Once the midday bell rang, Tuck would then take himself off and begin working with Frère Johan, and here he was relishing every moment. He'd done enough with Brother Ioan in the herbarium at Ewenny to have a good working knowledge of the standard cures, but here he was being treated to what amounted to an extended master class, for with the vast mix of people who came into the Hospitallers' care also came a greatly more varied range of ailments and diseases, not to mention serious injuries. And Frère Johan was quick to say,

"We're learning all the time from the Saracen physicians – they still have so much of what the Ancient Greeks wrote, you know, things we have long lost in the West," and more than once Tuck heard him then add, "I do not know what my counterparts back in the north would think of me now, but when I get a truly perplexing case, I have two local men whom I turn to. One is a Jew, who is unrivalled in his knowledge of herbs, tinctures and ointments. And the other is a Saracen, who knows more of surgery than I would once ever have believed possible. He will attempt things I would not even contemplate, and does so successfully, too. Ah me, Tuck, we have so much to learn, and at times I fear for the arrogance of our leaders, for these two men will work to save the life of anyone in a way that some of our most Christian brethren cannot find it in themselves to do."

"God works in mysterious ways," Tuck agreed, finding himself deeply drawn to such mutually beneficial coexistence, even to the extent where he began to wonder whether he wouldn't be happier actually joining the Hospitaller order. Here in the east it was often nigh on impossible to maintain the mental distance – and also what he was now beginning to think of as the blind bigotry – of Rome and the countries and dukedoms west of it. Blind hatred of those whom his brothers back at Ewenny would have clumped together as 'Saracens' was far harder here, particularly when you realised that living here in the east were many Christians who followed a different path to Rome, and who were no fonder of one another than they were of the Saracens.

Tuck had discovered four different sects of Christians out here, and that aside from the westerners like himself, most of the local Christians in Jerusalem followed the Byzantine Church. But over on the coast in the County of Tripoli, most were Maronites – followers of St Maron – and then to the north of them in the County of Antioch they were Jacobites – followers of St James. Despite his best efforts, Tuck could only grasp that these two sects loathed one another, even if they hadn't seemed to come to blows yet, over something about which a Byzantine emperor had made a decision over five centuries ago. And neither of these were fond of the Byzantine Christians and their patriarch in Constantinople, who in turn hated the Roman Church; all of which both baffled and infuriated him.

Why on earth did these four eastern branches of Christianity in the Holy Land argue with one another? Hadn't they got enough people to fight already? And that was before you added the Coptic Church in Egypt into the mix, because they too were fighting the Saracen forces, but were a wholly separate sect. It was deeply unsettling to a young monk who had grown up believing in the unity of his Christian faith to find it so subdivided. And it wasn't that he was remotely tempted to go and join one of these other branches of his faith, which worried him most, but the fact that it was so deeply divided at all.

And of course there were the Jews, of whom there were a great many living within Jerusalem. He had swiftly realised that they had a fund of learning of things long lost in the west, and his curious mind frequently meant that his trips to buy various herbs or spices on Frère Johan's behalf turned into whole afternoons lost in conversation with some Jewish merchant, who knew infinitely more about the applications of what Tuck was buying than he had even dreamed possible. Or he would stand mesmerised watching the Arab surgeon at work, totally forgetting why he had come for a while and what he was supposed to ask about, as he became lost in watching the man's dextrous hands cutting and stitching with a delicacy he had never seen in a westerner.

The sheer joy of learning new skills invigorated him like nothing else, and the pleasure of seeing someone recover after his treatment gave him a spiritual pleasure all of its own. Here, he felt for the first time as though he had found his forte, his purpose in life. He was even able to offer a couple of cures he knew of which were new to Frère Johan, and so he felt that he'd added something more than simply being a willing pair of hands.

He'd also persuaded Rhodri to bring the rest of the men into the infirmary each evening, just to help out with some of the heavy lifting of those patients too ill to be able to move themselves, for there were many soldiers who had come in who were long-term patients, and who needed to be turned regularly to avoid getting bed-sores. And to his satisfaction, he soon saw them starting to spend time talking to these bed-ridden soldiers, swopping stories of both fighting and of their homes as they improved with their understanding of the local language. It brightened the day for men who could do little but lie there and hope that their broken bodies would heal, and it gave his Welsh friends a much greater insight into the kind of warfare fought out here.

"*Duw!*" Hugh exclaimed the one night as they all sat down together afterwards. "You know that soldier I've been talking to? Well I saw his injuries for the first time today. He's burned all down his back and shoulders – and that's from his armour! No Saracen did that. All it took was some fool of a knight marching them out in height of summer in the midday sun, just before we arrived. The poor bastard looks like he's been boiled alive! His chain-mail shirt got so hot it even burnt him through his jerkin."

"I know the man you're talking of," Tuck said sadly. "Frère Johan's amazed that he lived. With those burns he was more likely to die, but somehow they've managed to stay clean, and the poppy-juice they doped him up with kept the pain down to bearable for the first few weeks. Frère Johan's not sure how long it's going to take to wean him off the poppy, mind you, because it's awfully addictive when it's been taken for as long as he has. But then he's not likely to ever be able to go soldiering again, either, because those burn scars are going to heal tight, even with the salves we've been making up."

It was a sobering illustration of just how different life out here could be. For a start off, whereas at home nobody fought in the winter because the roads got too muddy, and rivers too swollen, to easily move any large body of men around, here it was when much of the fighting picked up as the days got cooler.

"Do you think we'll be asked to fight?" young Owain asked worriedly one night, having spent his early evening listening to one of the native troopers – the turcopoles – telling him about how he and his knight had been ambushed out in the desert. "Saif said they were cut off from water for days and nearly died of thirst! Some men did, apparently, dried out and shrivelled like my old hosen! I don't fancy dying that way."

"I don't think we'll be asked to march out, if that's what you mean," Rhodri reassured him. "Most of the fighting men are attached to either one of the orders or to one of the great lords out here – and we're neither – so we wouldn't fit into their ranks. But if Saladin comes to Jerusalem …well, we might not have any choice in the matter then, which is why I want us to be at our best, not fat and lazy from having done nothing more than go with Tuck to pray every Sunday."

Knowing now that he had rather more time to visit the sacred sites, Tuck had taken to visiting one a week and taking the men with him. By now he had also realised that however much his friends might believe in God, there was only so much they could cope with in one go of religious observances, and so by measuring it out into manageable pieces, he was making sure that they got the maximum spiritual gain out of being here without driving them to distraction. It had helped that the Church of the Holy Sepulchre was literally around the corner from the Knights of St John's great *hôpital*, where they were living, and so that had been an easy place to take the men to as an introduction. And then there were the churches dedicated to St Peter, St Martin, St John the Baptist, St Anne, and St Mary Magdalene, all of which they made visits to, and even up to the Royal Palace within the great Temple Mount, although Tuck was warned by Frère Johan to be wary of the Templars who had taken over what had previously been the Al-Aqsa Mosque.

"They are not like us," he warned Tuck. "They follow St Augustine's severe rule like the Black Canons, and are prone to be zealots. Tell your friends to be cautious about being too familiar with them, for some of their jokes would be badly misconstrued by the Templars, and you might find yourselves in trouble! The Black Canons proper also have the church built on the Dome of the Rock itself, so be careful how you treat them there, too, Tuck. They won't welcome a Black Monk like yourself with open arms, not even here in Jerusalem! We who follow St Benedict are seen as indolent and corrupt."

"And this is on the site of the Temple of Solomon," Tuck sighed. "Where is the wisdom in all this conflict, eh?"

And indeed, once they had tramped into the confines of the elevated walled area within the city walls, Tuck could see why Johan had warned him. The Templars strode about as if they owned the place, even the lay brothers, and on several occasions they had to dodgy out of the way or get trampled on by groups of men who marched towards them with no intention of pausing or stepping to one side.

"Such arrogance will be their downfall," Rhodri muttered, to Tuck after the third such encounter. "They believe themselves invincible – and that's always a shaky place to start any fight from."

"I fear you may be right," Tuck agreed. "Pray that in the process they don't condemn Jerusalem along with them," never realising how close to being prophetic he had come with that statement.

Once the days had begun to cool as autumn came on, he even got them out through the Zion Gate in the south to Mount Zion and the church of St Maria that was on it.

However it was in the Church of the Holy Sepulchre, site of the Crucifixion, where Tuck felt a profound connection with something, although he struggled to say quite what. If he'd been expecting to feel the immediate touch of Christ – maybe as something powerful and energising – then this wasn't it, but he did feel incredibly moved by the sense of sorrow and suffering that he felt here, very much as he had done in the Coliseum in Rome.

What is it about me that feels so moved by these places? he wondered on their third visit, as the others simply enjoyed the peace and quiet after he had led them in prayers, for in a city of thousands of souls, 'quiet' was often hard to find for men used to nothing but the sounds of nature on the distant Welsh hills. *Is it that I sense the ordinary people who died on these spots in Our Lord's wake?* And in thinking that thought, as he looked around him he spotted Asser. Most of the week Tuck felt able to ignore the monk from Canterbury, for if he could not be compelled to acts of mercy by the sights within the *hôpital's* huge wards, then Tuck couldn't think of anything more heart-rending to move him to compassion; yet he had never seen Asser in there helping out as the others did. Where the other monk went to all day, Tuck had never bothered to ask, but something about being on this holiest of sites prickled at him to go and demand answers.

It was only as he got up to Asser, who as ever had been keeping as apart from the others as he could, that Tuck realised that once again Asser was crying his eyes out. And suddenly it dawned on Tuck that Asser had lost a lot of weight – not that he'd had much on him to lose in the first place.

"Whatever is wrong?" Tuck demanded, with rather less sympathy than he might have used with another. "You, a monk, are here in one of the holiest places on earth – surely that is such a blessing! Few others are granted such a chance. Why can't you rejoice?"

Asser turned tear-streaked cheeks up towards Tuck from where he knelt, his eyes blood-red from what Tuck now realised must have been weeks of crying. "You don't understand," he sniffed.

"No I don't!" Tuck riposted sternly as he squatted down beside him. "And that's not helped by the fact that you'll never tell any of us what's wrong. You can't expect much sympathy, Asser, when you trail around like a beaten dog all day, doing nothing to help others, and assuming the air of one of the martyrs without having died yet!" Mentally, Tuck then winced. That hadn't been at all tactful, but being tactful hadn't got him anywhere with Asser. And he felt even guiltier when Asser took a deep but ragged breath and made his reply.

"I cry because I mourn for my late wife and my children," he hiccupped. "I'm not a monk like you, Tuck. I didn't join the order out of any deep conviction. I did it because I had nowhere else to go and nothing worth living for."

Oh God forgive me! Tuck prayed. *What have I done? Why did I never make him tell me this before?* "Your wife and children?" he said aloud instead. "Why have you never mentioned them before? What happened to them?"

Asser gave another bubbling sniff. "I used to live up in the north of England with my wife and family, not far from Alnwick Castle." He heaved a heavy sigh. "We weren't rich. We were just freemen farmers like my wife's father had been before me. I thought our lives would go on undisturbed, and that my two sons would carry on farming there once I got too old."

Already Tuck was getting a dreadful sinking feeling over where this was going, and it wasn't helping his own feelings of intense guilt at so badly misreading Asser.

"I loved my Matilda," Asser continued, cuffing more tears from his cheeks. "It may sound odd to a man like you who never even looks at a woman, but to me she was the most beautiful woman on earth. I wouldn't have swopped her for the queen herself. ...And my boys ...oh, my lovely boys!" and he momentarily broke down again. "My William and my Edward were the light in my life, both of them so like their mother in every way."

God forgive me! Tuck's inner voice again screamed and feeling true remorse. *William? Is that why he was so fixated on the William we brought here? Lord grant me absolution for foisting the sins of some of my less-than-deserving brothers onto this poor man, and judging him when I had no right to! I must do penance for that act of arrogance on my part.*

Sniffing mightily, Asser was continuing. "All was well in our little home until the day two kings' fighting men rode over it three years ago. I don't know why the king of the Scots was fighting the Sheriff of Westmorland – I don't even care. All I know is that one day in July, all of a sudden there were fighting men everywhere, each lot accusing us of helping the other. I don't even know which side the men were on who set light to our home and sealed the door."

"*Dewi Sant!*" Tuck gulped, feeling his throat constricting in sympathetic grief. Had Asser seen...?

"I saw the place burn from where they had me tied up..."

Oh God, he had! "You actually saw it?" Tuck had to ask, appalled. What a terrible thing to have to witness.

Asser nodded, his face bleak. "I'd been rounded up by the sheriff's men, and it was only afterwards that he told them not to be so foolish and let the local men go. By the time I got back it was too late. ...Far too late. ...The roof had fallen in and it was just all smoke and ruin. ...After that I just started walking. Why not? There was nothing left for me there. ...I walked and I walked, first to Durham and then to York, and somehow I just kept going. By the time I got to Canterbury, my only thought was to spend the rest of my days praying for their souls. That's why I asked to join the monks."

Something nudged at Tuck's memory. "Hang on a moment, you were young William's tutor. So when did you learn to read and write, then?"

Asser gave a grunt. "*Hmph!* Don't you believe me?" The martyred expression was back in an instant, too.

"I didn't say that!" Tuck protested. "I apologise for my ignorance and for mistaking what you were, and are, going through, but I cannot read your mind and if I'm to help you, I need to understand. So it struck me that the average farmer, even a freeman, doesn't know his letters. That's normal. For pity's sake, Asser, there's many a nobleman who can't read or write, either! So I'm hardly maligning you by simply asking how come you *can*!"

Asser shrugged morosely. "If you must know, I'm the bastard son of a prior. My mother was his housekeeper. ...It was only a tiny place. Hardly worth marking on any map. ...In fact, by the time my father died he was the only one left there, but that meant that he had time to teach me."

"Ah, I see," Tuck said, forcing himself to sound sympathetic and understanding, even if Asser still irritated the living daylights out of him with his hang-dog ways. "Yes, there's been many a foundation set up by some well-intending lord, which has then simply died away for want of brothers to serve there, or the money to keep it going. I'm guessing that where you grew up was close by some manor house?"

"Yes it was. And so once my father died, my mother went to work at the big house, and I was put to work in the fields. They didn't need or want a man who could read better than the lord or his clerk could!"

Slowly Tuck was beginning to see what had shaped Asser into the miserable specimen he was now. A different sort of youth to Asser would have long since made his way into somewhere like Durham and offered his services to a merchant – and surely there must have been someone like that in a place as prestigious as Durham? Or if not there, then York certainly did. But Asser clearly only took what was offered to him, never going and seeking what else might be out there in the world; an eternal taker of the easiest path, despite how miserable it made him.

"But surely things were better in Canterbury?" Tuck asked, because by now the all-too-human side of him couldn't stop asking out of morbid curiosity, even though his higher self was telling him to stop and just leave it, and that such rummaging in someone else's murky past was unseemly for a man who had taken the vows of priesthood. It was a bit like watching a bolting horse and its cart, just waiting for the crash to come – part of you just couldn't look away. "Surely that was all you could have asked for? A chance to use your learning and to do as you wanted – to pray for your wife and sons, I mean."

Asser gave him a baleful stare. "No it wasn't. ...*Tsk*! Some of those monks! They were near illiterate, you know! So I tried to put them right… Why are you wincing like that, Tuck? They were saying the litany wrong. Surely it was my Christian duty to tell them so?"

God have mercy on me! Tuck thought fervently. *Please tell me I wasn't that arrogant, even in my youth? I may have thought the same, but at least I had the sense to never say so out loud! And I did value good monks like Brother Ioan, Brother Cadfan and Brother Rhys. I never thought* all *my brethren were a waste of space! I felt as sorry for the other novices who Brother Eustace persecuted as I did myself, and as a full brother, even in my naivety and youth I knew the bad ones were only the few — it was just rotten luck that they were the ones who had the most influence over my life. So I'm also sure that the couple of monks we met at the doors of Canterbury weren't typical of every monk in the place. Why would God allow it to be the most revered place in England if it was?* And that was a conundrum which had bothered him ever since, so surely there must have been some monks whom Asser could have confided in?

"I fear you stepped on some very proud toes there, Brother Asser," he said instead. "Indeed I do know what you mean, for I myself have come across brothers who seemed incapable of learning the proper forms of the prayers they said. And not through inability, but idleness, too. But do you not see how the other brothers might have thought it equally as proud and sinful of you to be correcting them, especially as you were so recently come amongst them?" Asser, after all, had been a grown man when he entered Canterbury, without the excuse of youthful ignorance.

In response Asser merely shrugged. "If so then that was their loss." He heaved another massive and rather — to Tuck's ears — self-pitying sigh. "So when the word came that a tutor was needed to go with some guests of the archbishops as they travelled back to their homes, I was the one they sent." Now his face fell into a mask of grief again. "But oh Lord, why did it have to be to a little boy called William? And one who looked so like my own boy did at his age?"

"That's why you were so distraught at William being sent away by his step-uncle," Tuck said, finally seeing what had eluded him for so long. "Oh Asser, that was a cruel blow. I do see that. But I've also seen how *that* William looks at you, and I have to tell you for the sake of your soul, that I fear you frightened him with the intensity of your feelings. I don't think he understands."

"But I told him that he reminded me of my own son!" Asser protested.

"Yes, I'm sure you did," Tuck ploughed on through gritted teeth, wondering how Asser could be so dense, "but did it never occur to you that that young William has never had such an… an… *affectionate* relationship with his own father? A nobleman like Lady Agnes' husband wouldn't have had anything to do with the day-to-day care of a little boy! Not like you would have done with your own sons. At best, the child would have been taken through to see his father to wish him goodnight, and probably not every night, either. And that may well have been the only time they saw one another. He may even have been a little frightened of his father if he was sent to him for punishments. The people who would have looked after William were his nurse and one or two household servants – people like Walter and Stephen – and they would have been people he'd known all of his life. You turning up out of the blue and then showering him with unfamiliar affection would have felt beyond strange to him – strange and worrying!"

"*Humph!*" Evidently Asser wasn't convinced, and Tuck was running out of patience. He felt terribly guilty that he had silently condemned Asser for a sin the man had clearly never had any intention of committing, but equally, Asser had never once stopped to consider how young William had felt about any of this. So now he said firmly,

"Well William is being well-cared for by the brothers here. He's happy with the other children, as you must know if you've taken the time to go and see him?"

"They won't let me see him."

Now it was Tuck's turn to tut. "*Tsk!* And did it never enter your head that that might be because William has told them that you scare him? Honestly Asser, you're hopeless! I feel for your terrible loss, truly I do, even though I have never had a family to love, much less lose. But this excessive grief over losing the other William is doing nothing but harm to you and to a little boy who is no kin to you. You have to stop it, and stop it now! Think of what you are going to do next. You don't have to go back to Canterbury if you don't want to, but you need to make some sort of decision.

"Are you going to join another monastery here? Is that what you want? Because you can't stay on with the Hospitallers after we leave – certainly not when you don't do anything to help the other pilgrims who are sick, or the wounded soldiers. If you do want to stay with them, then you need to wake up and start coming with me to learn from Frère Johan – they don't have room to keep a healthy man who is eating their food and yet giving nothing back in return. And if you can't think of anything for yourself, then by Our Lady, get on your knees here or in whichever church calls to your soul, and ask for divine guidance! But you can't go through the rest of your life just weeping and wailing over your fate."

"That's all very well for you to say," Asser muttered, getting to his feet and stamping off to the main door, which he just let go behind him, slamming and shattering the peace.

"What was that all about?" Rhodri's voice came at Tuck's elbow. "What bug bit his arse this time?"

Unable to keep his frustration out of his voice, Tuck explained what the real cause of Asser's grief had been, adding at the end, "And Heaven alone knows what he meant by, 'it's alright for you.' How is it alright for me? I'm hardly in any different a position, because I tell you, Rhodri, I don't think I can face going back into Ewenny Priory's cloisters any more than he can Canterbury's. But I'm not so daft as to not know I have to decide where I'm going from here; and so until I do, I'm making the most of what's been given to me here. If nothing else, I shall go back to Wales a much better healer than when I left, thanks to Frère Johan."

From Tuck's other side Sulien's sardonic voice said, "There's no cure for what ails Asser. He's just a miserable get who's never got over the indignity of being a bastard, Tuck. There's many a child who's fallen further from where they started, and yet made much more of themselves. We can all feel for him over the loss of his family. That's plain tragic, but he's not the first, nor the last, whom that's happened to, and if he's not encountered much sympathy, then maybe it's because he keeps on spitting in the eyes of the people who offer it? You can't help a man who won't help himself, Tuck, not even you. …Come on, there's that little wine shop just inside the gate. Let's go and get a couple of skins to share with the brothers tonight. There's not much that a drop of wine or beer can't put in a better light."

And much as Tuck wished otherwise, he realised that Sulien was right – Asser was no longer his responsibility. He would have to find his own path from now on. *But please, Lord,* Tuck offered up as a last prayer as they left the church, *if he wants to travel back to England, let it be with another group rather than ours!*

Chapter 12

Jerusalem,
November, the Year of Our Lord, 1177

However, only days after Tuck's encounter with Asser, events overtook them which drove all thoughts of the other monk from his mind. They knew that scarcely had they arrived before the greater *hôpital* complex had emptied of all the fighting knights and men-at-arms, for Frère Pascal and Nasir had marched out with them and they had missed their new friends; but the whys and wherefores of their departure hadn't really sunk in back then. They had been too new to the east, and the names mentioned at that stage hadn't meant anything to them.

But by late September word had already come back that Philip of Flanders had taken his army to join Raymond of Tripoli's, along with the Master of the Hospital, Roger des Moulins, with most of his Knights of St John plus some Templars, and also a huge levy of men from the region who had joined them – a huge force of over a hundred knights and two thousand men, such numbers staggering the Welsh, who had only ever fought in small raiding parties. At that stage, which was now already two months ago, this massed army had moved on the city of Hama, far to the north nearer to the County of Tripoli, and had besieged it, only relenting after an appeal for clemency from Bohemond, the prince of Antioch, whose lands lay even further north of there.

"I don't understand why they would just give up when they almost had the city," Frère Johan had said to Tuck at the time the news first came, as they pounded herbs together with honey and some of the sticky frankincense resin to make an ointment, one of their daily chores to keep the *hôpital's* medicines fully stocked. "Is this King Baldwin's hand we're seeing? He's so young, Tuck, and so he's not had that much experience. Oh that his father King Amalric was still alive. And worse, although nobody yet dares to say anything out loud at court, those of us healers who talk amongst ourselves have learned that he has leprosy, so he could already be too sick to lead."

"*Dewi Sant!* In one so young? How has that happened?"

Frère Johan had shrugged as he scraped the contents of his mortar and pestle into a glazed terracotta pot, which he then sealed with wax to protect its precious contents. "Who knows? Maybe a servant when he was a child? Someone who left the royal court before it became clear what they carried. But it's said that he feels no pain in his one arm, and it's spreading! You can't fault the boy's bravery, though. To have ridden out and so far in order to lead his army," he shook his head sadly, "that could be a courageous gesture that costs him dearly in his health. Campaigning is hard on a well man – for a sick one it could prove disastrous."

Another message in October then said that Prince Bohemond had called upon the army's leaders to help him capture a place called Harim, and that they had turned to head that way. And now Tuck saw the terrible problem of fighting in this land – word took so long to reach anywhere, that the results of actions had already taken place long before someone's allies could respond. For it seemed that Salah-al-Din had seen an opening with the Christian forces all moving north, and had decided to launch an attack of his own and he was already heading for Jerusalem!

"This is bad," Frère Johan's friend, Frère Bornhold, said having been one of the messengers who then arrived in November, and had come to the infirmary to have a nasty sword-cut on his arm stitched and bandaged. "The king's turned back and got as far as Ascalon – that's on the coast, Brother Tuck – but now it looks perilously as though he's trapped within its walls. As you know, Jerusalem has already been stripped of most of its troops, and though King Baldwin has called the *arrière ban* – which ought to call out every able-bodied man – what good will that do if Salah-al-Din turns his great army of tens of thousands towards here? How will so few defend the city if the king cannot get here? I got this cut when Salah-al-Din's vanguard attacked Lydda – and that's just a fraction of the men the Saracens could send our way if they wish. Be prepared to fight, my friends! You may be amongst the few here to defend the Holy City!"

"Let's get these pots out to the others," Frère Johan said, hoisting onto one arm a basket full of small pots filled with a honey-based balm which could be worked right into wounds, and grabbing another with his spare hand, Tuck doing the same. "Looks like we won't need to worry about these going bad – we'll be lucky if there's any left by the sound of it!"

Outside of the calm of the herbarium it looked like organised chaos to Tuck. In the course of one day, everything had changed. Lay brothers were setting up make-shift mattresses anywhere they could, while the more experienced healers moved the existing patients deeper into the *hôpital* or to the uppermost floor. And now for the first time Tuck saw the Hospitaller sisters, for normally these women and girls kept to their own part of the great building, assisting the women pilgrims and locals with specific women's complaints. Had he but known it, Tuck passed close to a young blonde-haired girl he would later come to know very well back in England, but in this intricate dance, which he mentally compared to what he'd seen bees do in a hive, telling one stranger from another was near impossible.

"If pressed, we can deal with two thousand souls," Frère Johan said, as he shouldered his way towards one of the wards, not boasting but looking deeply worried as if he could already see every one of these beds filled with wounded and dying. "Thank the Lord we're not busy with any pestilence just at the moment."

"And the sisters help?" Tuck couldn't help but ask, aghast. He'd never known women tend to wounded men, but Frère Johan nodded,

"Oh yes, and many of them are excellent. They can bandage and poultice with the best of us, and few faint at the sight of blood – well when you've delivered a few babes, what happens with the human body has few surprises left for you."

"Yes, I suppose that's true," Tuck said, desperately trying to quell his own rising anxiety. He'd never in his wildest dreams thought he'd see the kind of carnage these people were calmly preparing for. In truth he'd never even seen the aftermath of a Welsh raid, and suddenly he was hoping that he wouldn't disgrace himself and be sick at some sight, or worse, faint!

By the end of the day there was outright panic in Jerusalem, and as many of the people as could get there went to find refuge in the Tower of David, the fortification close by David's Gate, and about the only supposedly secure place not suffering from crumbling walls within the equally fragile city walls. As night fell, Tuck joined his Welsh friends on the roof of the *hôpital* as they all anxiously kept watch.

"You could go and join the civilians in the Tower," Tuck said, hoping he wasn't going to offend them by making the offer. "I'm staying here to help with the wounded, and Frère Johan says that Salah-al-Din is lenient towards those who care for others, so I'm likely to be alright, but you don't need to stay."

"*Nah*," Sulien replied, giving Tuck one his friendly arm-punches. "No room to swing a cat in that place! If I'm going down, I'm going down fighting, and that means room to use this quarterstaff. Can't do that surrounded by women and screaming kids, can I? And who knows, maybe Madog, Bryn and Llew' can even the odds up a bit with those big bows of theirs before the bastards get inside?"

The night drew on, and somewhere in it Tuck knew that he had dozed off, waking at least once to a night of clear stars up above and an eerie silence out in the city, only punctuated by the distant sound of wailing from the Tower of David.

Morning came, and the city was still intact, and by now the waiting was starting to tell on everyone. Nobody talked much, too tightly strung to be able to do anything but crack a few bad jokes, which no-one really did anything but give a few tight-lipped smiles over. The inhabitants of the *hôpital* checked everything was ready, and then checked it again, and still nothing happened.

Then just when they thought they would be in for another tense night, the first of the wounded started coming in, telling of a great battle at Mont Gisard near Ibelin. Salah-al-Din had underestimated the king, or was it Reynald de Châtillon who had led the army for the young king who was now severely ill? Whoever it was who had commanded the army, they had come out of Ascalon to join with the Templars of Gaza and caught the Saracens unawares. Some even said that they had nearly caught Salah-al-Din himself, though with the luck of the Devil, as they saw it, he had escaped to fight another day.

All that was somewhat secondary, though, in Tuck's eyes as he saw the first of the wagons pull into the courtyard with the worst of the wounded on it.

"You come with me, Tuck," Frère Johan had said, as soon as the batch of men who had arrived with them on horseback had been helped inside. "These can just about walk with some help. The ones coming in on the wagons will have to be carried, and that's where they'll need strong men like us."

And now Tuck saw the dreadful reality of war face to face. The wagon was filled with groaning men, and a couple who were ominously silent.

"Stay still, we will get to you!" Frère Johan instructed in both French and English, and another language which Tuck had learned was understood in the Holy Roman Empire. "Come, Brother Tuck! This man here by the tailgate is as good as any to begin with. Help me lift him across onto this stretcher." Being as gentle as they could, they lifted the man across onto a stretcher which had been put on a trestle table strategically placed by where the wagons had to pull up.

"Easier on our backs," Frère Johan had explained when they'd been setting it up, and now Tuck fully understood why. Taking hold of the poles at the foot end of the stretcher as Frère Johan took the head, it was infinitely easier to lift the man just the few inches to clear him of the trestle than it would have been to pick him up off the floor. This was experience showing, Tuck thought, as they carried him through into the first hall where some of the sisters waited.

A middle-aged sister bustled forwards and began a rapid examination of the soldier. "*Hmph!* Head wound," she declared. "Frère Wilhelm and Frère Gilbert, take him through to Frère Aimery."

But already Frère Johan was tugging Tuck to go back for the next man. "We have to keep moving!" he commanded. "Some of these men may be bleeding. They are our first concern. If we can't stop that, then there's no hope for them."

By the time they had got back to the wagon, another pair of the brothers had lifted the next man on the wagon onto a stretcher, and they passed them going in through the main door as they came out. And the next man proved what Frère Johan had said. The poor man was one of the turcopoles, but his arm ended in a ragged stump just below his elbow. The wound had been tied off with a binding which looked like it had once been someone's tunic, and as soon as they had hauled him inside, Frère Johan slacked the tourniquet off a little, and Tuck heard his sigh of relief as some blood began to flow.

"You can't leave it tied like that for too long," Frère Johan cautioned. "He might just live if we can get that wound cauterised."

"Indeed he might," the sister agreed, coming to their side and nodding in approval at what Frère Johan had done. "Surgical room for him," she told the next pair of brothers who came up, and who handed Tuck the stretcher they had clearly carried someone else through on, going by the way it already bore fresh blood stains.

Tuck felt his stomach give a lurch. *Please, Lord, don't let me puke!* he prayed. *Not here, not now.*

He hurried out and found that once again others had already come and taken more of the men. Those who were left were the two men who were worryingly silent, and this time Frère Johan got up into the wagon to examine them first.

"Is it bad?" Tuck dared to ask.

"We'll take these two through to my herbarium," Frère Johan decided. "There's nothing that can be done for them besides prayer and some soothing herbs."

"Will they die?" It shook Tuck that he suddenly found it mattered terribly to him whether these complete strangers would recover. What was the point of hanging on to these holy places if all that happened was that men died over and over for them? Where was the holiness in squandering such lives? *Surely, Lord, You did not give Your only Son to be the cause of others throwing their lives down in fights they cannot win?* his soul silently screamed, knowing that some – including sub-prior Humbert – would consider such questioning as heresy. Yet deep inside, Tuck believed that the God who had given him such faith would not ask such a thing of mere mortals.

As Frère Johan answered, "If God wills it," Tuck conscience rebelled at the thought.

"Would Salah-al-Din desecrate these holy places if we lost?" he found himself asking, as they gently placed the first man on one of the thin mattresses in the herbarium.

Frère Johan shrugged. "Why not? We did to their sites when we reclaimed the city. The royal palace was one of their temples, you know. I can't imagine that Salah-al-Din is overly pleased at the courtiers fornicating in his people's sacred site, or drinking their wine in there until they can barely stand and pissing in pots in some holy corner. So why wouldn't he want to do to us what we did to him?"

And if he doesn't, then maybe he's a better man than we credit him for, Tuck's wayward mind tacked on, never dreaming how prophetic his words would prove to be ten years further on. *Can one man be so utterly evil as that? For if he is, then would that not make him the Devil incarnate, and surely there is only one great evil such as that? What did Our Lord die for if not for the chance for mere mortal men like us to redeem themselves? Ah me, I seem to be forever finding more questions than answers. Is the fault in me?*

Two days on, he was past debating the rights and wrongs with himself, much less anyone else. Practically asleep on his feet, he had carried wounded men through to the different parts of the *hôpital* until his hands were sore and blistered from the poles, which were themselves by then caked with dried blood. The *hôpital* was filled with the cries and moans of the wounded, and by the end of the first day the only way to tell who were brothers and sisters of the *hôpital* was that they were the ones still walking around, because they were as blood-covered as the men they tended.

And for the Hospitaller sisters Tuck had found a new level of respect. Not once had he seen a sister falter while the brothers carried on. And watching the competence with which they treated the wounded, their skills had to match the brothers' in every way. *I don't know whether Our Lady was one such as you sisters*, he found himself thinking, *and whether it's that She's the one who crafts you in Her image here on earth, but there is nothing weak about any of you. So why is it that the only female saints we recognise are the ones who die dreadful deaths at the hands of men? Surely there must have been some feisty women like these amongst the early Christians whom we should revere?* And his thoughts turned to the tales he had heard back home in Wales. The Saint Brigit he had heard of – or rather Bríg, as her name was said there – had always sounded much more fiery, and he'd always thought that the fact that he'd seen her painted in some churches with a bowl of flames in her hand supported that. *Ah me, I just keep getting more and more confused*, he thought, as he sank to his knees beside one of the men in the herbarium.

He bathed the man's face, finally able to get around to removing the dried blood of others off him, and gently probing his skull to see if he could find any obvious head wound. Utterly absorbed in his medical quest and close scrutiny, it was only when he sat back on his heels that the man's features swam into focus and he gave a cry of distress. This was no stranger, this was Frère Pascal!

"Oh my dear friend, what happened to you?" he gasped, despite knowing that Pascal would not answer. "Oh no, this is too harsh. After all he did to help young William, that he should die here like this doesn't seem right."

"Tuck?" Frère Johan's voice came from behind him. "Is everything alright?"

Stumbling over his words, Tuck explained who this was, but then had it been possible for him to be more horrified, Frère Johan said with unbelievable calm, "I see. It's always a terrible blow the first time you see a friend in here."

"The *first* time?" Tuck spluttered.

"I have seen many of my brothers like this," Frère Johan confessed, "and several of them from amongst those who I called close friends."

"And you can carry on?" Tuck struggled to comprehend how that must feel. "How do you…? How can you…?"

"…Resign myself to their fate?" Frère Johan's fatalistic shrug which accompanied his words almost made Tuck want to scream. "It is God's will. How could I doubt that?"

Mercifully, a groan from the other side of the room drew Frère Johan away, and saved Tuck the problem of how to answer that.

"Why would God want you dead, my friend?" he softly asked Pascal's comatose form instead. "What possible purpose does that serve?"

He soon found himself called away again, for with the huge influx of wounded, nobody had the luxury of their own nurse, but whenever he got a moment, Tuck would slip back to the herbarium and patiently drip honey-water into Pascal's mouth. Everything he'd learned told him that if Pascal didn't wake up soon, then there was no hope for him, for a man's body could only go so long without sustenance, and even less without water. But Tuck hoped that if he could keep some liquid going into Pascal, that it would give his poor battered body the time it needed to heal. And though he found that inevitably his own body finally demanded that he get some sleep, while he dripped the sweet water into Pascal, Tuck prayed like he'd never prayed before.

In between, there were more prayers of a public nature, for although many of those who had died in the battle had, perforce, had to be buried where they had fallen, those who had been brought back to the *hôpital* in the hope of healing didn't all survive. And within a day the funeral services began to be held. Here Tuck was also much in demand as a consecrated priest, and time after time he found himself being called out to where the grave-diggers laboured, burying men several at a time out of necessity, for despite it being winter, and often properly cold at night with a frost, there was still only so long that a corpse could be left before it started to become a hazard to the living.

Over and over he recited the services for the dead, at first having to resort to a written prompt, which had been worryingly ready to hand when he needed it – how often had it happened that a visiting priest like himself had had to suddenly perform this office? But by the time the last of the immediate dead had been buried, Tuck knew that he would never again need a reminder of this service, the only mercy being that as yet he had not had to recite it for Pascal.

Standing by yet another dusty pit, and saying the words as the grave-diggers already began back-filling it over the bodies before night came, and the scavengers came out, Tuck recited:

"*...in terra invia et conficiente ac sine aqua sic in sancto apparui tibi ut videam fortitudinem tuam et gloriam tuam,*" from Psalm 62. But then his exhausted mind fell back into its old ways, and he automatically translated it approximately to, 'In a desert land with no way and no water, in sanctuary I come before thee to see thy power and thy glory,' before the meaning of the words fully hit him, and he faltered.

One of the grave-diggers looked up at him questioningly, and Tuck just about managed to gesture them to carry on while he stumbled over the rest of the words. But they had struck him hard, those words about a desert land without a path or water. Why had it never dawned on him before that all the psalms he so loved had been first written in a landscape such as this? It was so easy to say the word 'desert' when you lived in soaking wet Wales, and never begin to grasp just what a torment such a place could be. Never in all the years he'd recited these words could he have believed how hot it could get during the day, and yet be cold enough to freeze your marrow when night fell. Nothing had prepared him for the aridness of the landscape, either. Small groves of pistachios and almonds grew in certain places, but the deep undercover of a Welsh woodland in full leaf was never going to survive here, and the sheep and goats of the local farmer scavenged grass that to Tuck's eyes barely warranted the name. But it was the realisation of how hard a man's daily life must always have been in these biblical lands which had smitten Tuck so forcibly.

That night as he sat with Pascal, he began reciting the psalms again, but this time really taking the time to understand the words, and finding that their comfortable familiarity had vanished in a new wave of understanding.

"Their meaning has totally changed for me," he confessed to Frère Johan, when his mentor asked him why he was making such long breaks between lines, and admitted to his revelatory moment.

"Your Latin is good enough that you can do this?" Frère Johan asked in return, clearly surprised, but only to find an equally startled Tuck responding with,

"Yours isn't?"

"No."

"You've never put the Latin into your own tongue?"

"No, never."

"Oh!" Tuck didn't know quite what to say to that. He'd been mentally holding Frère Johan up as the infinitely more learned of the two of them, and to find such a huge gap in the brother's knowledge was somehow disconcerting. He was even more taken aback when Frère Johan asked him,

"Can you tell me what the words of Psalm 79 mean, then?"

"Yes, I'm sure I probably could. But why that one?"

Frère Johan gave an embarrassed shrug. "Well it started off being sort of adopted by the Templars, but we use it now too. But the thing is, Tuck, I've never known quite why."

Tuck took a deep breath to brace himself. "Well if you can give me the Latin, I'll do my best, but I'm afraid I don't know all of the psalms off by heart, and Psalm 79 isn't one of the ones I've said often enough to know it."

As soon as Frère Johan said the first line, "*Deus venerunt gentes in hereditatem tuam polluerunt templum sanctum tuum posuerunt Hierusalem in acervis lapidum*," Tuck felt a shiver run down his spine. "What is it Tuck? I know it mentions Jerusalem, but what else?"

"It says... errm... 'O God, the heathen are come into thy inheritance; ...thy holy temple have they defiled; ...they have laid Jerusalem on heaps.'"

"Oh!"

"Yes, more than a bit appropriate when the Templars' *hôpital* is right on Temple Mount, isn't it?"

Frère Johan looked a little shaken. He clearly hadn't thought it would be anything like that directly connected, and it took him a moment to give the next line.

After a moment's thought, Tuck translated, "'The dead bodies of thy servants have they given to be meat unto the fowls of heaven, the flesh of thy saints unto the beasts of the earth.' ...Bless me, that's a bit too close for comfort as well, isn't it, given what we've seen in the last few days!"

Frère Johan just about managed to give Tuck the third verse, "*Effuderunt sanguinem eorum quasi aquam in circuitu Hierusalem et non erat qui sepeliret*," but when Tuck translated that as,

"They have poured out their blood as water, around about Jerusalem and there was none to bury them," he waved Tuck to stop.

"...'None to bury them'? Are you sure, Tuck?"

"Erm, yes ...*sepeliret* ...yes, I'm sure that means to bury."

Frère Johan looked a little queasy. "If you don't mind, Tuck, I think I was easier in my mind when I didn't know that. It all sounds a little *too* close to our predicament here in these times – almost like we're wishing such a fate upon ourselves."

Not wanting to deprive Frère Johan of his sleep, Tuck desisted, but once he heard the brother's resonant snores from his pallet in the far corner of the herbarium, Tuck set his mind to the task again.

"Come on, Tuck, you can do this," he muttered to himself. "What kind of monk are you if you can't even remember the psalms? He's given you the prompt of the first three verses, surely you can drag up the rest from the depths?"

He was that absorbed in his musings, finding the academic exercise a blessed relief from allowing his mind to wander and linger too long on the mutilated souls he'd seen, that he wasn't really aware of his surroundings anymore.

"*Desolaverunt...*" he was muttering to himself. "Made desolate? Ah! Made into a waste, maybe? Yes, that would fit, 'they have laid waste his'... hmmm, his what? Or should that be 'to what is his'?" when a weak voice by his side said,

"How can you remember all that?"

Tuck blinked owlishly, then turned to see Frère Pascal's eyes just about opening.

"You've woken up! God be praised! Let me get you something to drink."

He hurried to find the mug of cold herb tea he had brewed and forgotten to drink for his own thumping headache, bringing it back to the pallet and helping Frère Pascal drink it slow sip by slow sip.

"I have prayed for you every day," Tuck told him. "I can't tell you how relieved I am that you've survived."

"God is good," Frère Pascal managed to whisper, before settling back into a more normal sleep.

"Yes, He is," Tuck said, going to stand in the herbarium door and drink in the cold night air as he looked at the stars up above. "Thank you, Lord, for the return of my friend, but I'm not sure that I'm cut out serve You here. If I had to witness many more days like this last week, I fear I would become as big a wretch as Asser, and that serves nobody, especially not You. But thank you for letting me see the reality of life here before I made the terrible mistake of committing to the Knights of St John for good. Instead, when the time comes I shall be very glad to go back home."

Chapter 13

Jerusalem,
Winter, the Year of Our Lord, 1177

When the king arrived back in Jerusalem, a great thanksgiving was arranged, but somehow Tuck hadn't the heart to attend.

"You go," he told Frère Johan. "I'll stay and keep watch over the men still here in the herbarium."

"Are you sure, Tuck? It'll be a grand event, a chance for you to see the great churches of Jerusalem fully lit and full of people. Who knows when such a thing might happen again? It's believed that Saint George took to the field with our men, you know, so surely that is something to celebrate?" Frère Johan had become rather worried about the effect of the wounded on his kind-hearted friend, who seemed to have lost some of the spring from his step.

As if confirming Johan's worries, Tuck replied wearily, "And why would Saint George do that? What are we to him?"

"His shrine is at Lydda – you know, the place my friend Frère Bornhold got wounded at? It seems the saint took exception to his resting place being disturbed, because he was seen fighting alongside the men at Mount Gisard!"

Yet Tuck didn't seem impressed, or if he was, Johan saw no sign of his old enthusiasm. "They saw him? Well then I suppose thanks are in order."

"They say the king has ordered a monastery to be built on the site of the battle, too."

"Has he? And how many men are going to have to die defending that place, if it can even get built if the Saracens decide to disrupt the works?"

"Tuck, what is bothering you so much?"

With a deep sigh, Tuck went and flopped down on the simple wooden bench that was outside the herbarium looking across the neat beds of herbs. "I'm sorry, Frère Johan. I don't mean to disparage these celebrations. It's just that I look at the hundreds of men lying in this place, and I can't help but wonder what we're fighting for?"

"The Kingdom of Jerusalem!" Frère Johan answered without a second thought.

"Yes, but *whose* kingdom? ...God's? Surely God doesn't need us puny mortals to protect Him? If he could part the Red Sea for Moses, He could smite the entire Saracen army with one blow if He wanted to. So what is He trying to get us to see here? That's been bothering me something terrible these last few weeks. Why is it that time and time again we win these seeming victories, yet at such terrible costs, but within months the places we have supposedly saved fall once more to the Saracens' might? Over a thousand men died at Mount Gisard. A *thousand!* With my friend Nasir amongst them, may God hold him in His eternal embrace. And nearly the same number again have passed through the doors of this *hôpital*, some of whom, like my friend Frère Pascal, will never be fit to fight again. Is it really *God* who demands such a waste of life, or is it the mortal men who wish to make their own great kingdoms in this barren land?"

Frère Johan looked at him, perplexed. "Surely you have bloodshed in your own land? That cannot be such a surprise to you?"

Tuck just about restrained himself from rolling his eyes in exasperation. "Yes, of course we do! But there's a difference. There I know that when men fight, it's for nothing more than earthly gain. It's inevitably one Welsh prince against another, fighting over some slight to their family's reputation, or a tract of land, or stolen cattle. Or if not, then it's the Welsh princes against the acquisitive English king, and for much the same reasons. Can't you see, Johan? It's all so very ...so *human!* So earthly. And the number of dead barely rises into double figures at any encounter, never, God be thanked, into the thousands who have died here!

"But here it's different. When I came here, I truly believed that we were fighting to restore the kingdom of God here on earth. But that's not what's happening, is it? If we were really going to do that, then all of the Christian forces would be focused on Jerusalem, along with enough of the surrounding area to be able to provide for that force. At a stretch, it would be extended to the line of the River Jordan between the Dead Sea and the Sea of Galilee, so that we could watch over Nazareth and Bethlehem.

"But I saw a map for the first time a week ago, and the scale of it revealed to me just how much land these great knights have tried to claim for their own. If you look at Monreal down in the south, and then up to the far reaches of Antioch, we're trying to hang on to a stretch of land as long as the coast from Messina on Sicily up to the Alps! No wonder we're losing! Antioch wasn't originally a holy place, its claim on the Church being the short-lived papacy there, and Tripoli certainly hasn't any ancient biblical connections as far as I can make out. So what on earth are we fighting over them for? Your own Order's fortress of Crac de l'Ospital is helping to defend Tripoli, too, yet I thought the Pope charged you with the care of pilgrims? Well there aren't going to be many pilgrims up there, are there? Not a holy place in sight!

"Oh, I'm sorry, Frère Johan," Tuck apologised hastily, suddenly registering the dismay on his friend's face. "I didn't mean to malign your fellow brothers who fight up there. It's just that from where I'm sitting, it looks like much of the fighting here has nothing to do with anything remotely holy."

"No, Tuck, I'm not offended. Rather, I'm shocked that you have seen so clearly what it never occurred to me to question in all the years I've been here. And I do see what you mean. Prince Bohemond has the Assassins in the east of his lands causing havoc, and beyond that the Seljuk Empire. Yes, Antioch itself was once the seat of one of the great patriarchs of the Christian world, but like Alexandria down in Egypt, our control of that went a very long time ago, and it's not as though there are any other holy places of the like of Bethlehem there, much less Jerusalem."

"And maybe that's why God is not giving us the great victories?" Tuck dared to suggest. "The kind of victories that come without such a terrible cost? We're not fighting for Him anymore, are we? We're fighting for the Raymond of Tripolis, the Bohemond of Antiochs, and the Reynald de Châtillons of this land, and what they want is *earthly* wealth. They're not content to wait for their reward in Heaven, they want it here, and they want it *now*."

The tolling of bells suddenly broke through their conversation.

"You'd better get going," Tuck said kindly. "Go on. Go and get what you can from this outpouring of thanks to God. But this is your world, my friend, not mine."

He let Johan go, then went inside to where Frère Pascal was sitting, at least now able to sit up enough to fed himself, even if it would be a while before he walked more than the few steps to the privy.

Pascal was smiling at him. "Dear me, Tuck, you really are a most disruptive influence."

"Me?"

"Yes, you! That wonderful mind of yours cuts through the fog of lies and misdirection like one of your Welsh friend's great arrows. Poor Johan didn't stand a chance once you started thinking about things.

…Oh, I'm not saying you have done anything terribly wrong!" he added hastily, as he saw Tuck's mortified expression. "We all need our faith testing from time to time, and it shouldn't just be by the strength in our arms, either. You've made me think, too, my friend, and I think I'm going to ask the Master to release me to go and work on one of our order's farms on Cyprus."

"Will he let you?" Tuck was worried that with the horrendous casualties of this last fight, that Roger des Moulins would be hanging on to every man he had like grim death.

"I'd just be taking up space an able-bodied man could fill here," Frère Pascal said with certainty. "So take heart, Tuck. If you are taking the first of the spring ships to Cyprus, I'll probably be travelling with you."

That consoled Tuck mightily. If he could save just one person, then that was something to give praise for, and suddenly he felt as though maybe he could go and join in these celebrations after all. After Pascal had assured him that, yes, he was fine to be left for a while, Tuck hurried around the block of buildings from the *hôpital* to the Church of the Holy Sepulchre. Easing his way in through the door, he was astonished to find that he could barely get any further than that into the church, it was so full. The great open space beneath the dome was lit with more candles than Tuck had ever seen in his life. And they had to be good quality beeswax ones, because if they'd been the cheap animal fat ones such as had been pressed into service in the *hôpital*, the stink of them would have been noticeable even through the rich aroma of the fine incense which was wafting around the church.

So this is where all the beeswax went to, Tuck's rebellious mind brought up, remembering how they had run out of the precious wax to use with turpentine to seal the bandages on certain open wounds. *Men may have died so that God can see his house here a bit better …really? …No, stop it!* he chided himself. *What's the matter with you? You're here to give thanks for the survivors. Just accept it and join in with the singing.*

On the far side of the great open space of the rotunda, and beyond it where a domed transept was also brightly lit, with his extra height Tuck could just make out the choir stalls, and that they were filled with monks. Lifting his eyes upwards, he saw the wonderful mosaics above him, and knew from the way they were reflecting the light that there must be more like them up towards the east end. He'd just never noticed them before, since it took the multitude of candles' flickering light to really bring them to life. And some of those mosaics must have been of pure gold. Or equally precious gemstones like lapis lazuli and garnets, which once again troubled Tuck with their excessive opulence.

And the incense! He'd already realised that here in the east their access to the precious resins ensured a much finer scent, and indeed even the stuff they burned in the herbarium to keep the insects at bay was better than he'd ever come across before, even at Canterbury. But today the Church was burning their finest, and there was something heady about inhaling the combination of finest grade frankincense and myrrh, with a hit of jasmine and rose, which was close to narcotic. And suddenly Tuck knew what he was going to do to appease his quarrelsome prior – he'd take some of this incense back with him to Wales. If the prior could boast that, even for a while, he was burning the same incense as they used in Jerusalem, he might even forgive Tuck just enough to let him have a parish of his own.

As he calmed to the atmosphere of the church, Tuck picked up on where they were in the Latin of the service, and for the most part was able to join in. He was so lost in the spiritual balm of joining in, that it was only when the service came to a close that he realised that people about him were looking at him strangely.

"I'm a monk," he managed to say in the local tongue, having by now managed to pick up enough to get by with. "Not from around here, though, from Wales," and he gave them his most beatific smile. Several gave nods of acceptance at his explanation, but a few who filed past him on the way out looked at him with something close to awe. It wasn't until Frère Bornhold came his way and said,

"Oh, that was you, was it! I might have known!" that Tuck got a clue as to why. "All of a sudden it was like there was this echo of the priests coming from the back of the church," Bornhold said with a chuckle, steering Tuck firmly outside. "Very effective it was! You must have been standing in just the right place for the dome to carry the echo of you, but let's get you away from here. At the moment the priests think that it was some angelic choir joining in, because from the transept it sounded more like several voices than one. But I don't think they'd be any too pleased if they found out that it was a giant of a foreign monk, in just a simple robe with herb stains all down the front! Rather takes away the effect of all their fine robes, you see. By St Lazarus, there was a lot of gold thread on display today, and no few jewels on the fingers of the leading priests as well. You do lower the tone of the place, Tuck," and Bornhold's amusement got the better of him and laughed out loud.

"Was the king there today?" Tuck asked him.

"No," Bornhold sighed. "He, poor soul, is too sick to rise from his bed. That campaign has taken it out of him. I think there's no doubt now that once his sister comes out of mourning for her late husband, and is delivered of her child, that she'll have to be married again to secure the throne. I don't think anyone can dodge around the king's illness with euphemisms any longer, they're going to have to face up to the fact that he'll never be able to sire an heir of his own."

"How terribly sad."

"Yes, I fear for the kingdom if it comes to a contest for the throne."

Tuck shook his head. "No, I just meant for him as a man, and a young one at that. How terrible to have to live knowing that your death is racing towards you before you've even had chance to start living it fully."

The following day, Tuck decided to go in search of the incense he wanted, and as he wandered around the various stalls, gradually working his way around the various traders of the city, he suddenly realised that he had come around to right by the royal palace. He stood back out of the way of the people milling about him and looked up at the great building which had once been a temple.

What are you like? he wondered. *What sort of young man are you, who controls this kingdom on the edge of the known world? Do all those deaths bother you? Do you lead them reluctantly? Or are you like our war-like King Henry's sons, who assume it's their God-given right to direct the small folk as they please, with never a thought for how they live or die?* He would probably never know, he recognised, but there was a part of him which felt terribly sorry for this king who was not even out of his teens yet, but who carried such heavy burdens. *I will pray for you*, he thought, *because someone ought to pray for you as just Baldwin, the man, regardless of where you're king of.*

And to his surprise it was here that he found purveyors of the finest incense.

"It is burned around the king to keep the air about him pure," one native trader told him in explanation, while a Jew a few yards further on added,

"They make him chew on the frankincense for its medicinal properties in the hope that it will help slow the mortification of his flesh."

Having handled some of the resin which the traders had passed to him to smell, Tuck's sympathy for the king's plight only increased, for the resin was hard and yet sticky, and he could imagine only too well how the stuff would stick to teeth and tug at them as you tried to chew. A man would have to be very desperate to resort to such an attempted cure.

He had very little money of his own, but the incense cost a fraction of what it would have done back at home, and so Tuck bought as much of it as he could afford. Over the months he'd been here, he'd discovered that one of his cough cures was more effective than the local version, and so he'd taken just a few herbs from the garden and made up some elixir to bottle, which he'd then sold, making enough from them to restock the small glazed-clay bottles for Frère Johan, and still have enough to buy the makings for more of the syrup with a little to spare for himself at the end. By his third batch he'd made enough that he could now afford the incense, and if his fourth batch had gone to soothing the sand-rasped throats of the sick soldiers, he was happy enough. Hopefully he would be able to get a little more incense before he left.

With the winter light fading fast, he made his way back to the *hôpital*, it suddenly dawning on him that it would soon be Christmas. "I'll be able to celebrate Our Lord's birth here in the very same land," he said out loud, cheered mightily by that thought. Now that was something to look forward to! What would the great churches look like then? And with the forthcoming celebrations being this time about something so purely Christian that there could be no ambiguity about them, Tuck felt able to join in wholeheartedly.

When Christmas Eve came around, Tuck made sure he had rounded up all of his Welsh friends, and had got them into the great church in plenty of time for them to be at the heart of things this time. He'd even given his robes a good scrubbing, recalling Frère Bornhold's words about the herb stains, and had made sure that his tonsure was neatly clipped. *I'm probably the only Welsh priest in the city, let alone in this church,* he thought proudly, *so I offer this up, Lord, not for myself, but on behalf of all Cymry!* And he joined in the office with joy in his heart, although keeping one eye on those around him. He didn't want to find himself being escorted out of the church for taking the focus away from its own priests.

"Now there's a thing to tell your grandchildren!" he said to Lord Hywel, as they all trooped back out of the church after the midnight mass. "You've celebrated Christmas right here in Jerusalem!"

And to his relief, Hywel's eyes were shining as brightly as he guessed his own were. "What a thing to see, Brother Tuck! Do you think we could ever get a craftsman to come and make mosaics like that on a church in Wales? I would dearly love to see that."

"Well, probably not from here," Tuck admitted. "That would be a huge journey for what would seem like an awfully small commission for them. But I'm sure there are such men in somewhere like Venice, for instance. That would be closer to home. And a painter might be even easier to find. Not everything in there was mosaic; some of it was fresco work."

"That would be lovely," Hywel sighed dreamily, but adding more loyally, "but we have as fine singers in Wales, do we not, Brother Tuck? They have wonderful music, but we could sing it just as well at home if we knew it."

Tuck grinned back at him. "Oh yes! You can't beat our own folk for singing!" *And that's another thing I could take back*, he thought happily. *I've an ear for music – I must make an effort to come to more of the offices, so that I've got the chants firmly in my head by the time we leave.*

Chapter 14

The Holy Land
Late Winter – early Spring, the Year of Our Lord, 1178

The remaining months of Tuck's stay in Jerusalem passed in relative calm. Whatever Salah-al-din was planning next had yet to become apparent; none of the warmongers amongst the kingdom's nobles got the bit between their teeth to cause trouble; and the king's sister, Sibylla, gave birth to a healthy baby boy between Christmas and the start of January, thereby securing the succession of the throne. Tuck himself devoted his time to attending the church services so that he could learn more of the beautiful chants sung there, and also to learning more from Frère Johan and the other wise men in the city. He spent whole afternoons with Benjamin the Jewish physician, and also with Sharaf, the Saracen surgeon, to the extent that he had to beg for scraps of parchment to write notes down on. And had it not been for the lingering memory of the aftermath of the Mount Gisard battle, he might yet have changed his mind about staying in Jerusalem, for he had now begun to make friends amongst the monks at the Church of the Holy Sepulchre too, and who were just the sort of holy men he had hoped would be in such a place. For if the Hospitallers took care of the physical care of pilgrims and soldiers, these monks were learned enough to make Tuck feel he had barely scratched the surface of his own learning.

Certainly his decision to leave wasn't made for want of trying to dissuade him on Frère Johan's part.

"You see, it's not all blood and gore out here," he tried to remonstrate with Tuck. "You could do so much good out here, my friend. Please reconsider and stay here. I shall be most sad to see you go."

But as the days started to lengthen, and his friends began to make preparations to move to Acre, in order to be there for the first voyages of the season westwards, Tuck knew in his heart that he would be leaving. However magical this place could be – and there were times when it could take his breath away and sweep him along with its fervour

– he knew that this was not where he belonged. Something was calling him back to the hills of home.

And to his joy he found that Walter, Stephen and young William would also be travelling with them.

"They are coming with me to Cyprus," Frère Pascal told him happily. "Walter and Stephen are not fighting men, but they know a lot about farming. So they are far better suited to coming with me and helping to cultivate the order's fields over there. And William can live with us as a normal child, with none of the pressures to be his father's heir – that is one kindness we can offer him after losing both parents."

That turned Tuck's mind once more to Asser. What would the morose monk do now? Would he try to follow William? Tuck sincerely hoped not. And as if someone above shared his worries, it was only a week before they were due to leave on the caravan departing for Acre, that he was summoned urgently into the hospital.

"Someone you know has been brought in!" the boy messenger told him. "He's asking for you."

Immediately worried in case it was one of Rhodri's men, or Heaven forbid, Lord Hywel, Tuck raced through the rooms of the hospital in the boy's wake until he was brought to a room at the back of the complex – and that made his heart give a lurch, because only the dying were ever put here in the normal way of things. Who had had such terrible luck as to be brought here just days before leaving for home?

But it wasn't one of the Welshmen at all. There, lying on the pallet was Asser, his face a bloody mess, and even under the blankets, his body looked somehow twisted out of shaped.

"*Dewi Sant!* What happened to you?"

A lay-brother melted out of the room's shadows. "He was brought in to us after someone reported seeing a man getting beaten by other men in an alley between King David's Tower and the Jaffa Gate. We've no idea what he was doing there, or why they attacked him, but when he came in he kept saying your name."

The priest in Tuck felt compassion for this man who was clearly in his last hours on earth, but the all too human part of him was silently screaming, *whose toes have you trampled on this time, Asser?* Certainly his fellow monk had a knack of upsetting people at every turn, and Tuck could imagine only too well a scenario where he had stuck his nose in where it wasn't wanted, or where Asser might have offered an opinion which was not only not welcome, but downright inflammatory. And while Tuck knew that if he was honest, he'd probably once been like that at times in his youth, he'd done an awful lot of growing up recently of the kind that seemed to have totally passed Asser by. Not that Tuck believed for an instant that even the haughty monks in any of these monasteries within Jerusalem would have done something like this, yet Asser had also not been noted for his ventures out into the wider city. But he could easily visualise a visitor to the Hospitallers taking umbrage at something said to them, and deciding to take matters into their hands outside the sanctified walls.

"How did this happen?" he asked again, crouching down to gently take one of Asser's thin and bony hands in his own massive paw. *Don't judge him until you know all,* he cautioned himself. *You got it wrong before! For the love of God, don't send the poor man to his grave with your misunderstandings weighing him down.*

Yet Asser's other hand came up and grasped at Tuck's sleeve with remarkable insistence. "Men …took William!" he managed to croak out.

"What?" Tuck's blood ran cold. "Who? Did you see them?"

Asser managed a flicker of his eyes in assent. With a feeble gasp, he struggled to say, "Been helping teach …children. …Let me speak to him." Tuck had no doubt that the 'him' in question was young William, but now was not the time to be saying that was unlikely to have been a wise move. "Was there when they came." He had to stop and draw several increasingly rasping breaths.

"Said …were …from …Tancred. …Lies!" he gave a cough, and Tuck was dismayed to see the trickle of fresh blood now running from the corner of his mouth.

"Wil… *erhuff,*" Asser weakly tried to spit a clot of blood, but it barely cleared his mouth and Tuck wiped it away with a cloth snatched from beside the bed. "Said …must ..go …with." Another even wetter and more wheezing few breaths. "I …followed. …Went …towards …Templ…"

Asser's grip on Tuck's sleeve slipped, and Tuck didn't need to see his hand fall limply to the bed to know that Asser had gone.

"May God bless you, Brother," he said from the heart. If what he was suspecting was true, then Asser may have more than redeemed himself by trying to stop yet another abduction of his former pupil, and had given his life to bring this warning.

"Take care of him, my friend," Tuck said to the hovering lay-brother. "I must run and warn the others. Something has gone terribly wrong unless I am much mistaken, and we may have very little time to put it right!"

Hoisting up the skirt of his habit, Tuck tore through the hospital, to the astonishment of the brothers and sisters working there. His first thought was to find Stephen and Walter, for if anyone was going to miss William, then it was them. But try as he might, he couldn't find them.

However, when he got to the schoolrooms, he found Sister Ermensend. Built along the same lines as himself, the huge and manly sister was never going to be considered either feminine or a beauty, but by now Tuck knew that her heart was as big as she was, and that she was the mother-hen to all the chicks in her care, knowing every one by name.

"William!" he gasped, knowing that she would grasp which lad of that name he was referring to. "Where is he?"

"Why, Brother Tuck," Ermensend beamed back at him in all innocence, "his uncle sent men to come and fetch him last night. Apparently it's all been a misunderstanding. Other members of the family have refused to acknowledge that his uncle has the right to the manor, and so his uncle has sent for him. They're taking him back to the coast as we speak – well, nearly. I believe you yourself will be departing with the same caravan, so you'll be able to see him then." Then took in the way Tuck's face was falling into ever deeper expressions of dismay. "Is there something wrong?"

"Oh, Sister," Tuck groaned. "It may well be that others in the family have refused to recognise Tancred's lordship of the estate on Sicily, at least while the son of the true line lives. But I fear those men who came here aren't going to take young William back – they're here to make sure that he never does! Once William is dead, there's less objection to Tancred taking what he wants. Please God and Our Lady that we find him in time!"

By now seriously worried, he raced back to find Rhodri and the other Welshmen, mercifully catching them just as they were heading into the stables for the morning mucking out.

"Asser's dead!" he gasped out, then proceeded to tell them what little he knew, adding, "And I can't find Walter or Stephen! That's got to be bad news."

"You think they're going to be silenced, too?" Sulien asked, as they all ran for their dormitory to collect their weapons, even young Lord Hywel.

"May St Issui intercede for me if I blacken men's names wrongly," Tuck growled miserably, "but would you leave potential witnesses hanging around? Men who are known in the community, and who might turn up a year or so later, swearing that William's body turned up in some ditch outside Jerusalem's city walls, and strangely just at the time when Tancred's men appeared?"

"*Duw!*" Rhodri swore. "A high-and-mighty Norman lord might not want to openly acknowledge that one of his own would resort to the murder of a child, but all of us have seen too much of what such 'fine' men will do to a Welsh child to doubt it." Then grinned wolfishly. "Well they picked the wrong men to try and hoodwink, didn't they? …Come on, Anian! Time to prove if those tracking skills of yours are as good as you're always bragging about!"

Armed with quarterstaffs and bows, and with Hywel, Rhodri and Sulien armed with locally acquired swords, they left the *hôpital* and went to the spot where Asser had been found, according to the lay brother who had spoken to Tuck. As they stood by the spot, casting around them, and Anian scrutinised the ground and everything around it, it was Hugh who stood and pointed down the long and fairly straight road that came in from the Jaffa Gate.

"I know it may sound daft," he said cautiously. "But do you think Asser might have been trying to tell you that William was taken to the Templars, Tuck? Because you can see straight up towards the Temple from here. Even if Asser was lying flat on the ground, he might well have seen those men dragging William off that way – might even have seen enough to realise that they didn't turn off at the first big crossroad?"

"Temple or Templars," Gryff agreed. "When they're both in the same direction, it's hard not to think that's what he meant."

"Boots!" Anian cut across him with.

"Eh?" several of the men said, turning to look at him as he stood up, brushing the dust off the knees of his trews.

"Boots," he repeated firmly. "I know a lot of people have already passed over this spot, but all of the locals wear those lightweight shoes. But there are imprints here on the ground of several men wearing proper, heavy boots. And you're right, Hugh, they head straight that way!" and he pointed to where they could see the complex of the Temple Mount rising above the lesser dwellings of the city.

Needing no urging, they all set off at the trot, being less than polite about forcing their way through the growing throng of people, as daily life began to pick up in the holy city with the brightening of the day. It didn't take them long to get right up to the great walls of what was now the royal palace and the *hôpital* of the Order of the Knights Templar, and Asser had only called out twice to report that they were indeed on the right trail. Now, though, as they jogged alongside the wall to head for the way into the great courtyard space, he called out just before they swung right to enter the complex,

"No, lads! Hang on! They didn't go in – look!" and as they all skidded to a halt and then came back to him, they could see what he was pointing to on the ground. "Someone came *out* of the Temple to meet them, "Anian said with certainty. "Look. Three horses. And they go off this way, with the men who were on foot on either side of them."

The small Welshman quested off after the tracks with all the determination of a huntsman's prize hound. "Ah! See? ...See those marks? They had someone with them who wasn't so willing! Somebody was being dragged back in amongst them." He bent down and squinted at the tracks. "Hmm... Not heavy enough for Walter, but could well be Stephen."

"Judas' balls!" Rhodri spat. "Where are they taking them?"

Tuck felt his gut turn over as he ventured, "I fear that if nowhere beyond it, that they're going towards the all-too-aptly-named Herod's Gate. *Dewi Sant*! I do not like that connection, by St Thomas I don't!" and he shivered as he felt a chill run down his spine.

"Connection?" Dai asked, looking worried but confused, and Tuck belatedly remembered that along with a couple of the other men, Dai's knowledge of the stories of the Bible were scant indeed. He'd worked hard to improve that over these last months, but even he couldn't condense every story in that time.

"Herod," he said thickly, as they all picked up the pace again, "or King Herod, if you care to acknowledge his title. He was the king of this area at the time of Our Lord's birth, but if what I was told is true, he was little more than a puppet of Imperial Rome's. St Matthew tells us that the magi visited Herod to enquire where Our Lady was with her infant son – you remember, they're the wise men I told you about who came bearing the three gifts – but then after they left, Herod feared that this new 'king' was a threat to him and his rule in this land. So he ordered the massacre of all Hebrew male children under the age of two years old." He had to gasp in more breath, but then shook his head as he added, "Nobody knows just how many children died, but it's believed to be in the thousands."

Dai looked as though he might be sick. "And it's *that* King Herod that the gate is named after? *Dduw drugarhau arnom*!" (God have mercy upon us!) Words which were echoed amongst the rest of them.

They surprised the sentries at Herod's Gate as they tore through, but then Anian again called a halt and changed direction.

"Bastards!" he muttered darkly. "They're trying to make sure they throw any followers off their scent! They're not going north at all, they're swinging around to follow the city walls."

Rhodri grabbed Sulien's sleeve. "Take Owain, Thomas, Iorweth and Gryff, and go and get us some horses! Tell Frère Josef we won't need them for more than a day, but we're never going to catch them, with the lead they already have, if we stay on foot. Tell him we only want the ponies, not the valuable horses! Go! Meet us by the Zion Gate."

As the five turned on their heels, Dai asked, "Do you know where they're going, then, Rhodri? Might they not turn off into the desert before then?"

But Rhodri was shaking his head. "No, *cyfaill*, I reckon not, and I'll tell you why: it's that Judas of a man, Reynald de Châtillon! Who else would so boldly use men from the Temple – because let's not forget that he has great influence with those knights – and yet be canny enough not to take anything too dirty inside there where the king might hear of it? Don't forget, lads, it's only just coming up to two years since that old villain got released from a Saracen prison to find that he was lord of sod all! He might since have swiftly married Lady Stephanie de Milly, which has made him Baron of Oultrejourdain, but you don't imagine a man like him is going to turn down a hefty bribe from someone like Tancred, do you? After all, he's barely got his marriage bed warm yet, so he'll want some money of his own until he can start bleeding Lady Stephanie's lands white."

Tuck groaned out loud with what little breath he had, for he was not built for running in the rising heat. "Reynald de Châtillon! Blessed St Thomas, how could I have forgotten him?" He gasped in another lungful of hot air. "But Oultrejourdain is on the other side of the Dead Sea, and that's where his great castle of Kerak lies. If he wants to be on his own turf before he risks killing them, surely we can catch him by then?"

"Kerak?" Rhodri snorted. "Oh, I don't think he needs to go that far, much less all the way across the River Jordan to Kerak, to do a spot of murder and slaughter, Tuck! *Duw*! He's not going to drag his captives that far! No, I reckon he's heading for Hebron, south of here, which he also owns. That's why I said to meet at the Zion Gate with horses, because I'd bet my boots someone has met them with some – they're heading south, not north! And I don't think they'll even go all the way to the castle – just nicely into lands Châtillon owns so that nobody will dare question a trio of shallow graves. "

Sulien had been nodding at Rhodri's assessment and added, "From what we've heard in the stables, Tuck, even if Châtillon's men are going to Hebron itself, that's only three days' march away if you pushed it. Well they've got the best part of a night's lead on us already. We can't let them widen that gap, because otherwise we'll certainly be too late.

"As it is, from all we've gathered, Châtillon is only treading carefully around the young king at the moment because he's still finding his feet after so many years in Salah-al-din's father's prison. Before he got captured, he was madman enough to spend six days raping and pillaging on Cyprus – and that's the Byzantine Emperor's territory! Someone who's enough of a mad dog to challenge the rule of such a powerful monarch would surely not think twice about a spot of murder on the side? So I think Rhodri's right. That son-of-a-whore Tancred has filtched enough money out of young William's estate to be able to offer Châtillon a nice sum for just a bit of throat-cutting by some of his men. Châtillon himself won't be there, of course. He won't risk that for such a lowly prize. It'll be some wretched little knight or sergeant, who's seeing his way to power by keeping his nasty nose wedged up Châtillon's arse, but who's expendable enough to Châtillon if he's daft enough to get caught."

Tuck gave a shudder. "Then I hope Sulien gets ponies that are fleet of foot!"

Yet when they had made the circuit of the city and confirmed that those they pursued had not turned off, but had mounted and ridden away, Sulien and the others were already waiting and with far better horses than just the work ponies they'd asked for. As they all mounted up, Sulien explained,

"Frère Pascal and Frère Bornhold were there when we got to the stables. They'd heard you'd gone running off, Tuck, and feared it would be something important. When we told them why, they insisted we be given decent horses. I don't think there's much love lost between our friends the Hospitallers, and the Templars. Frère Pascal took it almost as a personal insult that Walter and Stephen had been captured as well. Apparently they've already taken their vows to St John, so the Templars taking them is a case of them seizing another order's men, and that's just not allowed."

With the horses fresh and rested, they were able to keep to a brisk pace, and by the time the midday sun was baking down upon them, they could see in the distance the swirl of dust which proclaimed that a party of much the same size as theirs was not much over an hour ahead of them.

"Got 'em!" Anian snarled, reaching over to take the reins of Bryn's horse, as he in turn reached up and took his great bow from around his shoulders. Gryff and Dai were doing the same for Madog and Llew', the other two archers, and suddenly Tuck began to feel more optimistic. He'd already seen the range of the huge Wyche-elm bows, but now he was going to see them used in earnest!

Chapter 15

Early Spring, the Year of Our Lord, 1178
The Holy Land

"They're going to see us coming," Owain said with a sigh. "If we can see their dust cloud, they'd have to be blind not to see ours behind them. Surely at least one of them will look backwards before we catch up to them?"

"*Dewi Sant*, grant us some bloody rain!" Sulien growled, hawking another throatful of sandy dust up and spitting. "Nice sheets of Welsh rain we can hide in! These straggly bits of tired bushes wouldn't hide a rabbit from a hawk, much less us."

"Not even a decent hillock to creep up on them from," Madog agreed, his keen archer's eyes scouring the countryside for anything which might give him both some elevation and cover.

"*Yr wyf yn galw ar Dduw a'r holl saint i'n helpu ni!*" Tuck fumed in his frustration. (I call upon God and all the saints to help us). "*Issui Sant, chyfnertha 'ch gwas.*" (St Issui, help your servant.) He'd been praying for the cool of some rain ever since they'd got on the horses, both for the animals' sake and for him and his friends too. But now he felt a desperate longing for the swathing mists of home, which could cloak a man from sight at mere yards. Then something made him look towards the west, something flickering on the edges of his sight.

There, rolling in from the coast at speed, was a monster of a thunderstorm, and what had caught his eye was a lightning flash between the clouds.

"Look, my friends!" he called joyfully. "*Issui Sant* has heard us!"

For all that this was a desert kingdom, even here rain fell at times, and that was primarily during the winter months. Now they were at the start of March, just at the change of the seasons and had had a few dry weeks, but it looked as though that was set to change within the next hour or so. Unlike the steady Welsh rain, this was going to come in a massive deluge, possibly dumping a month's worth of rain in one go, but that didn't dishearten the Welshmen one bit. The only ones who would be inconvenienced were the archers, for it was necessary to keep the bow strings as dry as possible before use. But since the only way of carrying the great bows easily was to slip them into oiled-cloth sheaths, which had straps to loop across their shoulders – for no archer abused his strings by using them to carry his bow by – and these were the same cloths which had travelled all the way from Wales with them, all the three needed to do was slip their bows back in their carrying bags for now.

As the light turned a strange yellowish colour from the coming storm, the odd shadows it cast across the landscape suddenly threw the countryside into low relief, and Bryn called out,

"Look! Over to our left! …See? The road the others have taken curves to the right around those lumpy bits of rock. But there's a sheep track, or maybe a dried up stream bed, on the far side. If we follow that we'll temporarily disappear from their sight. We'll have to lie low on our horses' necks when we get there – those rocks aren't that tall – but the horses will be masked if we get down in that gully."

"Well done!" Rhodri praised him. "Yes, that will do nicely. By the time we come at them from behind from over there, the rain should be upon us. Come on lads! Time to ride hard and vanish before the bastards spot where we're going."

They heeled their horses to a brisk canter and swung off to the left well before they needed to, making it seem to anyone looking back at them that this was the direction they had always intended to go in, and that they had never been pursuing the other group at all.

It was a hard sprint for the horses, but as the great storm got closer the temperature dropped dramatically too.

"Come on you lovely big brute," Sulien said affectionately, as he glanced up at the rolling black clouds scudding towards them. "We can take whatever you've got – we're *Cymry* – but those in front can't!"

Sure enough, by the time they had rounded most of the ragged and sprawling outcrop of boulders, it was a good thing that they had slowed down a bit out of caution, for they suddenly heard the other group heading their way. Someone called out in the native tongue to the effect that they couldn't see anywhere to shelter yet, and the Welshmen knew that they had mere moments to set their ambush.

"Madog, Bryn, Llew'," Rhodir hissed. "Up there with Anian on that rock that looks like an old sow! Sulien, take Gryff, Dai and Iorweth and half of the horses to the left behind that clump of whatever plants they are. Lord Hywel, you go with them. Thomas, Hugh, Owein and Tuck, grab the reins of the other horses, you're with me! That gully will have to do for us."

The Welshmen scattered with the ease of being back into the raiding mindset they'd known since childhood. And just as they all slithered into their allotted places, fearing that the dust they'd stirred up would nonetheless give them away, great fat drops of rain began to fall. As the huge droplets hit the bone-dry soil hard, for a few moments they threw up individual little puffs of dust. But that only lasted moments and then the full force of the storm hit them.

The pelting rain soaked them to the skin in no time, and the horses briefly looked striped as the rain washed the dust off them in streaks, but after that man and beast were almost dithering in the dramatic loss of heat. In the negligible visibility, Tuck's group felt rather than heard or saw the three archers and Anian slide back down beside them.

"Give us the horses' reins," Madog said. "Can't see a bloody thing up there. We'd be more in danger of hitting one of you."

"Time for a bit of knife work," Anian said with rather too much relish for Tuck's liking, but then found himself having to hurry to keep in sight of his five friends who were now slithering forwards in the mud, quite disregarding of how plastered with it they were getting.

As the rain lifted briefly, they saw the men they were hunting all huddled together up on the track. They were an ambusher's dream, all clustered close to one another, and trying to hang onto their horses, who – unlike the Welsh's – were picking up on their riders' nervousness at being caught out in the weather, and were by now thoroughly spooked. Stephen, Walter and William were easily spotted by virtue of being the only ones not in native garb.

"*Tsk!*" Rhodri hissed in Tuck's ear. "Trying to make us think it's some rogue band of nomads, are they?" He sounded affronted that anyone would play them for such fools. "Never seen one of the desert tribesmen stomping around with spurs on!" and he tutted again.

Already the gully they were in was filling up with tiny rivulets of water, and then one broke into something a bit larger and faster moving, but the Welshmen didn't bat an eyelid. Used to crawling up fast flowing water-courses at home, this was nothing to them, and the additional noise of water only helped to mask their movements.

When the next brief gap in the rain came, they were right alongside the kidnapping party, and with a hissed, "Now!" Rhodri led his men up on the attack. From the other side, Sulien and Lord Hywel charged in with one of the other men, although in the sheeting water Tuck couldn't see who it was. Hywel was only distinguishable by his fancier sword, and Tuck guessed rather than saw in detail that it was Sulien in the lead. The other two men had to be holding the horses, just as the archers were doing for Tuck's group, but that still meant that including Tuck there were nine of them going in, and that gave them respectable odds against their adversaries.

As he used his fist to lay out a man who had to be a man-at-arms, Tuck realised that he could see none of the local turcopoles amongst the men on his side of the fight. Then he heard someone who sounded local still arguing with whoever the leader was, saying,

"No, not the boy! We didn't agree to that!"

With the element of surprise now over with, Tuck risked calling out to Rhodri and the others, "Don't kill the turcopoles!"

Out of the deluge Rhodri's face appeared close to Tuck's. "Why?" he demanded savagely.

"Because I just heard one of them protesting that they didn't know they were to kill William," Tuck yelled back over the din of metal on metal.

He used his weight to shove another soldier hard towards Anian, who already had his dagger up and ready, and then managed to grab the turcopole who appeared in front of him. "Don't fight me!" he yelled urgently. "I'm not going to kill you! We just want our friends back!"

Something in his voice must have got through to the terrified soldier and he dropped his long dagger's point away from Tuck's chest. Dragging the man back out of the fight, Tuck seized the front of the man's tunic and demanded,

"Whose man are you? Who do you fight for?"

"My lady de Milly," the man replied, and that, Tuck thought, said everything about what was going on here. The main culprits were no doubt in the pay of Châtillon, but as Rhodri had guessed, neither he nor his cronies were familiar enough with the lands Châtillon had just acquired to strike out across the countryside and still be sure of where they were going. They'd needed local lads for that, but those men weren't rogues – they were probably men with children of their own – and the killing of a child was something they wouldn't do willingly.

Even as Tuck turned back to call to Rhodri, both the fight and the storm stopped. It was as though whatever heavenly bucket had been upturned was finally empty, and the rain changed from deluge to spitting drops in moments, revealing only the Welshmen still standing, and Stephen, Walter and William huddled together while Lord Hywel and Sulien guarded them with swords still raised.

"How many of *you*?" Tuck asked the turcopole urgently. "You native men?"

"Him and him," the man said, pointing to two men who were on the ground.

"Rhodri!" Tuck called. "Those two and this man here – they're not the kidnappers. They're Lady de Milly's soldiers. They weren't part of the plot!"

"Bugger," Anian muttered darkly, but went to drop to one knee beside one of the men. After a brief check he looked up and said, "He'll live, but we'd better get him back to the infirmary."

The other turcopole, however, was as dead as the other men.

"Dare we take them back and try to confront anyone over this?" Lord Hywel wondered. "It doesn't seem right that only the 'dogs' get punished while the leaders get off."

Yet Rhodri was already shaking his head. "And who would we take this to, my lord? The Hospitallers have no authority over a man like Châtillon. And do you think their Master is really going to start a fight with someone who's a great lord out here over two lay brothers and a child? No, he might complain, but that's all that will happen."

"I fear Rhodri's right," Tuck said sadly. "And think on this, my lord: we still have to get our friends, here, to Acre. That's the only way they'll be safe. Better to leave things as they are." He turned to the turcopole. "If we get you and your friend to our infirmary, can we trust you to stay there until we have left on the caravan for Acre? After that you can go back to your homes, or wherever you want to go. I'm sure the Hospitaller brothers would back you in any claim that you could not go back to whoever employed these ruffians, because you were not well enough to travel."

"I do not know who that was, anyway," the turcopole said. "The only one I knew was that man over there with his throat cut. He came to me and said that a message had been sent from our sergeant that we were to guide them to Hebron. Something about them being men only recently come to these lands, and who did not know the way."

"*Hmph!*" Tuck snorted in disgust. "So several of these could well be Tancred's own men." He loosed the turcopole and went over to Walter. "I know this has been a terrible trial, my friend, but could you bear to look at the faces of these men and tell us if you recognise any of them from Sicily?"

Walter shuddered, and Tuck thought he looked as though he had aged ten years in as many hours, but with a huge sigh, Walter nodded and stepped forwards to where Anian had rolled a first corpse onto its back.

"Not him …yes, he's one …and that one …no, not him…"

It took no time at all to work out that eight of the men must be Châtillon's rogues, but that another four had clearly come from Tancred in Sicily, and with the three turcopoles, that had been the whole party. As far as the turcopoles had been concerned, Walter, Stephen and William were servants who were being taken to go and work at Hebron – it had only been once they were on the road that they had realised that the trio were destined to never reach there.

As they turned the horses back towards Jerusalem, Rhodri beckoned Tuck up to the front of the column with Sulien and Lord Hywel – who had to be made to feel as though he was in on the decision, even if Rhodri and Sulien would do what they thought best regardless of his opinion.

"I don't know about you," he began, "but I'm now very wary of going back into the city. Obviously we'll have to send the horses back, and that turcopole needs help, poor sod – I hope we can save him. But we can stick with the horses our enemies had, and go straight to where the caravan is assembling."

"I'm with you on that," was Sulien's immediate response. "I fear we're tempting fate to take Walter, Stephen and William back into the city. After all, we don't know for sure that those four were the only men from Tancred. It could be that there were one or two more, and maybe they got hit with the bad bellies we all had when we first got here? If they've been shitting themselves inside out for days, they wouldn't have been able to ride, but that doesn't mean they won't kick up a fuss when their mates don't come back, nor that they wouldn't be capable of looking out of a window and spotting Walter or Stephen out in the street."

"Exactly," Rhodri concurred. "The way things stand, nobody's going to be expecting those lads we left for the vultures to turn up inside of a week – because presumably they weren't intending to come straight back covered in blood? And with the caravan leaving tomorrow at dawn, we'll hopefully be halfway to Acre before anyone realises that their cunning plan has gone to Hell in a handcart."

Now, though, Rhodri turned to Tuck. "Yet someone has to go in with the turcopoles. The lads can sneak the horses we borrowed back into the stables, and our friendly brothers won't ask too many questions. But those two local men are going to have to have someone with them to explain how the one got so badly hurt. So I'm asking you: can you lie for us, Tuck? Will your conscience allow you to tell a story to the brothers on duty in the *hôpital* to quench any curiosity on their part? I know you'll want to go and bid farewell to Frère Johan if nobody else. But then he'll understand, so I'm not asking you to betray a friend's trust in you. It's the general frères and lay-brothers tending the sick who I'm concerned with. Men who might in all innocence think nothing of telling an inquirer of where we are and why."

Tuck smiled sadly at his friend. "Thank you for the consideration." He heaved a sigh. "And you are right, it does go against my inclinations, but I'm not the monk I was when I first joined you, either. I've seen too much of the world now to be able to afford such naivety, so yes, I'll have no trouble taking them in. In fact I've been thinking, and I think I'll just keep it simple and say we came across them outside the city walls. Everyone in the *hôpital* knows that I'm preparing to leave, so they won't question why I was beyond the city gates just at this point in time. In that sense our enemies have played into our hands, haven't they? By waiting until we were going anyway – on their part presumably to avoid anyone questioning where Walter and Stephen had gone – and spinning that tale about William, they've made things a lot easier than if they'd left us with weeks to try and hide our three friends away until we could go."

Lord Hywel looked at Tuck in wonderment. "Bless me! What a coincidence!"

However Tuck had a different view. "Really, Lord Hywel? After all this time in this holy place you cannot see the hand of God at work? Well maybe not God himself – I suspect He has mightier things to deal with than one small boy and a couple of serving men. But for every man who heeds the call of the Devil and does evil, there are others who try to do right, and somewhere along the way you often find that with a spot of Divine intervention, the latter counterbalances the first. So I think in this case our prayers for William to be able to go and live a quiet and normal life have been listened to by Our Lady, or if not quite such a divine person, then at least our own Welsh saints whom we pray to."

Rhodri chuckled. "Or if you can't quite believe in such direct divine intervention, my lord, then at least think that by trying to be so bloody clever and cunning, our enemies have ended up tying themselves up in their own complicated plot."

It was after nightfall when they made it back to the city, and while Anian and three others took the Hospitallers' horses back to their stables and settled them in, Tuck took the two turcopoles, with the injured man still slumped in the saddle of one of the acquired horses, around to the *hôpital*. He had been right to keep his explanation simple. There were enough poor souls who fell prey to thieves for the lay-brothers not to turn a whisker over yet another coming in, and once the pair were whisked away into the great warren of wards, Tuck led the horse around to the infirmary. His conversation with Frère Johan was more open but also filled with sadness.

"You have long said your intuition was telling you that you would have to leave," Frère Johan said regretfully, "but bless me, Brother Tuck, I never thought it would be so imperative for you to seem to vanish." He hugged Tuck warmly. "Go in peace, my friend. Listen to those instincts of yours, for I now believe that someone up above truly is guiding you towards something. I have never known a man like you, and if I don't have quite your talent for hearing what God wants, I still think that He has something very particular in mind for you, so have a care on your journey."

Blessing the fact that everything was already parcelled up, Tuck loaded his own pack onto the horse, and then went around to the dormitory and picked up the packs for the others. Then in the depth of night, he led the horse around to the Jaffa Gate, to where Anian and the others waited for him, and together they slipped out into the darkness, with only a couple of well-paid guards to close the gates behind them and forget that they had ever passed that way.

Chapter 16

Cyprus,
Early Spring, the Year of our Lord, 1178

All the way to Acre everyone was twitching at shadows. When they were camped for the night was the worst, for the arrival of the first of the season's caravans coincided with the breeding season for the scavengers, and so the darkest hours were often accompanied by strange rustlings, and the occasional traveller waking with a scream as some rat or other decided to try the taste of fresh meat. Rhodri swiftly allocated a rota for setting watch, if only because then those who weren't on watch slept more soundly, for after two days – and with having had no rest since the rescue of their three friends – everyone was practically falling asleep on the camels during the day.

Luckily, they had been able to join up with Frère Pascal once they were within the caravan, and were even more delighted when they discovered that Frère Bornhold had also elected to travel to Cyprus with Pascal.

"You're a bad influence, Brother Tuck," the big Hospitaller joked a couple of nights into their journey. "You've changed the way I see the Holy Land, and I no longer have the conviction I once had of the rightness of what we're doing. So I played upon my old wounds, and asked the Master if I might join Pascal at the grange on Cyprus."

"I'm very glad of that," Tuck confessed to Bornhold a little later when they were alone. "I can't help but worry that Tancred won't be so easily put off. The biggest problem to my way of thinking is that there are so few children who travel in these caravans. This time around we're lucky to have a couple of extended families heading back to France with us, but even so, their children are much younger or much older than William. It wouldn't take much for Tancred to discover that it's likely to be him who is heading for Cyprus. And I'd have felt a lot easier in my mind if we'd been able to determine whether Tancred actually *did* have any more men in Jerusalem or not – because once Sulien said that about somebody else being tied to the privies and unable to ride out, it's refused to give me any peace. Such a man could unravel all of our plans at a stroke. If Tancred didn't send more, then I think we can breathe easy, but by St Thomas, I wish we knew for sure. So I'm much relieved at the thought of two fighting men being at the grange, and not just Pascal on his own to defend the place."

"Do not worry," Bornhold had said confidently, "all will be well."

Yet in Acre they found that another party would be joining them on their ship, for the caravan from Jerusalem was sufficiently large for the travellers to be split across two ships. To Tuck's dismay, their own party was put with some small groups of men so that the larger families could travel together without being parted, but that meant that within those twos and threes, there were some whom Tuck didn't like the look of. One in particular seemed to be far too interested in what the Welshmen were doing.

Mercifully they hadn't had to wait for another ship to arrive, for many ships had wintered at Acre, but once on board, every time Tuck turned around he caught sight of a swarthy man with a wicked scar on his cheek watching one or another of their group. And it was only on the second day out of port that Rhodri came to join Tuck on the deck, saying softly,

"I see you have your eye on him, too."

Tuck's brow creased in a frown. "He watches nobody else, Rhodri. Nobody – only us. Of ourselves we're not *that* remarkable. I suppose I'm a bit of an oddity, being the only monk on board, but it's not just me he keeps track of. Oh, he's being careful! I'll give him that. He's making sure he doesn't stare too hard at Walter or Stephen, and he's making almost too much of an effort not to look at William. But he's taking an unhealthy interest in Pascal and Bornhold. It's almost as though he's assessing their weaknesses. How badly their old wounds might slow them down."

Rhodri was nodding along with Tuck's words. "I agree with everything you've spotted. Judas' balls! It's too bloody cramped on this ship to get him alone, as well. If we dragged him to one of the sides and threatened to throw him over, we'd then have to explain to the captain and sailors why – and we don't really want to have yet another group of people knowing why we're trying to hide young William. All it would take would be a couple of drunken sailors at the next stop on Crete telling the tale, and the whole of the Mediterranean could know before they even get to the grange!"

They were all grateful to disembark at Famagusta, and it was now that Rhodri announced that they would travel with their friends to the grange.

"It's not going to delay us by much," he told his fellow Welshmen, "and I think we'll all feel easier if we know our friends are settled and safe. And besides, if anyone is trying to track us, then if we're not on the next boats westwards, but the ones after that, then that should confuse the issue nicely."

It said everything about how they all felt that not even Lord Hywel objected, for all that everyone wanted to get home now. He had become very fond of Frère Bornhold in particular, because the older knight had taken the time to do a good deal of coaching of the young Welsh prince, and he was now a substantially better fighter than he had been a few months ago. And so with three newly purchased mules to carry their baggage, the party set off inland, following the road towards a town called Nicosia. However, when they were something like two-thirds of the way there, they turned off and took a much narrower road heading north. A day farther on, and they finally came to the grange, perched up on high ground and with a distant view towards the sea.

"Oh this is beautiful!" Lord Hywel declared in admiration, and indeed it was. A small but solid stone farmhouse nestled in a sheltered dip, and it was easy to see how self-sufficient the place could be. There was a good clean well for water, and plenty of pasture for the many sheep, who could be heard occasionally bleating out on the hillsides, not to mention a grove of olive trees and some vines. There were even a couple of lemon trees and an orange on the edge of the farm's courtyard.

It clearly needed some attention, for there were loose tiles on the roof, and weeds growing everywhere, but none of it was beyond the scope of the four men who would live there to mend or put right.

"I feel we have been blessed," Walter declared that night, as everyone sat out around a small fire pit, and watched the stars gradually coming out as the crystal clear night darkened.

Yet although Bornhold and Pascal readily joined in with their agreement, there was something in Madog and Anian's muted, "Hmmms"'s which made Tuck sit up. What had that keen-eyed pair spotted? Then he noticed the finger signals which were going back and forth between Rhodri and Sulien and them, and felt his heart sink. So they were not alone out here. And suddenly Tuck was angry. Really, really angry. What was it about poor little William that made it so imperative to hunt him down and kill him? Had they not made it clear enough to that thrice-be-damned Tancred that the child was never going to challenge him for his pitiful bit of Sicily?

Getting to his feet – for he found it impossible to now just sit there – Tuck began to stamp off towards the house, when Rhodri's voice called to him,

"What's wrong, Tuck?" yet in his tone Tuck could tell that Rhodri was fretting that he was about to give the game away.

"Belly ache!" he called back. "I'm not letting you cook again, Bryn!" That should signal to Rhodri that he had understood, for it had been Tuck himself who had cooked the meal tonight, with just a bit of help from Anian who had snared the rabbits. "I wouldn't follow me into the privy unless you have to," he added, and the others, realising what he was up to, backed him up with various ribald remarks.

Putting on a burst of speed just as he got out of the lit area, as if getting taken very short, Tuck briefly sprinted towards the privy pit, but then halted and moved much more silently through the darkness back to the house. Now he blessed all those hours of learning how to move covertly from his Welsh friends, and also Rhodri's foresight in seeing that one day prayer alone would not suffice. Hurrying to where the three archers would be sleeping, he already had their great bows out of their travelling cloths, and the quivers of arrows also ready to hand, when the trio slunk in through the door.

"Good man, Tuck," Madog said, as with a practised flip he strung his bow, then raised an eyebrow as he saw Tuck stringing the lighter Saracen bow that they had taught him to use. "Are you sure, Brother?" Then blinked in surprise as he saw the fury in Tuck's eyes.

"I've had *enough*!" snapped Tuck in response. "These ungodly Normans," he was practically spitting the words out in Welsh in his anger, "how dare they? How dare they choose to take a child's life over nothing more than *wealth* and *power*?" He made those two words sound positively filthy. "This isn't about having someone as the lord who can fight to preserve a place, as in the Holy Land – and even then, why not send the child heir into a monastery if you have to in order for others on a manor have a lord's protection? I know it's not for everyone, and I'm a clear case of that, but I lived! I survived. …Well no more! I'm not having us leave, and then not a day later have our friends slaughtered in their beds, just so some lord can now claim what was never his. We deal with this tonight!"

The archers grinned back at him.

"Come on, then," Bryn said. "It's up on the roof for us."

Outside again, it was easy enough to boost Llew' and Bryn up onto the shallow sloping tiles, and to then hoist Tuck up with Madog shoving from below. The four of them perched up on the ridge tiles and scoured the countryside for movement. A full moon would have helped in one way, but would also have given away their position, and so they were looking for any unnatural movement of foliage in the darkness, or the sound of a disturbed beast.

A faint rustle of cloth to his left alerted Tuck, and he turned to see Llew' going up onto one knee and taking aim at a clump of bushes close to the yard. With a gentle touch on Llew's arm, Tuck then signalled that he would take this one. His recurve bow hadn't the range of the big Wyche-elm bows, so it made sense for him to take the closer target. Nodding, Llew' crabbed sideways a little to allow Tuck the best shot, but only moments later found another target a bit further out in one of the fields.

"Now!" Madog barely breathed, and the four bow-strings thrummed as they let fly.

All Tuck felt was gratified when he heard a scream from the bushes he'd shot into. Got one! Then was glad that the true archers had pounded it into him to always have another arrow knocked and ready straight away, as another figure dived out of the undercover, presumably having decided that they had already lost any element of surprise, and might as well go straight on the attack. Tuck loosed his second arrow and was disappointed to realise that he had not made a proper hit, or at least not to kill since the figure did not fall hard. But that he had hit or clipped the man was clear from the howl of pain, and the way the figure began to writhe around, spinning around on the ground like a fly with one wing gone.

From up on the roof, Tuck then had a clear view of his other friends wading into the fight. There had to be half a dozen men or more down there, but it didn't take the Welsh long to subdue them, and then Dai and Owain appeared holding burning torches, and the scene below leapt into greater detail.

"Alright, who shot this one in the arse?" Anian called out, unable to keep the mirth out of his voice as he knocked out the man Tuck had hit in the yard.

"That would be me," Tuck admitted as he slithered down off the roof.

"Not bad going," Madog declared, clapping Tuck on the shoulder. "You winged the one in the bushes too. Good going for a novice archer," and now Tuck saw Gryff holding onto a man who was on the ground with an arrow sticking through his arm, and another bad cut on his leg.

"Right, tie them up and stick them in the barn," Rhodri declared. "If they live until tomorrow we'll question them then. Four men to stand watch over them at a time. I'll lead the first watch, then you, Sulien; and Anian, you can lead the last one before dawn – sort yourselves out, lads."

Tuck chose to sit watch with Rhodri, not least because just at the moment he didn't trust himself to not do something drastic, like throttle one of their prisoners if they provoked him, and he was far too wound up to sleep. His insides felt as taut as a bow string. With them were Gryff and Hugh, two others who were steady lads, and Tuck found their calmness easing his own turbulent feelings. Even so he found himself fidgeting, until Rhodri finally asked,

"What on earth is the matter, Tuck? Are you sitting on ants, or something?"

"Ants in my soul, more like," Tuck confessed. They were speaking in Welsh, so there was no chance of their prisoners understanding what they were saying, and he felt able to talk openly. "What is it about this boy, Rhodri? This…" and he waved an arm in exasperation at the world in general, "…this is all so *extreme*! He's one child, may Jesu save him! What is it about him that makes him worth all this effort?

"By St Thomas' sacred bones, even our savage King Henry doesn't hunt his enemies like this! Have we had a single instance where we've felt that young Hywel has been hunted once we set foot in France? No, not at all. For all of our worries, even in Rome there was nary a hint of anyone on the lookout for stray Welsh royals, and you couldn't ever call King Henry forgiving, or one to forget! So what is it about young William that engenders such …hatred, for want of a better word?"

"*Duw*, Tuck! You've hit it on the head. I've had this feeling, niggling away in the back of my mind, ever since we had to go chasing out of Jerusalem after him, but we've been so busy getting ourselves set to head for home that I couldn't work out what it was."

"Do you think Walter or Stephen know?" Hugh asked thoughtfully. "I mean, it's hard to think that they would not, given that they've known him since he was a babe."

Rhodri gave a disgusted snort. "It'd be bloody hard for them not to, I would have thought."

"I wish they had trusted us sooner," Tuck sighed, suddenly finding his emotions shifting from tetchy to sad. "After all we've been through, surely we've proven our worth?"

"Don't take it so hard," Gryff consoled him. "It's taken all these months for Walter to grasp enough of that weird local Greek dialect to be able to converse much with anyone, and he's still far from fluent. Even we learned it faster than him, and we aren't learned men like you. And his own Sicilian dialect is too far from Latin to help even you much, either, going by the way he could guess at the Arab words better than some of ours. I don't think he could tell us much that was complicated even if he wanted to. And you can't blame Stephen if he was bowing to his father's wishes. In a way it says a lot about him that he respects his da' that much."

Tuck huffed a great sigh, releasing more of his tension. "Thank you, my friend, yes, that makes a lot of sense, and it's an explanation I should have thought of. Ah me, I'm just all out of sorts this evening. I never in my wildest dreams thought I would ever actually *want* to kill someone, but out there …out there I wanted to skewer those evil swine so badly I could almost taste it."

Hugh gave him a playful punch on the arm. "Just proves you're a proper Welshmen," he said with a wink. "You've got some of our Celtic fire in your belly after all. You couldn't be *Cymry* and not be able to get a touch of the red mist a few times in your life – that's what my ma' always says, anyhow."

Of all the things anyone could have said to Tuck, that was something which resonated deepest within him. *I am Cymry!* he thought with no small sense of pride rising, too. *I'm no barbaric Norman. But I can be moved to fury over injustice like any of my fellow countrymen, and I accept that, Lord – not so much as a fault, but as a good trait which proves I know right from wrong.*

If I get back to my old home, St Issui, I vow that I'll be as vigorous a defender of the weak and powerless there in your valley as I am here. I'm not a cold-hearted killer – never have been, and please God, I never will be – but I've grown up enough now to know that sometimes you have to fight fire with fire unless you're prepared to be a martyr. And that's fair enough if it's just you you're making that decision for, but these days I'd not be remotely happy dragging some other poor soul to their doom just because I was presuming a saintliness of soul for myself. That'd just be plain arrogant. Setting myself up to be stuck full of arrows like poor St Sebastian would be nothing less than hubris, and I've learned enough humility to never want that.

For now, though, he got up and walked to the huddled group of prisoners.

"Who sent you?" he demanded, hoping that at least one of them would understand, for he knew most spoke a kind of Greek, but that some Arabic was known here, too, as well as some French and also Latin from the Church. He tried his question in French for a second time, blessing Stephen for having got his command of that language significantly better in the months they'd been together, and then in Arabic as best he could, having learned as much of that as he could too. Then as one of them tried to spit at him, put real anger in his voice as he added in French once more, "I am a priest, full and proper! So if you don't want me to cut you off from God before you die, I would think very hard before you show me disrespect!" He saw that sink in, and guessed that in the flickering torchlight several were suddenly seeing that he was tonsured for the first time.

"Old Imad, the Arab down at the docks," a voice said thickly through burst lips and broken teeth. "He recruited us. Paid us well. Said there'd be more when we brought him the boy's head. Somethin' about proof needin' to go back to the man who'd put up the money."

"And do you know who that was?" Tuck demanded, still standing over them and glowering fiercely.

"Naah, don't be daft," a more cynical voice came from further along the group. "We don't get told and we don't ask."

"You overheard nothing?" Tuck persisted. But by the various grunts and sniffs, the answer to that was no. "You pathetic examples of humanity," he lashed back at them, losing his command of French in his anger and reverting to Welsh. "By *Dewi Sant*! If the Lord made us in His image, then he must have made you from the last scrapings off His immortal arse! You villains were ready for the Devil to pluck for his own before you even finished suckling from your poor mothers' teats. Shame on you! Shame on you all! I'll offer none of you absolution at your last if you don't live through this," and he turned his back on them.

"*Duw*, Tuck, that was going a bit strong!" Hugh said in awe. "You really are angry, aren't you?"

But now Tuck's face fell. "I can't believe I've been so moved to anger as to blaspheme like that." He shook his head miserably. "I'm going to go and stand outside and look at the stars and pray very hard for the Lord to forgive me that outburst. Call me if you need me," and he stamped off out through the door.

Rhodri looked worried and made to get up and follow him, but Gryff and Hugh held him back. "Let him go," Gryff advised. "He needs to sort his thoughts out for himself."

"Aye," Hugh agreed. "It was going to happen sooner or later – I'm just surprised it's taken this long for Tuck to feel the temptations which come on all of us at some point. Don't worry, Rhodri, Tuck's not going to go bad on us. He'll probably see it as God testing him when he's calmed down; but we see it as him getting to see life as it really is. He'll be a better priest for it, you know. Tuck's always had enormous compassion, but this will give him a genuine understanding of soldiers, and who knows what good might come out of that when he gets home, and has someone like us come into his church?"

Rhodri sat back down with a faint smile. "Wise words, Hugh. Yes, Tuck will be a wonderful priest in some parish, and they'll be lucky to get him." But deep inside he still offered up a few prayers of his own that Tuck wouldn't be permanently scarred by this experience – and Rhodri wasn't a man who prayed hard very often.

Come the morning there were decisions to be made, the first of which involved their prisoners. After much discussion they decided that they would march them overland to another port and shove them into the hands of any galley captain who needed men for his oars, but that that port would not be Famagusta. Whoever Imad the Arab was, he could remain in suspense for as long as possible. Sulien and Anian were sure that he wouldn't worry enough to search for the missing mercenaries when he still had the money he should have paid them on completion of the assassination.

"He'll put it in his pocket and swear that it was the men who tricked him, if asked," Anian assured Tuck with a knowing wink. "There's one like him in every port – a man with a finger in every dirty pie going, and with a knack of making sure that the blame falls elsewhere when things go wrong. Imad's the least of our worries."

A less pleasant conversation was the one with Stephen and Walter. Poor Stephen looked as miserable as they had ever seen him, and in the furious conversation which went on between him and his father in their own obscure dialect – after Tuck, Rhodri and Lord Hywel had made it clear that they wanted the truth and were in no mood to be fobbed off – the others didn't need to understand every word to know that he was saying, 'I told you we should have trusted them.' Walter still looked doubtful when Stephen turned back to them, but despite Walter plucking at his son's sleeve to try and pull him back, Stephen jerked his arm free and took a deep breath.

"I am most truly sorry," he began. "We've kept this secret for so long it's become a habit. For my part, I wish we had told you right back when you helped us with Lady Agnes, but my father made her a promise to tell nobody, and I hope you can forgive him if you know that he saw it as his sacred duty to keep that promise."

Tuck immediately turned to Walter, and speaking slowly so that the older man would understand, said, "It does you much credit that you've kept your word to your lady this long. But, oh my friend, how I wish you had thought more of the consequences. It was our soldier friends' good instincts that made us come here with you. And I hope you can see now that had we not come, you would not have woken to see this morning, and William would have died alongside you." Tuck saw no reason to distress Walter with the detail that William's head would have been cut off to take as proof. The old man didn't deserve that.

"So who is he?" Rhodri demanded, not prepared to relent until they had the full story this time.

And Stephen's answer of, "He's related to the King of Sicily," landed in their midst like a rock launched from a trebuchet.

Chapter 17

Cyprus
Early Spring, the year of Our Lord, 1178

"He's *what?*"

"He's *who?*"

"William? Surely not…" echoed in differing variations around the camp as the shock hit them.

"I think you'd better give us the whole story," Sulien said, being the first of them to recover.

Stephen turned and said something to his father, who got up and went to where William was stroking the nose of one of the mules, drawing the lad off with him towards the olive grove. "He doesn't really know who he is," Stephen explained, "and he doesn't need to hear this. It's not like he's going to be part of that world ever again, and what he doesn't know he can't let slip by accident."

He took a deep breath and then began again. "I'm sure by now that you all know that the Hauteville family are our leading lords on Sicily, and that our King William is married to your King Henry's daughter, Joanna – well, not *your* king, Frère Pascal and Bornhold – but I believe the English king is also related to King Baldwin of Jerusalem?"

Pascal nodded. "Cousins, I understand."

"So you know that all these high-born Norman families interconnect? …Good, so you need to appreciate that once upon a time there was a separate Norman duchy of Apulia, which is now part of the greater Kingdom of Sicily, and that the title of duke of Apulia has been used off and on in recent generations for the oldest son and heir presumptive of the king of Sicily. It's a bit like King Henry's third son, Geoffrey, now being duke of Brittany because it's part of the Plantagenet's Norman lands." He coughed and added apologetically, "I'm afraid I have to give you something of the family tree of our kings or this won't make much sense to you.

"So our current King William is the son of the old King William, who was himself the son of King Roger II. Now old King Roger – our king's grandfather – had six sons, so you'd think he wouldn't run out of heirs, wouldn't you? But his oldest son – another Roger – who was given the title of Duke of Apulia, died six years before his father and leaving no legitimate heirs of his own, so he never inherited the crown. Keep that in mind about the legitimate heirs, because there was a bastard son.

"Now going back to old King Roger, his next son, Tancred, similarly died a full sixteen years before him; and the next son, Alphonso, four years even before that. So old King Roger had lost three of six sons many years before he died. The fourth son was William – our current king's father – and as you've obviously guessed, that William became king after Roger. But there were two other sons. The youngest, Simon, died in the same year as his father, but the other one, Henry, lived on."

Stephen took a deep breath. "Henry was Lady Agnes' husband, our lord, and young William's father."

There was a stunned silence and then Owain broke it with, "God's hooks! That makes young William what? The current king's cousin?"

"That's right," Stephen sighed. "The current King William and our little William's father, Duke Henry, were brothers, both sons of old King Roger. Well that wouldn't have mattered much in the grander scheme of things. Let's face it, with the English Queen Eleanor having given King Henry so many children, we have every expectation of her daughter giving our king as many heirs. We'd have to be very unlucky for him to die without heirs like so many of his brothers did."

"But there's that bastard," Rhodri said suspiciously. "I'm not liking where this is going, but would I be right in guessing that the Tancred who's been hunting us with such a passion is that illegitimate son of …was it the oldest brother?"

"Yes, he is." Stephen shook his head and said in disgust, "Power hungry doesn't even start to describe Duke Roger's son, and for some reason which my own lord could never fathom, Tancred sees it as his right and due to become Duke of Apulia. In his eyes it was his father's title, and so it should pass to him. But there are two things against that. Firstly, and most obviously, is his illegitimacy. But a close second is that for all that our king doesn't have a direct heir of his own, he nonetheless already had an heir in his legitimate brother. So while he lived, my lord, Henry, was the actual next in line – not that he was bothered about becoming duke of Apulia, because it's not exactly been handed down from father to son unbroken. It's more a discretionary gift in the giving of the king, and King William hasn't given it to anyone. But now my dear lord is dead. And young William is his very legitimate heir…"

"...Oh shit!" Anian exclaimed. "So in effect he's the heir to the king until he has sons of his own!"

"Then why, by Judas' balls, did the bloody king not take better care of William?" fumed Sulien.

"Because he didn't realise he needed to," Stephen explained. "After all, a bastard like Tancred is never going to be in the running for king, is he, and that's foremost in the king's mind. Where William currently stands more in Tancred's way is over this matter of who gets to be Duke of Apulia. He knows full well that his bastardy is an issue with regard to him inheriting the kingdom, and I think he's too sharp to press that claim hard at the moment, and that's why he's not done anything to openly give the king cause for concern. He's played it very craftily. Tancred knows full well that even if the king acknowledged him, he would never get the backing of King William's enfeoffed lords and supporters; and therefore that he'd never hold onto the throne even if he unexpectedly inherited it. So from the king's point of view, Tancred poses no threat at all, and he's enough of a Norman lord to believe in his ability to sire sons once he married, so being young and healthy, he's probably not given a second thought to finding an heir beyond his own children.

"But the duchy is another matter, and all the more Tancred's to claim, in his eyes, because he's Duke Roger's only surviving issue, Duke Roger having been the last holder of that title. And he's cunning enough to pursue that claim well away from the king's court until he's sure that all King William needs to do is simply acknowledge what to all intents is a *fait accompli*."

"Blessed St Thomas! I see it now," Tuck gulped. "As the *only* legitimate heir of the last of the king's brothers, in Tancred's eyes little William could well be made the duke ahead of himself. And of course, once the king has made little William duke of Apulia, even if the king and Queen Joanna have a whole tribe of sons, while an existing duke lives, they can hardly take back the title and hand it on to their own child. ...Well they might ...but it would set a worrying example to their other enfeoffed lords, and wouldn't go down well at all. And they've probably thought no more about it than as something to hand on to their own child. ...But where Tancred's concerned, there's a good chance that the title of Duke of Apulia could once again have some standing in its own right, should William then have a son of his own to hand it on to. Bless me ...and that's just what Tancred thinks should happen for him, isn't it?

"But …oh, *Duw*, Tancred can't afford to hang around now, can he? That's what we've been missing – what we didn't see. It's that urgency about all of this, isn't it? Tancred can't afford to linger now, because if the queen starts having children at the speed our Queen Eleanor did, then before this year is out, he could be seeing his prize vanishing out of his hands and into *their* baby son's. Or if not this year if she has a girl first, then soon after. And that's also why the King hasn't worried about William – if he even knew he'd gone missing – because with his own marriage he must have expectations of heirs. Our William is just the child cousin who he's probably never even met, so why would he care? It's only in Tancred's warped mind that the duchy is up for grabs."

"*Dewi Sant,*" Rhodri breathed. "Of course! We're only in March, but if the queen is already pregnant – or gets pregnant within the next month or so – then by Christmas it could all be over for Tancred to get his hands on the title. I'm presuming that it's lucrative?"

"I don't know that you'd call it lucrative," Stephen answered. "It's hardly a fertile part of the land, but what it does include are the two ports of Bari and Brindisi, and if Tancred can get hold of them…"

"…Then he gets his hands on an important part of the pilgrimage and crusading routes to the east," Rhodri concluded.

Sulien whistled. "That'd be a nice little earner! Can you imagine it if our Prince Richard gets to take the Cross, as he keeps pestering King Henry to be allowed to do? How many men would pass through those ports then? The taxes alone would make Tancred a very wealthy man."

"And poor little William is standing in his way," Tuck said sadly. "If he doesn't die soon, then by Tancred's way of thinking, the dukedom and all that money will be gone forever. Never mind that the king has shown no sign of handing it on to his brother, let alone his heir. And he hasn't, has he, Stephen?"

"No, not at all. Not to my Lord Henry, and in the time since his death, nothing was ever mentioned to Lady Agnes about William having it, either."

"So this is really all in Tancred's head?"

Stephen nodded miserably. "All a fancy of his own making, I fear. I can't imagine King William letting such a tactically important part of his kingdom fall into someone else's hands, and that's what it is – tactical. All that you said about pilgrims and crusades holds as true for the king as it does for Tancred."

"Hold on, though," Tuck said, suddenly brightening up. "But all of this means that as soon as the queen announces that she's with child, then William becomes of no use to anyone, doesn't he? So we're not looking at the poor mite being a hunted man to the end of his days. He's just got to survive until Christmas, or at least hopefully not much beyond that. A couple of years at most, for surely the king and queen will have an heir by then?"

Stephen puffed his cheeks as he thought furiously. "Hmmm… Put like that, no, he won't be looking over his shoulder for the rest of his life."

"And we have got breathing space," Anian added. "Think about it: this fool of a bastard lord is still waiting to hear back from his hired assassins, isn't he? So it'll be a while before he has chance to put another plan into place."

Madog nodded. "You've got a point, my friend. …In fact, we've been caught on the hop a bit by this, so we haven't thought it through properly. But now I'm thinking that there's no way that Tancred can have heard of us leaving the Holy Land. I mean, it's just not feasible, is it? We left on the first ships to depart from Acre after the winter. So think, lads: this has to be something Tancred put into place last autumn at the very latest, and probably a lot earlier."

Yet Rhodri and Tuck were already shaking their heads, even as Pascal said, "But then that doesn't explain Tancred's men in Jerusalem, does it?" Prompting nods of agreement from both men, and Bornhold groaning, grabbing a handful of his hair with both hands, and growling,

"Blessed St Lazarus! Why didn't I see it? No, there weren't any of the *ordinary* ships in the harbour, aside from the ones that had wintered there, but there *was* one of the Templars' ships! It was re-supplying as we boarded our ship. *That's* how those men arrived! Tancred offered the Templars money for his men's passage! They came on the first ship *east* from Cyprus – probably on one that wintered either there or on Crete."

"And *that*," Rhodri said emphatically, "is why these men were so prepared for us here on Cyprus. They hadn't been sitting on their arses all winter waiting for the first boats to come westwards. They've had all winter to think about the different possibilities, and while they couldn't have known about us and the fact that we'd be returning westwards, there must have been one part of the plan which always allowed for Walter and Stephen to come back off pilgrimage. Tancred had to have given his men money to use however the thought best, and part of that is what bought the services of Old Imad – whoever he is – and this bunch of wastrels he paid for, even if initially it was only to watch the port and listen for news. And I can't imagine he had to pay them much, from the little they've said. I doubt whether any local lords are queuing up to hire their dubious services, so they probably came cheap as men already only just staying one step ahead of getting caught for their previous crimes."

"But that brings us back to what we're going to do about William just now," said Tuck with a sigh. "If Tancred still has him firmly in mind, then I'm not sure it's safe for anyone to stay here over the next few months. We're still far too close to Famagusta. It'll only take word to get back that the Hospitallers have new men back on this grange for the wrong people to put two and two together."

"Tuck's right," Rhodri agreed. "I think the best thing to do would be for all of you to come with us to the western coast of Cyprus. Let's make sure that we have these trouble-makers stowed in the belly of some galley under the lash of a tough captain, for a start off. That'll be one lot of tongues that won't be wagging in the local market places. And I know you don't want to let your order down, Pascal and Bornhold, but this place looks to me as though it's been in want of some care and attention for quite a while now. Those sheep out on the hills have clearly survived under the care of some local shepherds who nominally would answer to you, so let's leave them as they are. A few months won't make a ha'penny's worth of difference to them. In fact, they probably think of the sheep as more theirs than yours, anyway, and no doubt trade more than a few lambs to supplement their income that the Hospitaller order never get to know about."

As Pascal and Bornhold looked askance at this blithe acceptance of illicit trading, Tuck couldn't help but laugh. "You should see what the Norman Marcher lords on the Welsh borders go in blissful ignorance of," he said to them cheerfully. "It's amazing what slips under people's noses when they stick them so high in the air. Rhodri's talking from experience, here," and the other Welshmen were all nodding sagely, which only raised the two knights' eyebrows even further.

"But it all means that you can come westwards with us – all five of you. By the time you're turning back to return to this place, you'll have convincingly thrown men off your trail. It'll give Old Imad time to send more men up here to look around and find nothing, and I doubt he enquire later on unless he's paid again to do it. And with that in mind, we leave no bodies. Grim though it will be, we need to carry the corpses of those four who have died in the night away from here. There must be no trace that they were ever here left for others to discover."

"Blessed St Thomas, Brother Tuck!" Lord Hywel said in admiration. "You've become quite the practical conspirator in your time with us! My father would be proud of me if I came up with something like that."

"It's our bad influence rubbing off on him," Dai said with a wink Hywel's way.

"You can take the man out of Wales, but you can't take being *Cymry* out of the man," Madog declared. "It's in the blood, my young lord. You just have to let it have its head!"

All the Welshmen chuckled, which only had the two knights and Stephen shaking their heads in further awe at this wholly alternative way of viewing the world. And yet they had convinced Stephen enough for him to ask,

"So you think that if we come back here in a few months time that we'll be safe?"

Rhodri sniffed. "I wouldn't go as far as to say 'safe', but I do think that as long as you're careful, and do things like go to the markets in the other direction to Famagusta, for instance, then it's unlikely that Old Imad will stir himself sufficiently to send more men after you. Tancred would really have to grease his grubby palm with substantially more than he's done so far to get him moving – unless I've totally lost my touch with reading men like that, and *Duw* willing, I haven't."

"Then the sooner we get moving, the better," Sulien declared. "Madog, take three of the lads and remove everything which can be buried or hidden away from the farmhouse until they return. Take Stephen and Walter with you so that they know where things are. We'll have to use the mules for the bodies – there's no way around that. We'll cart one body as far as we can, by switching it between mules so that they each only have short stretches of carrying two bodies, but then that might have to go down a ravine and hope that the local scavengers can render it beyond recognition before it's found."

Gryff sucked his teeth thoughtfully and chipped in with, "Might be even better if we dress him up in some of Walter and Stephen's clothes. Who's going to poke around at a three-week-old corpse? As long as it roughly looks like one of them, I doubt anyone will search much further."

"Let's dump two of them, in that case," Rhodri decided. "If we throw a bit of William's clothing down with them, they might even think a scavenger has dragged the smaller body away? I can't imagine that decent trackers would be working for Imad. He'll only have the dregs of the docks to hire, so it wouldn't have to work for someone as skilled as Lord Einion's man, Tysilio, who we had to fool that one time – *Dewi Sant*, he could track a ghost through fog, he could! So let's make it seem like our three Sicilians have died not far from here.

"When we get to the far coast, Pascal, if you and Bornhold start asking around for news of two of your brothers who have gone missing between here and there, who's going to know that you are them? And that will further muddy the waters for anyone trying to track you. We'll try and time it so that you can sneak out of town just as we're about to get on a ship, so that it looks as though you've left with us. Walter, Stephen and William won't be able to come into whichever port we find, anyway, because that would just wreck all our careful sleights of hand. So we'll leave the mules with them."

Tuck agreed. "The one thing we mustn't do is let our prisoners see what we're up to at any stage," he concluded the discussion with. "So let's get them marching out under guard before we start doing any of this changing clothing and the like. You and most of the lads take them on ahead, Rhodri. Just leave the three archers with me and we'll do the rest."

The plan worked better than they could ever have dreamed. Not a day away from the farmhouse, Tuck and his party passed a nasty cleft in the land, where the edges crumbled dangerously, and so the first two corpses got shoved over the edge there, a pair of William's shoes he was outgrowing getting thrown over as well, along with a suitably torn shirt besmirched with some of the dead men's blood. By the time it got found, nobody was going to be able to tell that the blood had already been drying before it got rubbed into the cloth. And then within the day, another prime spot allowed them to dispose of the remaining two other dead mercenaries in fake Hospitaller garb, all of which allowed Tuck's group to then catch up with the rest of the group on the second day after that, covering their late arrival with declarations of having to bury the bodies back at the farm – just in case any of their prisoners had enough of a grasp of the *lingua franca* of the Holy Land to know what was being said when the Welshmen were talking with Pascal and Bornhold and the three others.

They deliberately avoided Nicosia, and instead made a leisurely march down to a small port called Paphos, by which time two more of their prisoners had died – something which even Tuck could not find it in himself to mourn. These men had regularly taken lives with scant regard for most of their adulthood, and it was hard to think there would be anyone who would miss them. At Paphos they found some local fishermen who assured them that they knew some of the feared galley captains who came their way from south of there along the north African coast, and within a couple of weeks, two of the sleek, oared vessels came into the harbour and gladly took the remaining prisoners on board. In return, they offered to transport the Welshmen as far as the southern coast of Crete. They would not put into the well-used crusader port of Candia on the northern side, being engaged in what could only be described as acts of piracy, but by now the Welshmen were rather glad that they were taking the circuitous route. Anyone trying to track them this far would have to be very good indeed.

And so they bade a fond farewell to their five friends, who would now take a gentle march back to the farm. It was a wrench to finally part from Stephen and Walter, and even more so from young William, whom they had all become very fond of. But it was also harder than they had expected to leave Pascal and Bornhold behind. So much of what they had been through in the Holy Land had been shared with one or other of these two, and it was these men that Rhodri and Sulien found it hardest to leave behind.

"If you can't live peacefully here, come and find us in Wales," Rhodri told Bornhold as they clasped hands at the quayside. "Ask for Lord Cadwallon of Elfael, we'll not be far from his lands. It's wet and cold, and there's always a fight going on somewhere, but by *Dewi Sant*, you know who your enemies are – not like this skulking in the shadows."

By the time they reached Sicily once more, it was almost August, and they saw the countryside scorched by the blazing heat again. Their diversions had cost them dearly in terms of time, but at least they had been able to say farewell to their five friends safe in the knowledge that they were unlikely to get any further trouble from Tancred's paid ruffians. But at this point even the most cynical of them couldn't help but believe as Tuck did, that there was someone on high watching over them. For at Mesina they were able to catch their next boat straight away, never stopping even for one night, meaning they would not risk someone having a good memory and linking them with the same party of Welshmen who had come through before. And that boat took them not to the mainland, but onwards, first to Sardinia, and then onto the port of Marseilles – nominally in the hands of the Holy Roman Emperor at this time, but also just beyond the official boundaries of his lands. It placed them nicely to retrace their tracks back up through the Duchy of Burgundy and on through France proper before autumn fully set in.

Just the sight of the greener fields as they tramped northwards brought on a great longing for home in all of them. Everyone had missed the rich green tapestries of foliage of home, but to at last see the multitude of greens, and smell the vibrant and clean scents of woodland and fields in the rain, had all of them moving that bit more briskly in anticipation of getting back.

"We'll be home for Christmas," Lord Hywel said, so full of emotion at the thought that he wept.

"I want to see my wife again," Rhodri confessed emotionally. "*Duw* but I've missed her so much. I shall be begging Lord Cadwallon not to send me far from her side again. I'll even take a demotion to just one of the men he calls from the fields if needed, if it will save me leaving again."

"Then you'll be around to stand by me when I ask Mistress Nest for her hand," Anian said, then added worriedly, "as long as bloody Emrys from across the valley hasn't beaten me to it while I've been gone. That is."

"Don't worry," Sulien said, giving Anian a playful swat, "Emrys couldn't keep his trews up if his life depended on it, and Nest knows that. She wants a man who she can trust not to be off chasing the first bit of skirt that catches his eye after she's married him. She'll be waiting, Anian." And that set everyone else off in a flood of memories of people they couldn't wait to see again.

Yet for Tuck there was a sudden rush of wholly different feelings as they finally stood on the French coast on a crystal clear morning, and saw the outline of the English coast on the horizon. There would be no welcome home for him from the monks. Nobody would be rushing out to greet him and clasp him to them with cries of joy at his safe return. And worse, he would be separated from these men whom he had come to think of as brothers in the familial sense, not just as fellow inmates, as he had the ones he'd shared the dormitory with at Ewenny. If the others were truly going home, then his own fate was once again most precarious.

Chapter 18

Abergavenny,
The Year of Our Lord, 1178

"So you came back."

It was hardly the warmest of welcomes, and Tuck had only got as far as the priory gate. This really didn't bode well for his continued reception.

"Who's prior?" he asked, feeling faintly sick at the sensation of prison walls closing in around him, once more pounded in on him. *Please God, don't let it be Humbert,* he found himself praying.

"Prior Durand," the gatekeeper said with a smirk which did nothing to quell Tuck's misgivings. "But you won't find him here. He's up at the castle with my lord de Braose."

"And Humbert?"

"*Sub-prior* Humbert is still here – so don't think your exploits aren't known by the new prior."

Tuck managed to wring out a ghost of a smile. "Oh, my 'exploits' have expanded considerably."

"I'm sure they have. Took your time getting back from Canterbury, didn't you?"

"Canterbury?" Tuck exploded, suddenly angry. "Is that what you lot think? Well you can scuttle on back to the rest of them and inform them that not only did I continue on to Rome with Lord Hywel – we've been all the way to Jerusalem!" He fished into the belt bag he wore and produced his pilgrim tokens, brandishing them under the supercilious gate-keeper's nose. "See? Proof! So who's the degenerate amongst us now, eh? I have helped tend the wounded at the Hospitallers' great *hôpital* in Jerusalem after one of the battles out there, and I have learned much of healing and cures – enough to be able to pass on a great deal to Brother Ioan!"

"Brother Ioan's dead," the gate-keeper said, his face suddenly falling into misery. "He went out to tend to a sick man at the castle, and some drunken soldier stuck a knife into him."

Ioan dead? Tuck felt what remained of his attachment to this place fall away. Not a single soul remained here whom he gave a tinker's curse for, and part of him wanted desperately to take to his heels and run after Rhodri and Lord Hywel. They had left him early that morning to continue on their own way home, but quite what they were returning to was another question, since they had heard of feuding between the local Welsh princes from the farmer they had stopped with last night. At least they were all friends together, though, and Hywel had declared that he would ask his father if he could keep this band of men for his own. A dozen men out of his father's substantial levy of fighters wasn't enough to give him enough men to challenge his father's authority with, but plenty to help keep him safe, and now Tuck was wondering whether Hywel might run to having his own priest?

Then he realised that the gate-keeper was saying, "…and that's why the prior is with my lord de Braose to decide the punishment for Ioan's murderer."

"So this happened recently?"

"Only two weeks ago. They were just waiting for sheriff de Braose to get back to the castle."

Dewi Sant, why did we take our time? Tuck grieved. *Two weeks, that's all it would have taken, and then I might have been the one going to the castle, and after all I've been through, I might well have survived the attack.*

"I'm going to the castle," was what he said to the gate-keeper instead, and without giving the brother chance to protest, turned on his heels and strode off towards the looming bulk of de Braose's fortress.

When he got there he had no trouble getting in, simply by saying he was a monk from the priory come to see the prior – it wasn't a lie, after all, and they didn't need to know what he needed to see him for. Striding into the hall, he took in the scene being played out before him. Up on the dais, a man who could only be the prior, going by his rich gown and tonsure, was sitting at de Braose's right hand, while the son – also a William de Braose – sat at his father's left. The three were drinking wine and deep in discussion. Meanwhile over to one side of the hall, a man who was practically swaying on his feet was being watched over by four other men in the garb of de Braose's soldiers. They were hardly guarding this man, though, and the looks on their faces were ones of pity rather than loathing.

Curiosity piqued, Tuck went first to them rather than the prior, and as soon as he saw the man he knew what had happened. By now he had seen those haunted eyes before. This man was no cold-hearted killer. He was someone who had seen too much killing and had been scarred in mind if not body by the experiences.

"I'm Brother Tuck," he introduced himself softly to the nearest guard. "May I take a look at this man?"

Something in Tuck's tone and manner made the soldier blink. Clearly he'd been expecting condemnation from one of the monks, not sympathy. But Tuck stepped in and gently lifted the man's face so that he could look into his eyes.

"You have nightmares," was more of a statement than a question, but he got the faintest of nods. "Do you sometimes see people who you thought were dead?" Another nod.

Tuck turned to the soldiers. "I've just returned from the Holy Land, and I've seen many men out there who have been affected like this. He's not a bad man, and I truly believe that if he can be allowed to go and live somewhere quietly, he'll be of no further danger to anyone."

"Well good luck convincing those three of that," one of the soldiers said bitterly. "He's my uncle – not that any of the high and mighty here bothered to find that out before they asked me to guard him. Uncle Emrys is sick. He's never hurt a soul before."

"That was the trouble," another said. "He was forced to join one of de Braose's raids where they slaughtered everyone they found. He's not been right since."

Squaring his shoulders, Tuck marched up to the other side of the great oak table at which the lords were sat. He was so close that they couldn't avoid being aware of his presences.

"Who are you?" the prior demanded, looking him up and down and taking in the travel stained habit and tonsure. "I don't know you!"

"No, my lord prior, you don't. I was sent on pilgrimage with Lord Hywel before you came. My name is Brother Tuck, and I am come here direct from *Jerusalem*."

There was a moment's silence as the prior looked at him as if he had dropped to earth from a passing cloud, like some grubby angel who had fallen from grace and landed minus his wings. Then the prior's innate sense of superiority kicked in and he waved Tuck away with,

"Then get back to the monastery – I'll deal with you later."

"With all due respect, my lord, that's not why I'm standing here." The prior's eyes widened at Tuck's blatant disregard for an order, but had no chance to speak before Tuck continued, "I'm here because that man over there is sick. I've seen this before in the great Hospitaller wards in Jerusalem. He cannot continue in my lord de Braose's service, that is obvious, but his actions were not deliberate, and I am begging you for mercy on his behalf."

"*Mercy*? Mercy!" the prior spluttered. "Do you know what he did?"

"I do, and I counted Brother Ioan as one of my friends, so do not think me indifferent to the loss of a good and kindly brother. But hanging this man won't bring Ioan back, and there is such a thing as forgiveness, my lord. He did not know what he was doing at the time. There was no malice aforethought in his act. He is a man haunted by the ghosts of the past and deserves our pity."

The two de Braose men were snorting in disgust at Tuck's words, while the prior turned a strange colour at being so lectured to by someone he perceived as being of so little consequence. A mere monk like Tuck should be seen and not heard, except in the church – and preferably not seen too much, either!

"He hangs tonight!" the senior de Braose declared, and sadly, given that de Braose was the sheriff of Herefordshire but even more of a law unto himself on this side of the Welsh border, Tuck realised he had failed.

To gasps of shock at his lack of respect, Tuck spun on his heels and marched away from the table, never bothering to look back. As he reached the soldiers, he said firmly,

"Bring him with me! There must be a chapel somewhere in this Godforsaken place?"

As he strode out of the door, with the prior's receding, "Brother! ...Brother, *come back here*! ...Do you hear me? ...Come back! ...Brother? ...*Brother*!...." following him, one of the guards caught him by the sleeve, saying,

"De Braose won't let the ordinary men into the chapel. That's for the family only."

"Then who sees to the men?" Tuck asked, appalled that he had never thought to find this out before. How much had he taken for granted back in those days? What else had he failed to do in his naivety back then?

"There's a small chapel out on the hillside on the edge of the village, only a small wooden hall. The prior sometimes sends one of the priests out to that for us ordinary folk."

"Then show me where it is," Tuck said firmly. "You can come with us to guard him so that there's no question of him being let free – although I can't say I'm not tempted to do that. Unfortunately, I suspect that if we let him go, in the state he's in he would only stand there and not run, for I doubt he even knows where he is anymore. Mercifully, I am a priest. So I shall pray with your uncle there until they come for him. If I cannot save him in this life, I shall do all I can to ensure he enters the next in the best possible way."

"Thank you, Brother," the man's nephew said, "but you know you're going to get into trouble for this?"

Tuck snorted in disgust. "I'm afraid I was destined to be in trouble the moment I set foot back in this valley! It was only ever going to be a question as to over what, and I can think of no better reason than this."

At the small chapel, Tuck dug into his pack and found a stub of a candle, which he set on the simple wooden table of an altar. But then his hand found the pack of incense tucked away amongst the few spare clothes he had.

"Can one of you get me some charcoal?" he asked. "I only need a small amount, and something I can burn it on."

"My cousin's the smith here," one of the other men said. "I'm sure he'd let me have a little," and wearing a puzzled frown, disappeared out of the door.

He came back faster than Tuck had anticipated, and with company. Clearly the villagers were none too happy about what was about to happen to the man Emrys, and were intrigued by what the guard must have said. Certainly there was no sense of hostility coming from them that Tuck could pick up on.

When he got the charcoal glowing on the small piece of flat metal that had been brought in with it, he carefully dropped a few grains of the precious incense onto it, and within a few breaths he could smell the rich aromas of frankincense, myrrh and rose beginning to waft around the tiny chapel on the drafts which blew in. He'd shoved his pack over into the darkness out of the way, and so it was far from obvious where the wonderful scent now appeared from. As he then began to pray as he had prayed over the dying soldiers in the *hôpital* in Jerusalem, it was as if he had brought some of that sanctity back with him. Not a mouse stirred as the villagers all watched in awe as he prayed over Emrys.

Tuck had no idea how long he had been at his work, but when he heard the heavy tread of more men-at-arms, he helped Emrys to his feet and led him to the chapel's door, only to realise that dusk had come, and full night wasn't far away.

"Do not fear," he said gently to Emrys, "I will come with you as far as I can."

They got as far as the gatehouse to the castle, at which point the sergeant said almost apologetically to Tuck, "I'm afraid my lord says you're not allowed into the castle tonight."

Yet there was no pleasure in the sergeant's manner as he led the rest of the little contingent inside, and Tuck could tell that this wasn't sitting easy with any of the castle's guards. All of them were no doubt thinking that there, but for the Grace of God, could have gone any one of them. As the last men headed in, Tuck hissed urgently, "Where's the nearest spot to where he'll hang on the outside?"

Emry's nephew pointed through eyes full of tears to the right, but another villager caught his arm and said, "This way!"

The man led Tuck to a spot by a high stretch of blank wall. "He'll be behind there," he said, his voice choked but angry.

"I need my pack!" Tuck suddenly realised.

"I'll go!" a lad volunteered, and ran off into the night.

"More charcoal, please, as well," Tuck asked, and the smith went to get some without question.

All of a sudden he remembered the effect of the echo back in the Church of the Holy Sepulchre, and the rebel inside him immediately wanted to reproduce that effect in defiance of these arrogant lords. A few experimental hums soon found a spot where there was something like a resonance off the stone walls, if not a full echo, and as he and the small crowd which had gathered around him heard the pompous tones of Prior Durand start up, he fanned the charcoal, dropped more incense on, and began to sing. He dredged up every one of the beautiful chants he had learned over the months in the east and sang them from the heart. And it was only when he felt the urgent tug on his sleeve from one of the villagers, and them hissing,

"You must stop, Brother! Emrys is dead and the sheriff's men are coming!" that he realised that it all must be over.

"Quick! Come this way!" someone said, and it was only as he found himself within the darkness of the forge that he realised that it must have been the smith who had guided him.

"You must be silent, Brother," he whispered softly. "Stay here behind this – it's a piece of leather I have hanging up to stay smooth to cut and put onto sword handles. It won't move in the breeze if anyone opens the forge door. I shall be in my house next door, and I'll come for you when it's safe."

For what must have been the next hour or so, Tuck could hear the occasional stamping of feet, and the muffled voices of men sporadically drifting through the forge's walls. Eventually, though, all went quiet, and a little while later the smith reappeared, this time with a candle.

"You must run," he told Tuck. "The de Braoses are furious that someone defied them like that. Go! Go west and keep going."

However Tuck had had time to think, and he was determined not to give these men such an easy victory over him. And there were people here whom he could see needed his help; people who were being failed by those who were supposed to be seeing to their spiritual welfare. He had been one of those blind and ignorant ones before he had left, but no more, now he knew better, and his spiritual crime would be all the greater if he ignored their plight now.

"Don't worry, my friend," he said with a reassuring pat on the smith's shoulder, "those two will have to get up a lot earlier in the morning to catch me out!"

Taking his leave, he walked briskly back up to the monastic enclosure. Once upon a time he would have been daunted by how to get inside, but not now. Going around the perimeter wall, he came to where there was a gap where the waste water flowed out to drain into the nearby river. Taking off his boots, he waded in, then went barefoot over the path to where he recalled the washing area was. He cleaned his feet off and dried them on the end of his habit, then put his boots back on.

With care he crept around to Ioan's herbarium and was pleased to discover that the hiding place he remembered up under the reed-thatch roof was still there. In it he hid his recurve bow and the handful of arrows he had, and also the oiled-cloth pouch with the precious incense in it. Nothing would persuade him to make a gift of it to the priory now. They didn't deserve it in his eyes. He would save it up for those times when he felt it was right and proper, not squander it on fools. And he did think that this new prior was a fool – not stupid, but so wrapped up in his own self-importance that he would make ridiculous decisions with a blithe disregard for any he saw as beneath him.

For now, though, Tuck wanted to keep this Norman prior off-balance, and so he made his way through to the priory church, taking his place in the choir stalls and waiting for his fellow monks to come in for the depths of the night office of Matins. It had to be later than he thought, because the next time the brothers filed in, it was to observe Lauds – Matins must have come and gone while he was hiding in the forge. Too weary to take much notice of anything, his fellow monks stumbled through the office and then dragged themselves off to bed once more. They would only have a scant hour or two before they would be roused from their beds again to observe Prime, at which point their daily routine would begin.

So Tuck slipped through into the dormitory area behind them, glad to see that it was the ghastly Eustace who was still keeping an eye on everyone at this point, and that he was actually nodding in his seat throughout the office. Clearly Humbert and Durand declined to get up for the night time offices these days, and that suited Tuck's plan very well. And so he lay down on the simple bed which was kept for visiting monks just outside the main dormitory door. It would ensure that whoever came to rouse the monks next would have to go right past him.

He felt his actions at the castle had been blessed when it turned out to be Brother Edgar whose turn it was this time to come and wake his fellow monks. Edgar was hardly the brightest of monks, but he remembered Tuck quite clearly – perhaps because Tuck had often intervened to save Edgar from being bullied by the other novices when they had been young oblates together.

"*Ooh*, Tuck! You're back! When did you arrive?"

"Late yesterday," Tuck told him. "I went to the castle and the prior told me to come back here, so I did. Bless me, Edgar, it's been a while since I had to get up for Matins and Lauds! I can barely keep my eyes open."

He saw the words sink in, and knew that if asked, that Edgar would now repeat his words as if Tuck had actually been there at both offices, as well as the coming Prime. He reinforced the notion by adding, "I see that Brother Cedric hasn't got any better in the year I've been gone – still keeps making a mess of the Latin." For again, as if by divine plan, it had been the idle and useless Cedric who had led the brothers' prayers at Lauds. Cedric, whose mangling of the daily offices even the less able students still found grating, which meant that everyone would recall that he had been there, and so if Tuck knew that, then he must have been there also. It did not require anyone to have to say they had seen Tuck in person to confirm his presence.

It was past the breaking of their fast in the refectory before word must have reached Prior Durand of Tuck's arrival, but after that it didn't take long before Eustace came for him. Yet if Eustace had been a little wary of Tuck before, one glare from Tuck as Eustace tried to cuff him forward, soon had him backing away and just gesturing to the prior's office.

Inside Tuck submitted to the anticipated interrogation. Yes, he had been with Lord Hywel the whole time. Yes, because of the fear of Hywel being taken hostage by the king, they had gone all the way to Rome. That had to be repeated several times before it was believed, along with production of the pilgrim tokens – although Tuck was careful not to let any of those go for fear of them being whisked out of his possession and into the prior's, for the looks he gave them were deeply covetous. But by the time Tuck had told of his months in Jerusalem, cheerfully boring the prior and Humbert with lengthy descriptions of every one of the great churches within the Holy City, and the gory details of the infirmary, even they had to acknowledge that Tuck could hardly have made that much up.

And that put them in a terrible quandary. What to do with Tuck? Even a pair as cynical and ambitious as Durand and Humbert nonetheless believed devoutly in the redemption of a pilgrimage. Any pilgrimage carried its own considerable benefits, they had to concede, but while they might have been less than in awe of a trip to Saint David's, Tuck's journey to Canterbury put him on a level with both of them; while his continuing to Rome and then Jerusalem took him to a whole higher level again which they could not ignore. They also fully believed that such an act conveyed a considerable blessing upon the pilgrim, and Tuck had done far more than just go to the holy places. A man who had followed in Christ's footsteps by washing and tending to the poor and sick could not then, by their own belief system, be a total miscreant. It simply wasn't possible for him to be both at the same time by the very measurements of worth that they subscribed to and upheld. Yet at the same time their wholly normal human reactions towards him as a man were ones of loathing, and they could not disguise their deep antipathy to the merest thought of having him back amongst them.

Nor could they quite bring themselves to ask outright if it had been him outside the walls of the castle last night. For if they did that and Tuck answered yes, then they would be in the even worse complication of having to find some way to punish this awful monk that would not bring divine disapproval down on them – because would God not be looking down on this scruffy monk, who had nonetheless managed to accrue such a wealth of spiritual honours, and judge their own actions? And yet they also still had to appease the earthly terror that was the de Braoses. Better, then, to just tell the brute of a sheriff that their errant monk had been back at the priory at the time, as witnessed by their own monks, and not ask too hard about how the timings matched up! After all, as men of the Church, they ought to believe in the ability of a heavenly choir to manifest itself, even if the de Braoses thought them naive for doing so – and the elder de Braose was reaching an age when he was starting to worry about his time in the afterlife rather more than he had in his belligerent prime, so upsetting the one group of monks who might pray for him was something he was becoming less willing to do.

Therefore it was with barely disguised sighs of relief that they finally heard Tuck say,

"What I desire most now is to be able to minster to a small flock of my own. I do not ask for a place of any importance. Rather, I believe that God has guided me towards the care of the poorest and most humble."

"Clodock!" Humbert squeaked, almost tripping over the name in his anxiety to prompt the prior. "We need a priest for Clodock, remember, Father?"

"Ah yes, Clodock. I think that might suit you very well, Tuck. The last brother who went there came back disturbed in spirit and mind. He had a bit of a rough time with the soldiers from Longtown Castle, you see. But you? You've been mixing with soldiers for months. I'm sure you'll cope."

And if it's by Longtown, then it's a long way from here, Tuck thought, struggling not to grin. *You do want me as far from here as possible, don't you!* But he answered meekly, "I would be blessed to tend to the people of Clodock. Thank you, Father Prior."

What he wasn't expecting was for the prior to want him to start for there that same day. That was going to complicate things, for he could hardly go and retrieve his hidden items when there was a brother at his heels at every turn. He managed to finally get them to agree to him spending some time in Brother Ioan's store to collect some small quantities of simple salves and ointments that he might need until he could start making his own. That gave him chance to rescue the incense and to throw the bow and arrows over the priory wall, hoping and praying that nobody would chance by and spot them.

By the time the Nones bell rang out, summoning the brothers to prayer once more, Tuck was being ushered out of the priory gate, and heard its bar being dropped into the cups behind him once again. This time, though, he was a very different man to the youth who had left two years before, and he had none of the same qualms over heading out into the relative unknown. *Oh well,* he thought, *at least they aren't going to be watching me set out on the road. I can go and get my bow without them wondering why I'm heading in the wrong direction.*

He found his bow and arrows, and shouldering them with his pack, decided to give the castle as wide a berth as possible. He felt he ought to thank the smith, though, and so worked his way through the village by the back tracks until he came once more to the forge. Like all such places, it stood a little separate from the rest of the village, for any craft which involved as much fire as smithing did was always a danger to any houses close by, but that made it easier for Tuck to slip in unseen.

"Oh, it's you, Brother," the smith said, putting down the heavy hammer he was working with.

"I came to thank you for last night," Tuck said gratefully.

"No, Brother, it's us who are thankful. Emrys was one of us – not one of the men de Braose drags in from who knows where. He was never a soldier, should never have been forced to be one. It was just his misfortune that he was a big man, and that caught de Braose's eye, and even then it wouldn't have mattered if the sheriff hadn't lost so many men in the last few fights against the Welsh princes."

"I thought they swore fealty to King Henry at Oxford?"

"Oh they did. But that hasn't stopped there being the odd raid at the local level. It's in the blood of folks around here, been doing it for generations. It'll take more than some king far off in London to stop them altogether. I doubt the king takes much notice of us most of the time. He'd rather forget about us. A bit like that poor sod he's got de Braose holding onto as a prisoner."

"Oh yes?" Tuck asked, his curiosity piqued. "Who's he then?"

The smith snorted in disgust. "One of the Welsh princes he took back in '65. Only a lad back then, he was. One of the ones that brute of a king had blinded, our Maredudd who works at the castle says. I bet the king doesn't even remember he's still here, but de Braose won't let him go, just in case the king ever asks. So he sits in a room and moulders his life away. What a bloody wicked penance to put on to anyone, let alone someone who wasn't old enough to be guilty of anything in the first place."

"What's his name, does anyone even know that?"

"Maelgwn, I believe."

Tuck was thinking furiously. "Do you think the local lads who get left here, when the family moves on to one of their other castles, would let me go in to see him? As a priest, I mean?"

The smith blinked in surprise. "I can't see why not. As long as it doesn't get them into trouble. There's no love lost on the de Braoses here."

It was only about nine miles from Abergavenny to Clodock, not far for a man who had walked as many miles as Tuck had, but plenty far enough for the prior to think twice about sending a brother to check up on him regularly, so Tuck knew he'd be able to get away without any trouble. If by any misfortune someone from the priory came looking for him while he was gone, well he'd just have to have a sick parishioner up in the hills to visit. Few of the brothers would try to follow him there. And so he said with a smile, which was echoed by the smith's,

"I'll be back, then, as soon as I hear of the de Broases heading for Brecon. I'm sure someone will bring me word to my new chapel at Clodock when they come back from markets here. If you'd find me a compassionate soul amongst those who are left behind who'll get me in, for I'm sure that de Braose will be taking the tougher soldiers with me, I'll see what can be done about soothing this poor unfortunate's soul."

And suddenly Tuck knew that he had found a purpose in life again quite beyond tending to the people of Clodock and its surroundings. There was an innocent victim here who needed rescuing, and if Saint Issui would heed his prayers, he was going to find a way to get this Maelgwn out.

THE END … But if you want to find out how Tuck rescues Maelgwn, pick up a copy of the first book in the Guy of Gisborne series, *Crusades,* which you can purchase from the same place where you found this book, or follow one of the links from my website page.
There's a taster of *Crusades* for you to try following the Historical Notes.

Thank you for taking the time to read this book. Before you move on to the notes which give you a bit of background to the story, I would like to invite to to join my mailing list. I promise I won't bombard you with endless emails, but I would like to be able to let you know when any new books come out, or of any special offers I have on the existing ones.

Simply go to my website www.ljhutton.com and follow the link there. You will also be offered two free eBooks.

Also, if you've enjoyed this book you personally (yes, *you*) can make a big difference to what happens next.

Reviews are one of the best ways to get other people to discover my books. I'm an independent author, so I don't have a publisher paying big bucks to spread the word or arrange huge promos in bookstore chains, there's just me and my computer.

But I have something that's actually better than all that corporate money – it's you, my enthusiastic readers. Honest reviews help bring them to the attention of other readers better than anything else (although if you think something needs fixing I would really like you to tell me first). So if you've enjoyed this book, it would mean a great deal to me if you would spend a couple of minutes posting a review on the site where you purchased it.

Thank you so much.

Historical Notes

Tuck's original monastery of Ewenny at Abergavenny still exists, but nothing of the building of his time remains, so anyone visiting it should not expect it to look as I've described. That Norman building took a beating in the rebellions of Owain Glyn Dŵr in 1405, and consequently the extensive rebuilding work which went on in the 17th, 18th and 19th centuries wasn't exactly destroying valuable medieval remains. Therefore although the nave these days might look Norman, it's not. And strangely for such a prestigious church, we also do not know for certain when it became a fully monastic foundation beyond that it was somewhere between 1154 and 1189. I therefore freely admit to picking a point for that which sits well with the story at hand, because I wanted Tuck to enter the monastery as an oblate – a child gifted to God – so that he would have learned Latin at an age when it would have become almost a second language for him.

However, Abergavenny excepted, there are some stunning early medieval churches still surviving in that area if you want to visit any of them, and I have modelled Tuck's monastery church on such places as the magnificent Brecon Cathedral, which has only become a cathedral in modern times, but is a stunning example of what a large, Welsh monastic church would have been like in terms of its size and layout.

https://www.breconcathedral.org.uk/gallery/brecon-cathedral-gallery/

Likewise, St David's, Llantony, which was also attached to a monastery and where, although the windows have been enlarged, the nave is still thoroughly Norman. And if you want to see some breath-taking carvings, do visit another Grade 1 listed church on the Welsh borders at Kilpeck. http://kilpeckchurch.org.uk/ They have carved dragons, but also the most wonderful corbel table (the roof support) which is carved all the way around the church with grotesques and weird and wonderful creatures, not to mention a hound and hare that could have walked straight out of the Disney studios – someone knew and loved their animals to get that much personality into two tiny stone heads. If you do visit, please remember that this church is heading for a thousand years old and the stonework is now fragile.

St Issui's at Partrishow is very real and almost unaltered, although you need to go prepared with a very good map to find it. Don't even try it with a sat-nav, even though five miles north of Abergavenny doesn't sound difficult! You'll end up getting lost in dead end tracks in the Black Mountains! But if you do get there, also look for the holy well just down the track, which still gets many votive offerings. St Issui's is a gloriously peaceful little spot and the church just delightful – this is its website   address: http://www.cpat.demon.co.uk/projects/longer/churches/brecon/1693 1.htm

It was never a symbol of wealth or heavily decorated, but if you want to visit somewhere that still has that special something of an air about it, then this is the place to go to. Please respect it, and be kind enough leave something in the way of a donation to help the very small community it ministers to to keep it going – ancient buildings can take a lot of upkeep.

The lack of learning of many of the monks is also not fiction. Right from back in Alfred the Great's day some four hundred years prior to Tuck's, people bemoaned the lack of understanding of much that the monks would recite on a daily basis, and although there were repeated attempts to reform the Church, inevitably in between reforms there was substantial backsliding. The most recent of those attempted reforms for Tuck would have been that of St Bernard of Clairvaux and his founding of a new order at the abbey of Cîteau, near Dijon, in 1098. Already Cistercian monasteries were being founded in England by Tuck's day, including the famous ones at Rivaulx, Fountains, and Jervaulx, all in Yorkshire, but also one which Tuck would have known of, Tintern, on the banks of the River Wye in Monmouthshire – although again, not the buildings which survive today, which are over a hundred years later at their earliest. However, senior Benedictines (the Black Monks) in the twelfth century would have taken a very dim view of any within their ranks suggesting that the Cistercians might have had a point about their corruption!

Anyone of rank within what we now call the Benedictine order by the later twelfth century was inevitably nobly born, and many were forced into the Church very much against their will. That even extended to King Henry's illegitimate son, Geoffrey, who had to be hurriedly ordained in order to take up the role of archbishop of York some decades later – a role he took up most grudgingly. So the Church did not promote on merit, and I am far from maligning the religious institutions of the day by painting them as corrupt. Many of those higher-ranking medieval churchmen could have shown the mafia a thing or two! Yet at the same time, given the lack of science to provide alternative answers to things like why people fell ill and died, or such things as earthquakes, everyone in the medieval period was a believer in one faith or another, and to an extent that we in our secular world might sometimes find surprising. So a brutal man like William de Broase, or Raynald de Châtillon, might do what we would regard as unspeakably awful things, and yet still hold a firm belief that if he paid for enough masses to be said, that his soul would beyond question be saved. It would never have entered their heads to question what we might regard as contradictory opinions, convictions or beliefs. In that sense, the medieval world was very different to ours.

The heavy-handedness of King Henry II towards the Welsh princes is not fiction, and neither is the role of the de Braose family. The massacre of Seisyll ap Dyfnwal and his family is true, and so is the taking and blinding of hostages by King Henry. And although the Maelgwn who appears at the end of the story isn't a real surviving prince, there were separately both other princes named Maelgwn, and also other survivors who lingered on in prisons right to the end of King Henry's reign – my character just joins up a few dots for literary purposes. Many readers will know something of the murder of Archbishop Thomas Becket by three knights, supposedly doing what King Henry wished, but may not be familiar with the spectacular act of atonement he then performed at Canterbury. Even kings might fear for their immortal soul back in those days, so I have not had to stretch the truth for reasons why King Henry might have been acting with less violence towards the Welsh princes who met him at Oxford, even if he still chose to behave as if he was their overlord by right – something which was far from true for all of Wales, when parts of it had never felt the Norman yoke on it. It would take until Henry II's great-grandson, Edward I, before the Normans would establish the chain of great stone castles across Wales, whose ruins you can still see today, and that was a full century on from when this story takes place.

Canterbury cathedral nowadays is also nothing like the church Tuck would have seen. The great Gothic church we still have part of, rose out of the ashes of the great fire of 1174, and the first rebuilding phase took ten years to complete, while the shrine to Becket wasn't finished until

1220. At the time when Tuck visits, the east end was indeed square and it was a building site, and it wouldn't be until 1180-4 that the new apsidal Trinity Chapel would be built in its place. If anyone wants to see what an early Norman crypt and ambulatory would have looked like, one of the best survivors is at St Wystan's Church, Repton. This is the website and just follow the link to the crypt for more information:

http://reptonchurch.uk/index.htm

As for Rome, you have to remember that much of what we see of its churches today have been built since the Renaissance. Virtually none of the standing churches have anything much other than small parts of their interiors dating back to the medieval time when Tuck visits. San Giovanni in Laterano was, and still is, the cathedral of Rome and an incredibly impressive building, but only its baptistery and Byzantine mosaics would be recognisable to Tuck, the rest being very much 15th to 18th century work. What is correct is that up until 1309 the palace adjoining this church was the home of successive popes, and until 1870 the popes were crowned in San Giovanni – not St Peter's as you might expect! It would be a century later before the complex of the Basilica of Constantine (in part of what is now the greater Vatican complex) began to double as a residence for the popes alongside the Lateran Palace. There is nothing left of the old St Peter's which existed from the fourth century up until 1506, by which time it was falling down. The nearest you will get to anything from this era are the catacombs beneath the modern Vatican.

If you want to see what Rome might have looked like to Tuck, my best recommendation would be to visit Ostia Antica, just outside of Rome itself and once part of the great port of Rome. It is easily accessible by buying one of the day trip public transport tickets that go out to the next limit beyond the city, then taking the underground (the Metro) to Pyramid station. From there you take the ordinary train out to the Ostia Antica station, and the huge archaeological site is just a short walk from the station. Do take plenty of water or other drinks! It's an enormous site to walk around. But the great joy of this is that few tourists find it, so unlike the crush around the Forum, you can wander at will. Here you will be able to explore old Roman houses and streets, which haven't changed in thousands of years – there's even a shrine to Attis and Cybele which features in another book of mine, *The Room Within the Wall!*

I'm guessing that many readers will have seen the film *Kingdom of Heaven*, and while I'm a fan of the film – not least for its beautiful portrayal of how sumptuous the eastern court was, and also for the way it visually highlights the massive disparity in numbers between the few crusaders and Saladin's force – it also has some huge historical errors in it. By the time of young king Baldwin IV's reign, the real Balian of Ibelin was well into middle age and married to the king and Sibylla's step-mother, Maria Comnena – not only widow of King Amalric (who had succeeded his brother, Baldwin III), but herself the daughter of the Byzantine Emperor and therefore an incredibly politically powerful figure in the east.

Reynald de Châtillon, however, was every bit the warmonger he was portrayed as. There is some question as to whether the great victory which young King Baldwin had over Saladin was in reality led by Reynald, and certainly he was a much more experienced a fighter than the young king would ever be. However, since the contemporary Arab sources for the battle credit the young king, and Reynald was sufficiently loathed by them even then for them to have made much of it had he led, on balance it seems likely that it was indeed young King Baldwin's victory, despite the torment he must have suffered to go into battle in armour when he was already seriously ill. The great Hospitaller fortress of Krac de Chevaliers only became know by that name in the nineteenth century, and not to be confused with the other great fortress of Kerak, which Châtillon acquired upon his marriage to Stephanie de Milly. To the men of the time it was known as Crac de l'Ospital, and that is the name I've had Tuck use.

As for the huge storm I've had Tuck and the Welshmen getting caught in, you may think it fantasy, but in fact such massive storms do strike in this area. That has been starkly illustrated at the archaeological site at Petra, where large concrete blocks had to be installed across some of the gullies leading down to the Siq and Treasury (of *Indiana Jones* fame!) after it became clear that tourists were being killed by flash floods when storms hit higher up in the area. When you look at the height of these modern barriers you realise just how dangerous these flash floods can be. But there still survives a dam built by the Nabateans – the people who built and lived in Petra from the 6th century BCE to the 1st century CE – to protect the Siq and beyond, and who also installed water drainage pipes and a tunnel to carry flood water away from the city. So having Tuck and his Welsh friends caught in a deluge out in the desert has its basis in fact.

The leading family on Sicily at this time was indeed the Hauteville's, and the relationships within them and the marriage of King William to Joanna (or Joan) of England is true. The only adjustment I have made to them is in the survival of the king's brother, Henry. He's very poorly documented – which made him ripe for using – but undoubtedly died before his father just as most of his brothers did. Certainly there's no evidence of him leaving an heir behind, but then that made it all the easier to gift him with William who then disappeared. With the ruler of Sicily having control of what we now regard as the mainland of Italy, pretty much from Naples down to the far south, he was a powerful force in that region, and the dukedom of Apulia was sometimes used as a title for the king's direct heir. And surprisingly, the real Tancred actually became king of Sicily in his own right from 1189-1194, despite being illegitimate, such was the lack of heirs within the family by then, and he was succeeded by the remaining sister – something rarely heard of in those days.

If you would like to hear some of the lovely music of Tuck's era, there are some examples recorded of what survives, and some of them are on YouTube.

https://www.youtube.com/watch?v=_p9WQlyVPrA   This one is by Leonin, a composer based in Paris in the late 12th century. And this is another example of 'western' music at the time, https://www.youtube.com/watch?v=lbzw3B6jklU

However, this next example is of music from the crusader states, and you can hear that it is quite different – although this particular piece comes from a little bit later with the fall of Edessa.

https://www.youtube.com/watch?v=6mxCilXRaWY

Tuck appears again in the Guy of Gisborne books, which are also based very much in the real twelfth century, even if they follow the exploits of some legendary characters!

Confiteor

I confess to Almighty God... to all the angels and saints, that I have sinned exceedingly in thought, word, deed:

My name is Gisborne, Sir Guy of that same. You may have heard of me. Most of it will have been lies or tall tales. I care not. I shall tell my version of events now, for my confessor insists I hold nothing back for fear of imperilling my immortal soul.

I know what his abbot thinks I shall confess to, here and now when my deathbed looms. I wish I could write this all in my own hand so that for once, at least, the full tale will not be edited by those who lack the courage to hear the truth. Instead I shall have to trust to my scribes' vows and honesty, and in God, that in his mercy he will allow the truth to come out. May Dewi Sant and Saint Issui intercede on my behalf one last time.

No Brother Gervase, do not look so askance. You have no idea of what I shall tell, so do not judge me yet. If other readers like it not, that is for them to argue over with their confessors and their consciences. Mine is clear. If you think I lie, well then, you may believe me condemned in the afterlife if it comforts you. I, however, have no such doubts of what lies ahead. This is the truth, as I swear to it by Almighty God, who has seen all already and knows my fate better than me. I entrust my soul to his care, and once that has fled my body, what happens to this frail shell is of little consequence. If some wish to dance or even piss on my grave I shall be past caring.

So, where to start? I know what you, my confessor Gervase, and any other reader who later on digs this out of the dusty monastic scriptorium, wants. You want to hear about him. About Robin Hood. It is nothing less than I expected. After all, to all of you our stories are intertwined and his is the legend – I only catch your interest for his sake. But I have a mind to make you wait a little. We shall get to him soon enough! You must bear with me and my story for a while yet. First you must hear about how it all began, what happened to our family – oh yes I do say our, dear Brother, for a connection is there – and what set us on the road to unexpected infamy. Only then may you judge whether I deserve my reputation – a reputation, I might add, which has only come about long after the events happened, and from the mouths of those who were never there.

Yet one point I must dispel before we start, for it irks me mightily. In these latter days a foolish rumour has arisen that the great outlaw was also a great earl. Some even hint that he was of noble Saxon lineage, although surely even the most cloistered monk knows that no lords of the former English retained such power and office by our day. No! A pox on such nonsense! ˜Robin Hood˜ was never an earl! What need would such a man have had for taking to the green-wood? Even in the days of my youth those great men were never simply ˜Englishmen˜ any more than they are now when our French lands have been long lost. All the men of such rank and substance also held lands in Normandy, Brittany or Aquitaine, quite aside from their estates here. Even in more recent times when King John in his folly lost our lands across the water, they could still easily retreat to France by the simple expediency of swearing fealty to the French king when they fell foul of their English one – which many did over the years.

Or if they lived nearer the borders, then the Welsh princes and Scottish kings were also only too willing to welcome the enemies of their powerful neighbour – as my father witnessed and suffered for. Did not King Henry I move against Robert of Bellême, Earl of Shrewsbury – the son of Roger of Montgomery – for just such an alliance? In 1112, if you recall our not so distant past, after imprisoning the rebel earl, he seized not only Bellême's land on the Welsh border but also the family lands of Mortain in Normandy. And Mortain you should know of as staying in royal hands, since John was Count of Mortain long before he was king! If ˜Robin Hood˜ had been such a man, do you truly believe that even absent King Richard's hapless governors, let alone the more resident King John, would have left him to be dealt with by a mere local sheriff? No! That tale is utter nonsense!

And as for being the Earl of Huntingdon, ah me! Do not make me laugh, for it makes me wheeze these days. Have you no memory for such things? The true Earl of Huntingdon was brother to the king of Scotland, no less. Indeed, David of Huntingdon, with his brother King William of Scotland, and the king we never had – Richard and John's oldest brother, Prince Henry – took control of Huntingdon early in the great rebellion of 1173 to '74. Ah, I remember that well, being very disgruntled to be left behind when my not much older cousins went off to fight.

But you are distracting me already! Patience, Brother Gervase! Recollect what happened then, for it is all pertinent. King Henry II sent his army north and resoundingly defeated the lot of them, with King William of Scotland being sent to the leonine Henry at Northampton in chains. That is what happens to earls who defy kings! It took ten long years for Earl David to get his hands back on the Huntingdon estates, and then only after King William had bound himself to Henry and acknowledged his over-lordship of Scotland. Do you seriously think that even in his dotage Henry, or his lion of a son, Richard, would have stood back for a heartbeat while such a man defied their family again? And in nigh on the same shires, no less? For truth, no! And do not forget, our legend was well established long before

John took the throne and had to deal with his rebellious earls. Robin Hood was not, nor ever could have been, this man or his heir. Besides which – just to throw you a bone to tease – I met and came to know David of Huntingdon, so I can tell you from personal experience that he was nothing like ˜Robin Hood˜ in looks or manners!

There, I have had my say on that matter. As for the rest, will you believe me? Or will you think I am simply lying to make myself seem a better man at this last stage of my life? This whole saga an aggrandisement of myself at his expense? Me, the dreaded Guy of Gisborne. Gisborne the jester stealing the king of Sherwood's crown in death, as I could not do in life? Or will your mind remain unclouded enough to read these words and sense the truth behind them? And will you recognise him when he first appears? Will you see him as I saw him, before the legend entwined itself around him? So I challenge you, my reader, now that I can no longer ride in the lists and take up challenges by right of arms. I challenge you with the point of my quill pen – ha, there is a pretty image! I challenge you to read this with an open mind. Only when a line has been drawn beneath the last words may you say Gisborne lies and is no better than you thought him.

So, dear brother, we will begin in earnest in the morning, and you may judge my unshriven soul for yourself.

Welbeck Abbey, Nottinghamshire, in the reign of Henry 111.

Ah, I dreamed such a dream last night, Gervase. It must have been your exhortations to tell all and tell the truth, for when I lay down in my bed my mind was all of a whirl. Either that or it is the effects of this dreadful ague I suffer, after the drenching in the cold and rain I received coming here! For you should know that while I am deeply grateful for the attentions of your infirmarer, I would not willingly have come back to stay in this area where I lost so many of those whom I held dear. My intent was only to spend a

single night near to Nottingham and then return north to my home. Indeed, had I not felt it incumbent upon me to honour the last wish of another of those cherished few, at my age I would not have made the long journey and be here now. The years weigh heavily on me in this familiar landscape, and already I feel that if I could just walk out of here and turn a corner, I would walk through an invisible veil and step back to those years of my prime. So as I scoured my memories in those last moments of wakefulness, here in this bed, they shifted into dreams which took me back all those years to when it began – before the legend wrapped itself around us, and, had we known it, when we were all standing on the brink of the greatest adventures of our lives.

In my dream I was riding like the wind through that Derbyshire vale, the winter landscape sharp and crisp around me, and down below me I could see the fight unfolding. Little John was facing Robin Hood with swords drawn, and there had clearly been an exchange of blades already. Then Robin went flying backwards as his heel caught on a fallen branch. His sword flew out of his hand and Little John closed on him, although I knew that John would never maim, much less kill, unless he had no other choice. Then a thrown knife from Will Scarlet's hand skittered along John's blade right by the guard and John dropped his sword too. I remember digging my spurs into my horse's side, determined to get there and stop this madness, and vaguely registering that there were other men surrounding the fight, all of them mounted. Up with me, two other horses were pounding alongside mine, and I recall their smell on the crisp winter air and the sound of their hooves breaking icy puddles as we plunged down the slope.

I recall thinking as we rode, and the freezing air blasted my face,

˜There are three of us here with a boy, and three more of mine down there. Can we take six experienced fighters like them if it comes to a fight? Sweet Jesu, we have to! I have to take them. I cannot tell the sheriff I let so many well-armed ruffians go free to ravage as they pleased! ˜

I saw Robin roll and come up with a knife from his belt in his hand and make a swipe at Little John. I remember thinking back then,

˜By Our Lady, he means it! Blood will be spilled this day!˜

And so it was in my dream, so vivid, so fresh!

Someone off to their side tried to dismount to join in the fight, and an arrow from one of my men stopped him in his tracks.

˜Good for Thomas˜ I heard one of my fellow riders give praise, and gave thanks myself for the range and power of the great wyche-elm longbows.

I saw Brother Tuck reach out and restrain one of the other strangers, but we were still too far off for me to see how successfully or not he was in holding on to the man. However I heard him call out in his strong Welsh voice,

~Stop! In the name of God, I command you, stop!~
And then I was shouting as loud as I could,
~Stop in the name of the sheriff of Nottingham!~
As a forester and a man of the sheriff, I had full authority there and intended to use it against these vagabonds. Whether that would be sufficient, or whether I would end up making an utter fool of myself, I had not the time to consider.

I rode up to this man I was to come to know as Robin Hood, standing there tall and dark, with a soldier's readiness to pounce, and looked into dark brown eyes as feral as a wolf's and every bit as dangerous. I heard another great bow sing and felt the thump of another long arrow hitting the ground nearby. Another warning shot no doubt, but I was not so foolish as to break my gaze upon this outlaw to turn and look. If I could not subdue him, then those arrows would soon be taking flight in anger!

~How dare you attack my men! ~ I snarled at him, and he stood his ground and stared back at me with insolent arrogance. He was not in awe of any sheriff's man then any more than later.

I recall Little John getting up and backing off from him but watching me warily too, as did the others in my party, all waiting for my signal to attack these sunburned strangers, who had the appearance of Templars even if they were acting like outlaws. Experienced fighters every one, they were the most dangerous men I had seen in years. Not since my time fighting the Welsh had I seen soldiers of this calibre.

~I will not tolerate you marauding your way through this shire!~ I threatened them, and hoped it would be enough, for I can still recall the feeling of my pulse racing and the blood singing in my veins, as it does when time seems to slow in that moment before chaos erupts, and when everything changes.

I see us all still, both in my dreams and now in my memories, frozen in time there amongst the trees like in some religious tableau. Me up on my big horse. Robin full of fire and fight on the ground before me. Little John standing a few paces off but no less ready for a fight, and Tuck on a shaggy carthorse trying to bring a calm to the situation and yet still ready to join in if things turned nasty. The four of us and the man you know of as Will Scarlet, plus others who would be part of the famous outlaw gang, all lined up as if for inspection by some unseen divine being who was still contemplating what to do with us all.

These dreams still come to me, Brother, and in them I cannot help but feel a higher guiding hand even if that thought scandalises you. Wise men have told me that dreams and visions are closely related, and that just as in the religious vision, a dream may illuminate the workings of the divine to mankind in a way we would not see in this real world. I do not claim *saintliness for myself or those others, Brother, so you need not purse your lips so hard in disapproval. No, I am saying that in those dreams and in the memories they refresh for me, I now see a force outside of ourselves pushing us in ways we might not have gone of our own accord. I believe that Robin Hood, the legend, came to be because someone more than mere men decided that there needed to be someone like him. That greatness was thrust upon him and those around him, and that is why the tales have lingered so in the minds of folk who have never even been to Sherwood or Nottingham.*

However, to return to my dream of last night, you need to hear much more of our earlier lives in order to see that divinely preordained confrontation in the same light as I do now. To see how we came to that point when Little John and Robin Hood were having their first encounter, and that it was a fight where one or other of them might have died if things had gone differently! You see? Such are the pivotal moments legends are made of! So let us begin while I still have breath to tell the tale.

About the Author

L. J. Hutton lives in Worcestershire and writes history, mystery and fantasy novels. If you would like to know more about any of these books you are very welcome to come and visit my online home at www.ljhutton.com

Alternatively, you can connect with me on Facebook

Cover image © L. J. Hutton
Photo of monk iStock, background image iStock.

Printed in Great Britain
by Amazon